CRIMSON SIN

REBEL HEART

BOOK 1

TRINA M. LEE

CRIMSON SIN

Copyright 2015 by Trina M. Lee
ISBN 9781723712425

All rights reserved. No part of this publication may be reproduced, stored in a retrieval system, or transmitted in any form or by any means, electronic, mechanical, recording or otherwise, without the prior written permission of the author.
Published in Canada

Published by
Trina M. Lee

Editor
B. Leigh Hogan

Cover Art
Covers by Christian

This is a work of fiction. The characters, incidents and dialogues in this book are of the author's imagination and are not to be construed as real. Any resemblance to actual events or persons, living or dead, is completely coincidental

Chapter One

Many ages ago one of the greatest of offences was committed by a faction of God's angels. They became enchanted by the women of man and took many of them as lovers. The results of these illicit unions were hybrid offspring. Abominations. The nephilim.

Blessed with the gifts of their angelic fathers but cursed with the mortality of their human mothers, the nephilim are offered a choice: live a human life or take your place among your father's kind by serving either the light or the dark. Sounds simple enough. If only it were.

Those nephilim that chose to live as human were stripped of their gifts. And then they were hunted and killed. The angels of the dark, the demons, wouldn't stand for rejection by those they considered to be rightfully theirs.

The undecided nephilim were also an unfortunate bunch. The gift of free will meant being able to make one's own choice. Because of this the undecided were heavily sought after by the dark. Lucky me. I was one of them.

* * * *

"I'm on my way, Jett. Soon. I promise. I just have something to take care of first."

I did my best to reassure my best friend, Jett Savage, that I wasn't ditching out on practice. Our band had been selected to participate in the annual Battle of the Bands event held by the local rock radio station, The Fox, at The Spirit Room. Jett had been a real drill sergeant about it since we'd gotten the good news.

"What could be more important than being ready for the first night of the competition? We're the only chicks playing this thing,

Spike. We have to wipe the floor with those guys." The sound of a lighter being flicked was followed by a deep exhalation of breath as Jett lit a cigarette.

I bit back a curse when a man, rushing down the sidewalk past me, almost knocked me into the street. Clutching my phone tight, I said, "Since when do you worry about being better than the boys? We rock as hard as any of them do."

A glance at the street sign on the corner revealed that I was just a block away from my destination. I wasn't really sure what the hell I was doing. Apparently I was following the orders of an angel who enjoyed giving the vaguest descriptions ever.

"Chicks always have to prove themselves in these male-dominated industries. It's fucking bullshit." Her tone dripped acid. I knew her dark eyes would be flashing with the fierceness of her wolf.

"Tell me about it. Try being a female nephilim. I'm sick to death of hearing how rare and special I am. Special? What the hell does that even mean?" Having a werewolf for a best friend meant I could say such things.

"I know, right?" The slam of a car door echoed in the background. "I'm heading over to the jam space now. Don't be late, or it's your turn to buy booze."

She hung up before I could toss a quip back at her. Just as well. She was distracting me anyway. I stuffed the phone back into my cute little purse. It was a heart with black bat wings, one of my favorites.

Turning my attention back to the street ahead, I scoured the people milling about, searching for the woman I'd been sent to find. According to Cinder, I would know her when I saw her: red hair, provocative clothing, a working girl. She was in trouble, and I was here to try to encourage her not to make a huge mistake, one that could cost this woman her life.

I was putting a lot of trust in Cinder here. He insisted I could do this.

Sure, that was easy for him to say. He was an angel. What came easily to him did not come so easily to me, especially the confidence needed for such a task. I wanted to help though. Really, I did. Growing up being able to see and feel angels and demons had made it impossible for me to live in ignorance of their ways. Officially I had yet to pick a side to serve. I did my share of bad shit on a daily basis, as we all did, so I always jumped at a chance to help Cinder when I could.

He was a good friend. He'd been there for me when I thought I was losing my mind in the hard teen years. When I hit my twenties, joined a rock band, and started partying way too hard, he was still there. He still believed in me. And I didn't want to let him down.

I slowed as I drew closer to my destination. Scanning the street, I didn't see anything amiss. A convenience store on the corner was relatively busy as was the liquor store next door.

This wasn't the best part of town, and soon a john pulled up beside me. "Looking for a date?" barked the middle-aged guy in the minivan.

I barely repressed a shudder. My gaze went to his hand where there was a very obvious wedding ring indent. The car seat in the backseat made me want to vomit. Cinder always said it wasn't our place to judge, but how the hell could I not?

"Hell no," I said with a sneer. "And you shouldn't be either from the looks of it."

I nodded toward the empty car seat. The guy looked momentarily embarrassed, then he scowled and flipped me his middle finger before speeding off with a screech of tires.

I glanced down at my attire, wondering if I looked like I was selling myself. A black, knee-length skirt paired with a Halestorm tank and black, knee-high boots summed up my rocker-chick look. It was badass, and I was offended that he'd seen it as an advertisement.

"Says more about you than it does about me, buddy," I muttered beneath my breath.

Then I saw her, a ginger-haired woman that looked to be a few years older than my twenty-four years. She wore a tiny, tube-like dress that barely covered her ass. Leaning against a bus shelter, she stared into a small makeup mirror and reapplied bright red lipstick.

Nerves stopped me in my tracks. What the hell was I supposed to say to her? Cinder had only told me that I needed to encourage her not to get into a black sports car without infringing upon her free will.

I took a few deep breaths, but my heart pounded hard inside my chest. This sure hadn't been how I'd expected to start my evening when I rolled out of bed this afternoon. Being self-employed made it way too easy to stay out late with Jett and the girls. Sleeping the day away was such a waste, but it felt so good.

Fear of failure made my mouth dry. Too many what-ifs danced through my head. The worst kind of fear starts with "what if…" So I took another deep breath and started toward her.

My plan was to engage her in conversation. What to do from there, I had no clue.

Before I reached her a black car pulled up to the curb beside her, ignoring the fact that it was bus parking only. She eyed the driver who leaned over to speak to her through the passenger window. When he passed whatever silent test she was putting him through, she sauntered over to talk to him.

I quickened my pace, ready to break into a full-out run if I had to. I reached her as she grabbed for the door handle.

"Wait, please," I gasped, skidding to a stop beside her. "I need to talk to you."

She looked up in surprise, which quickly turned to hostility. "Who the hell are you?"

I wasn't sure what to say. The man inside the car looked pensive, trying to decide if my appearance was a good or bad thing. However, it was the demon, standing a few feet away and watching, that made the blood rush from my face.

Nobody else could see him, but he knew damn well that I could. The fact that I could see him meant that he was a lower-level demon. I couldn't see the higher ups unless they wanted me to. However, that didn't make him any less dangerous than the others. He stood there waiting to see what I would do. With arms crossed and black wings tucked in against his back, he wore a mask of malice.

"I'm Spike," I said. "I was sent here to talk to you. Can I buy you a coffee? Or a drink?"

Her gaze narrowed in suspicion. "Who sent you?"

"A friend. You don't know him, but he knows you, and if you will just trust me—"

"I don't know who the fuck you are, but you better get the hell off my corner before I gut you. Tell your friend to fuck off." She elbowed me aside and opened the car door.

I grabbed hold of her arm and jerked her back. It was desperate. Maybe I was crossing a line, but I panicked. She whirled around to give me a shove, but I stood my ground, refusing to let go.

"Get the hell off me, bitch."

We scuffled there on the sidewalk in front of a john and a demon. She tried to shake me off, but I wouldn't let go. Pleading with her to listen only made her angrier. The demon was laughing, enjoying my impending failure.

When the scuffle began to attract the attention of passersby, the guy in the fast car sped off. I was elated to see him go, so much so that I wasn't ready for the fist that pounded my face.

"Bitch, do you know how much money you just cost me? That was a well paying trick you just chased away." The woman didn't look tough, but she knew how to throw a punch.

I backed away before she could hit me again. I tasted blood and discovered it came from a gash on the inside of my lip.

"Look, I just wanted to help. I'm sorry but if you would just let me explain—"

She hissed, "If I ever see your face down here again I'll curb stomp it until you're unrecognizable." With a glance at those watching our exchange, she spun on a stiletto heel to storm away.

"Come on, Gina, please. Just listen to me." The name popped out of my mouth unbidden. It stopped her in her tracks.

She turned back to me, her eyes wide. "How do you know that name?"

I had no friggin' clue. I was as shocked as she was. "I told you, I was sent by a friend."

My words had the opposite effect of what I intended. Rather than calm her, they only seemed to rile her up even more. The demon drew closer. His black eyes were like two sunken pits as he studied us closely.

"I don't know who sent you, but you can tell them to stay the fuck away from me. I want to be left alone." Gina's shout was shrill. Clutching her tiny handbag tight, she made an awkward retreat, walking backwards until she was far enough away to turn and run without me at her back.

She wouldn't get much speed out of those high heels, though I had no intention of giving chase. I'd been told to try to keep her from choosing to get in the car, and I'd done what I could. Cinder had said that sometimes our lives were steered in certain directions by higher powers because it was best for us, even though we often couldn't see that until after the fact.

I watched her go, and the demon watched me. When there was nobody within earshot, I acknowledged him. "You don't intimidate me."

"I don't need to," he replied with a voice as smooth and creamy as soft butter. "That wasn't my job."

Intimidation certainly seemed to be their job most times I encountered them. "Your job was to make sure she got into the car?"

"No. Merely to make sure she had the choice."

The lack of emotion on his face was unnerving. He exuded this eerie calm that made my palms tingle, which they only did when I felt defensive and was about to use my occasionally useful angelic gifts. The last thing I wanted to do was throw down with a demon though his threatening proximity made me wary.

His admittance made it all sound so simple. Perhaps it was. He'd come to exploit a broken woman's free will, knowing it could end in death.

"I had a job to do too," I said, though I wasn't feeling particularly thrilled about my victory. It felt like a blundered outcome. The look on Gina's face when I'd said her name came from a place of secrets and horrors. I felt sad for her. The demon stared down his angular nose at me and smiled. "Yes, well, sometimes when you win, you lose."

Chapter Two

The riff that screamed out of my guitar was perfect. It was strong and powerful, a sound that could bring me to my knees. The rush I got when the music flowed from my fingertips was better than sex.

The song was new and still coming together, but so far it was falling into place like the last few pieces of a puzzle. The sound reverberated through the rented storage facility that my band, Crimson Sin, used as a jam space. It was therapeutic, a place where I could just let go and forget about the demon whose words haunted me.

"That sounds fucking awesome, Spike," Jett gushed, a cigarette in one hand and a microphone in the other. The stack of Marshall amps pounded the sound out with a volume that would make the average person cringe. Jett absorbed it like a dry flower absorbed water.

My long, black locks fell forward to hide my face. They were a far cry from the punk rock mohawk that had earned me my nickname, but the name remained just the same.

Laying back on the second-hand store couch we'd shoved into the corner, Jett dragged on her cigarette. I played through the riff one more time before joining her.

I plucked the smoke from Jett's hand. "Where the hell is Tash?"

"She's on her way." Rubi beat out a rhythm on the drums that sounded like jungle tribe music. "One of her classes ran late. Or so she says."

"Boring." Jett helped herself to a beer from the small, hotel-style fridge. Our jam space was small and bare, but stocked with booze and a couch, we could have lived there. And we certainly spent more than a few nights there working through a song until it felt just right.

"Well, one of us should have a fall back plan. Who else will support all of our asses when we're old, dried-up rockers? It might as well be Tash." With a Cheshire Cat grin, Rubi shrugged. Even though she too was a university student, she didn't quite share Tash's intense level of dedication. Although I was willing to bet Tash was late because of other reasons, the boyfriend kind.

"Agreed. Tash it is." Raising her beer to that, Jett tossed a purple lock of hair out of her eyes. "Do you guys think we should try the new song this weekend? I wish we had a little more time, but I think it's great. We should do it."

The door burst open, and Tash rushed in with a large guitar case housing her bass slung over her shoulder. "I'm here! Sorry."

Jett smirked. "You were with that douchebag Mr. Country again, weren't you?"

"Screw you, Jett. Just because you think all boys are toys doesn't mean the rest of us do." With a roll of her eyes, Tash plugged in her bass.

I raised a hand and cleared my throat. "I do. You know, just for the record."

After the many times I'd been burned, I was done with guys. Sure they were good for a few things, but being trusted with my heart wasn't one of them. Not anymore. Of course, that was easy to say when there was no current hottie on my radar.

"Fine. Spike, you and Jett can have all the toys you like. Just because my boyfriend prefers country music doesn't mean he's a douchebag." Tash stuck her tongue out, and Jett threw an empty beer can at her in response.

"Actually, Tash," I snickered. "Yes it does. And when you get tired of his big dick, you'll accept that."

"Whatever, bitches. Are we jamming?"

Jett snickered and lit another cigarette before picking up her mike. "Yeah, let's run through 'Vegas Baby' a few more times. I think it would be a good opener for this weekend."

We were just a day away from playing the first night of the battle of the bands, a four-part event that kicked off this weekend. The winning band would get the opportunity to record an album with a well-reputed rock record label and open for one of their headlining rock acts when they visited the city on tour. It was a chance we couldn't pass up.

"Yeah, I like that one. Nice work, Jett." The sound of my guitar was fantastically loud as I tuned it down a step. "I'm surprised you remember enough of Vegas to write a song about it. I think you were wasted from the time the plane landed until take off four days later."

Jett replied, "That's what pictures are for. To fill in the blanks."

The opening riff poured from my sweet Gibson. The drums came in next with a sudden crash. Both Jett and Tash came in together, the vocal starting with the first bass note. The sound was just as good as anticipated. As different as each of us were, we all brought something to the table that made Crimson Sin the powerhouse it was. A take no shit badass, a wild child looking for a thrill, a born musician, and even the good girl, we were a colorful assortment, and we had a hell of a lot of fun doing it. And only two of us were human.

Jett sang her heart out. Her throaty growl and raspy voice packed each lyric with such energy and emotion. Most people would never have guessed that she was a werewolf.

Looking around at my girls, I couldn't have been happier with my band mates. Tash's red hair was a scarlet flag, whipping around in time with the music. With our combined differences and similarities, we were able to bring out a sound that could never have been achieved without the four of us together.

It was a damn good thing that the jam space was in a warehouse district that operated primarily during the day. We owned the night in this neighborhood.

Just past one in the morning, we called it quits for the night. We packed up our gear, talking excitedly about the upcoming battle. Jett and I hung back when the others left. She stared at me with a fierce, take no shit expression.

"So? Did you save the day?"

I nodded. My good mood soured. "I think so. I mean, I did what Cinder asked, but the demon who was there, he said something that made me think maybe I fucked up."

"Well, yeah, of course he did. He wants to make you doubt yourself." Jett pursed her glossy lips and studied me. "Honestly, Spike, finding your place in this fucked up world doesn't sound like a bad thing to me. Not yet anyway. You're special. Embrace it."

"Yeah, real fucking special. I'm not even supposed to exist. And now this?" I fumbled to light a cigarette, seeking comfort in that first drag. "Something bad is going to happen to me. I just know it."

"Stop being such a fucking cynic." She snatched the cigarette from my hand and stuck it between her lips. A plume of smoke filled the space between us. "You're half angel. Do you have any idea how friggin' cool that is? You gotta own it, girl."

"And if I don't want to?" I peered out at her from behind a curtain of black.

Being a nephilim was something I'd accepted long ago, mostly because I hadn't had a choice. My mother had feared the demons would come for me, so she told me the truth as soon as I was old enough to understand that my father was an angel. Together they had committed one of the greatest crimes, a forbidden romantic union that resulted in a forbidden offspring. Me.

My father may have been an angel at the time of my conception, but of course that changed everything for him, causing him to fall from grace. Now I was the one who had to choose between the light and the dark. To be honest, I was terrified of both sides. But then again, I had serious commitment issues.

Jett blew a series of smoke rings. "You don't have a choice. Trust me. I've been there."

"You have not. You love being a werewolf."

"We bust our asses to stand apart. To proclaim through our image and sound that we're not like everybody else. Because we really aren't. And that's fucking rad."

I laughed at her ridiculous use of the word rad. I slipped into my comfortable, worn leather jacket and slung my guitar bag over my shoulder.

Satisfied that everything was turned off and secure, I followed Jett out the door. The moon hung high overhead, a sliver against the backdrop of the city sky. It drew her gaze.

"One thing I can tell you, Spike, is that it only hurts worse if you fight it."

An uneasy feeling captured my attention. I felt like there were unseen eyes upon me. "Thanks for the pep talk, all knowing one. I'll see you tomorrow. You bring the beer money."

Flashing me a peace sign, Jett darted across the parking lot to her swanky new Mustang convertible. It had been a birthday gift from her deadbeat dad, a guy who was never around enough to notice the changes in his daughter. But he'd given her a fat trust fund and now a car, so she saw it as a chance to focus solely on music instead of getting a real job like the rest of us. She squealed out of the parking lot with a screech of tires and a heavy bass beat.

I took my time getting to my old 1971 Chevy Nova. Jett had given it the nickname: The Piece. As in, the piece of shit. That beater had been one of my first serious purchases. It was loud, reeked of oil and other fluids, and was in serious need of a paint job. But I loved it. The Piece had caught my eye one day during a lengthy and unbearable bus commute. Sitting in an overgrown yard in a sketchy neighborhood, it hadn't moved for months. Passing it everyday, it began to grow on me. Then a for-sale sign stuck in the window got me thinking.

Logic was against the purchase. When I picked my way through the dandelion-laden yard to the screen door that hung ominously off its hinges, I knew I was going to regret it. Some guy in a stained bathrobe answered the door. He wasn't even sure The Piece would start. It did. Barely. The rest is history.

As I crammed my guitar case into the spacious trunk, I resisted the urge to watch over my shoulder. When Cinder appeared beside me, I still jumped even though I'd been aware of his unseen presence.

"Dammit, Cinder," I scolded. "Don't do that shit when I'm alone in an empty parking lot in the middle of the night. Are you trying to give me a heart attack?"

The angel had the nerve to laugh. Then he plucked the cigarette pack from the pocket of my jacket and waved it in my face.

"These are going to stop your heart long before I ever do." He let me swipe the pack from his hand. Studying me while pretending he wasn't, he added, "I was sure you sensed me. Your body language changed. You tensed up."

I slammed the trunk closed and turned to face him. Nothing about his appearance gave away his identity. Other than the wings, of course. Those, however, were invisible to the mortal eye unless he wanted them to be seen.

With his short but slightly shaggy haircut and his chiseled good looks, Cinder wore the illusion of the average college-aged guy. I could never decide if his hair was light brown or dark blond. At times it seemed a little of both. His nose was slightly too big for his face, but it gave him an edgy look as opposed to being purely Abercrombie & Fitch. Adding to that edge, a two-inch scar slashed down his forehead and through his right eyebrow. Naturally I was curious as to how an angel could be scarred. I always wanted to ask, but he seemed reluctant to discuss it.

"I did sense you." I peered past him into the dark. "I couldn't tell it was you though. As soon as I get that feeling, I can't help but be paranoid that it's one of them."

Them. Demons. I'd spent my entire life living in fear of them. My mother's deep-rooted terror of the dark ones had infected me at an early age. She'd always feared they would come for me. And they had, eventually. In a manner of speaking.

Cinder's smile faded, and a graveness overtook him. "I won't let anything happen to you, Ember."

I flinched at his use of my real name. Nobody called me that other than my mother. And unfortunately, Cinder. Ember Evans was the name that appeared on my legal documents but nowhere else.

"That's not something you can guarantee, and you know it. Now if you don't mind, I'm going home to a hot shower and a comfy bed." I tugged my keys free of my pocket with a loud jingle. "I feel like I fucked things up with Gina. I may have trampled her free will somewhat by grabbing onto her so she couldn't get in the car. The demon there, he made it seem like I botched the whole thing."

"Self doubt is one of the most destructive forces in this world. He can plant the seeds, but only you can make them grow." Cinder's wise advice put things into perspective, as it often did. I couldn't argue with that. He reached to gently touch my swollen lip. "You did good tonight, Ember. You will learn all you need to know. In time."

The door of the Nova creaked as I opened it. The noise was an assault to the ears, especially in the quiet of one a.m.

He continued, "You would make a valuable addition to the light." When he leaned against the car and crossed his arms, his casual stance didn't match his reason for coming. "Have you given it any further thought?" Great, more pressure to make my decision.

He spoke as if I hadn't been thinking about it for a while already. Cinder had come into my life on the night of my sixteenth birthday, just over eight years ago. Introducing himself as my friend and guide, he'd said that it was in my best interest to take my place as my father's daughter among his kind, that I was a rare female in the densely male nephilim world, and that a special path was laid out before me.

I wasn't so sure. Despite having angelic parentage, I'd never considered myself one of them. I was mortal, paranoid, and as far from perfect as one could get. It seemed ridiculous that I had a place among the angels. Of course, choosing the light or the dark had its perks. Not only would I be protected by the side I chose, but my supernatural gifts would grow.

On the other hand, living a human existence would mean giving up my inborn link to the supernatural realm entirely. No longer distracted by angels and demons, I could focus on my music career, or lack thereof, and work on growing my graphic design business. Maybe I'd find time to get The Piece a tune up.

Given my alternatives, the choice to join humanity seemed easy enough. But I would always know what I'd given up, and of course, there was always a catch. Choosing the human route didn't mean I was free and clear of my angelic heritage. The dark sought to exterminate those who chose humanity. I would be a dead woman walking.

"I spend all of my free time thinking about it. It's not exactly breaking news, you know. But I'm just not ready yet, so don't pester me about it." I lit a cigarette, needing to do something with my hands other than jingle my keys.

Cinder grimaced in disgust and wrinkled his nose. "It's dangerous to put it off. You can't do it indefinitely. Sooner is better than later."

No rule stated that we had to make our choice by any specific time. The choice was entirely mine. I wasn't being forced into anything more than saying yes or no.

But I understood where Cinder's concern came from. It was dangerous to remain undecided, thus sought after by the dark. They weren't quite as respectful of free will as the light.

It should have been an easy choice, but it wasn't. Between work and writing music, I spent most of my time partying and screwing around with my friends. The girls and I had made some fantastic memories. On one hand, I wasn't sure I could trade that for fighting demons and darkness. On the other, I didn't want to be a piece of shit who achieved nothing of significance. And besides, was there really a place for a rock n' roll junkie like me among the light?

"Sooner is better than later." I nodded, sucking smoke into my lungs. I blew a cloud up toward the sky and got into the car. "Got it."

Cinder stopped me from swinging the door shut. A frown creased his brow. "Ember, I don't think you appreciate the gravity of the situation. I'm not here to convince you either way, merely to guide and inform."

Cigarette hanging between my lips, I fumbled with the radio. Maybe he was right; maybe I wasn't taking life's possibilities seriously enough. But I'd spent my entire childhood with a mother who lived in constant fear. If I couldn't shrug off my fear of demons, I would turn into the same anxiety-riddled basket case that she was. And I already had enough issues.

"Trust me, I know this is serious shit," I assured him. "Do you think it's easy for me to make this choice? I haven't exactly led a normal life so far, you know."

Plucking the cigarette from my lips, Cinder dropped it on the ground and crushed it beneath his heel. He leaned down so I was forced to look into his pale violet eyes. The color was so pale that they could be mistaken for grey. I'd seen them in the sunlight. Definitely violet.

He looked grave as he said, "There's more to it than just serving the side you feel you belong with, light or dark. Most importantly, you must follow your heart."

Chapter Three

So many bands rarely played the same stage on the same night. The current band launched into their next song with a crash of symbols and the scream of guitars. It was loud, powerful. I was impressed. And because I'd been watching their entire set, I was also worried. Molly's Chamber was our biggest competition.

I studied each band member in turn, lingering on the black-haired singer commanding center stage. Everyone in the local rock scene knew of Arrow Lynch. Something about him struck me as familiar because he was like me, a nephilim. I couldn't decide if this ability to sense one another was good or bad. It seemed to be both, as our kind were greater in number than most might think.

I'd seen him around. We had never spoken, and I hoped to keep it that way. Unfortunately, most nephilim chose the dark, which spelled danger for anyone who wasn't part of the darkness, human or otherwise.

I turned to Jett and shouted to be heard over the music, "What do you think?"

She pursed her lips, scrutinizing the guys on stage. "I think I need a cigarette. Let's go."

We both knew that Molly's Chamber was the second best band in the competition, after us of course. However, we were the only all-girl band, and as shitty as it was, that meant we had something to prove.

Smoking was prohibited in public places in Edmonton, so we headed outside for one of several smoke breaks we would take tonight. Tash and Rubi were upstairs in the dressing rooms that the participating bands shared. I'd been more interested in checking out the competition than drinking backstage.

As we stood up to leave, the song ended with the drunken cries and the applause of a crowd who just wanted to rock. The singer shouted encouragingly to the rockers gathered around the stage, getting them all worked up. He was smooth and poised, exuding an arrogant confidence.

However, the bass player sparked my personal interest. He rocked a vibrant blue mohawk. The front was long enough to hang in his eyes, with the rest spiked up. In a leather jacket and tight black jeans, he was easily the hottest guy in the room.

"Come on." Jett tugged on my arm before following my gaze to the stage. "Oh, no you don't. Yeah, he's sexy and all. Right now, he's also the enemy. Besides, I thought you'd sworn off guys for a while."

I let her pull me along outside. As our set time drew closer, I began to get a case of the nerves. That always happened right before a show, but this time was different. The stakes were higher. We had to kick ass.

A group of people loitered along the street outside the nightclub, smoking and talking in loud, obnoxious tones. We walked away, heading down the block.

Jett fired up a joint, took a pull, and handed it to me. I accepted it absently, hoping it would calm my nerves. I felt disappointed when it only heightened my anxiety instead.

"Stop stressing out, Spike." She nudged me with an elbow. "It smells sour. Don't doubt for a minute that we'll win this."

"Gross, dude. Don't smell me. That's creepy."

"Shut up. I can't help it. It's the wolf. You wouldn't believe the shit I can smell. It's not all cupcakes and roses."

We passed the joint back and forth, talking as we walked. I considered telling her about seeing Cinder but decided this wasn't the best time to bring it up. That wasn't the way to calm my racked nerves. Since his mildly unpleasant visit, I'd done my best not to think about it.

Instead, I said, "One more band after Molly's Chamber, and then it's our turn. Try not to do anything that will end up on the internet." I laughed, recalling the time Jett threw a beer bottle into the crowd at a heckler.

"Hey, that video got a thousand views the first night and drove traffic to our website. I know what I'm doing."

We stopped at the end of the street, far enough away from the cluster around the door to allow us to talk and smoke in private.

A series of hoots and whistles from the crowd around the door announced the arrival of the Molly's Chamber boys. Friends, acquaintances, and wannabe groupies praised their performance with loud expletives and hand slaps. They drank in the compliments. And who could blame them? They were one of the best bands in town, and they knew it.

"Look at those cocky bastards." Jett scowled down the street at them. "I bet they think they've got this thing."

"Fuck 'em. We've got this. What matters most is that we beat Something Like Sorrow." Holding the joint between my lips, I adjusted my boobs, shoving them around inside my push up bra and Ramones top. "Does my cleavage look even?"

"Yeah, your tits are amazing. Stop showing off." She plucked the joint from my lips and sucked down the rest of it. "And don't say that name again. You know it's forbidden."

Something Like Sorrow was Jett's ex-boyfriend's band. Though they'd broken up more than six months ago, she was still holding a grudge. I didn't consider them much of a threat. They were mediocre at best, a power-chord band really.

The Molly's Chamber boys made their way to the bus stop bench near the club. Their voices were loud, carrying down the street toward us. They carried on about how great their set had been, how they were going to win this thing.

"Gotta admire their confidence," Jett mused, her heavily painted, red lips pursed in judgment. "I hope it doesn't scar them too badly when we kick their asses."

I smirked, but my snarky reply was interrupted by the vibration in the back pocket of my jeans. I retrieved my phone and read the text message from Tash demanding we get back inside immediately.

"Tash is having a fit," I said. "She wants us back inside."

"Yeah, yeah. We'll get there. Tell her to have a drink. It's the best way to numb out the nerves."

I typed a brief reply that we were on our way. We had plenty of time until our turn to play, but Tash always got antsy right before each show. On stage, once the low, heavy tones rolled out of her bass, she was all good.

I watched as a few girls walked by the bus bench, receiving a few catcalls and whistles. One of the guys called out, "Hello, ladies."

All of the girls ignored him but one. She called back with a flirty, "Hi, Sam."

Without waiting for the girls to move out of earshot, Arrow nudged his buddy and loudly said, "Didn't you bone that chick after The Pretty Reckless show last month?"

"Yep." Sam chuckled. He had the tact to wait for them to move on before saying, "She got all weird and started calling me Daddy about halfway through. It was kind of fucked."

The hot bass player with the mohawk laughed, spewing a stream of smoke from between his lips. "And yet, you know you'd do it again."

Sam laughed as if his friend had told the best joke. "Well, yeah. What can I say? She was eager to please."

"Classy bunch of guys," Jett muttered, tossing the remains of the joint aside. "Let's go back inside before Tash has a meltdown."

I studied the bass player. His smile lit up his face as if a light were shining within him. It made him look a little less badass, like he might actually be a nice guy.

"Go ahead. I'll catch up."

Jett gave me an appraising glance and nodded, her smile sly. "Ah, I see. Looking to get your world rocked, Spike?"

"Possibly. Doesn't hurt to keep my options open." My smile was more playful than sly.

"Just remember, he's the enemy. For now anyway. No pussy for him until it's all over."

"Jett!" I protested, loud enough to draw Arrow's gaze my way. Our eyes met, and for a moment, everything froze. He looked away before I could, a disconcerting relief.

We walked back down the street toward The Spirit Room. Jett continued inside while I fished a cigarette from my pocket and strutted up to the bus bench. Ignoring the other three guys present, I focused my attention on the bass player. I wasn't about to be chased off by his nephilim friend.

"Got a light?" I asked, holding up my unlit smoke.

"Yeah, no problem." He fumbled in the pocket of his tight pants and produced a lighter.

"I saw you guys play earlier." I tossed my long, black bangs out of my eyes and leaned down so he could light the cigarette for me. I eyed the tip of a black tattooed feather that peeked out from beneath the collar of his jacket. "I liked it."

I smiled, a flirtatious tug of my red lips. Ignoring the others who watched the exchange in amused silence, I enjoyed the way he looked me over with obvious interest. His eyes were a heart-stopping, fiery, amber gold. His gaze traveled over me, lingering on my cleavage before returning to my face.

"Thanks. I like that you liked it." He watched me stick the cigarette between my full lips and take a drag.

"But as good are you are, we're going to kick your ass." I blew out a plume of smoke, watching it disappear into the night. "Seriously though, at this point, I think you guys might be our only competition."

"Oh yeah? Well forgive me if we don't take it easy on you."

Arrow scoffed and snickered but didn't say anything. I ignored him, feeling uneasy so close to him. The weight of his stare was intended to intimidate me. Well, fuck him.

"I'm Spike." I offered the hottie a hand tipped with perfectly polished, black nails. That would only last until I picked up my guitar. Then it would become a flaky mess. "I'm the guitarist for Crimson Sin."

"Rowen Cruz. I've heard good things about you guys. And I guess you already know that I play bass in Molly's Chamber. This is Arrow, Sam, and Greyson." He took my hand and gave it a warm squeeze while gesturing to his buddies with the other. "So… may the best band win."

Goosebumps rose up on my arms. My stomach flipped. It could have been the natural response to a cute guy eyeing me up, but it felt like something else, like my subconscious was trying to communicate a message that my conscious mind didn't want to receive.

"Most definitely." I nodded a greeting to his friends, finding it hard to meet Arrow's eyes. Being in such close proximity to him gave me the fuzzy sensation of static electricity. "Thanks for the light. Maybe I'll run into you later. You can buy me a drink."

Turning on a heel, I gave Rowen a flirty wink and sauntered off. Right away his friends started in on him, making inappropriate jokes. I could feel them watching as I went. Arrow's gaze felt heaviest though.

Suppressing a shudder, I disappeared into The Spirit Room.

I joined the girls in the dressing room just upstairs from the back of the stage. It wasn't the biggest, most luxurious dressing area, but it was divided into two rooms, one of which Rubi and Tash had claimed as "girls only."

We spent the next thirty minutes psyching each other up and putting last minute touch ups on our hair and makeup. I peered at my reflection in the mirror that lined one entire wall. Scrutinizing the heavy, black-and-silver shadow framing my greyish-blue eyes, I decided it was in no need of work. I reapplied my favorite cherry red lipstick and spritzed on the citrus perfume that I loved but Jett hated. Leather cuff bracelets adorned my wrists. A spiked collar around my neck and giant hoop earrings made up the rest of my accessories.

"You should've worn something that shows off your wings," Rubi said, catching my eye in the mirror as she ran a brush through her short, dark bob.

Wings were not a feature the nephilim were born with, much to my great childhood disappointment. According to Cinder, they manifested after one chose a side, when a certain level of maturity had been reached, or whatever. I didn't really understand how it worked.

At the age of eighteen I'd been feeling rather dramatic about the whole awkward identity thing. So I'd gone out and gotten wings tattooed on my back. They were beautifully done. The black, precisely detailed feathers ended low on my back, on the curve of my ass. The only other tattoos I possessed was a small dragonfly on the side of my leg and the word 'truth' in a lovely script on the back of my neck.

Other than my ears, I was piercing free. Tash was the least modified of the group, having no tattoos or piercings at all. Jett was covered in ink but lacked piercings. They weren't werewolf friendly according to her. The most notable tattoo she bore was the crescent moon on the left side of her neck, which marked her as a member of the local Doghead wolf pack.

"I was feeling mysterious tonight." I turned to show Rubi the tips of my wings that peeked out through the space between the hem of my top and the low-slung waist of my jeans.

When we were all draped in leather, lace, and a hell of a lot of eyeliner, we headed downstairs to set up our gear. Jett conveniently disappeared to the bar. Singers were so spoiled sometimes.

We ran through sound check while a DJ kept the crowd occupied with some hard rock tunes. I tuned my guitar, plucking my way through the strings until they sounded just right. Jett returned right on time, with a waitress carrying a tray of shooters trailing her.

"Pre-show shot time," Jett announced, swiping something pink and creamy from the tray and downing it without waiting for us to join her.

I helped myself to a Gladiator. The mix of Amaretto and Grand Marnier was one of my favorites. After a few of those, my nerves began to numb out. Tash grabbed one as well while Rubi abstained. She preferred to do her drinking after we played.

The stage lights dimmed, and the emcee stepped up to the mike. We got into position, ready and thrumming with anticipation. I stroked a hand lovingly along the neck of my lovely, black Gibson Les Paul guitar. It was my baby, the one thing I could not leave home without.

The emcee had barely said our name when the drums thundered into a steady rhythm. I joined in, and the sound was sudden, loud, and extreme. The stage lights came on, and we all but blew the roof off the place.

Our music was raw and in your face, but it was also catchy. The crowd was definitely into it. It tickled me when a handful of people crowded around the stage to sing along. They knew our original material, and a few of them even wore Crimson Sin t-shirts purchased from the merchandise booth run by Tash's sister. Playing around the city for the past few years was starting to pay off.

Jett's vocals were rough and gritty, her voice raspy and sexy but melodic as she sang:

Don't tell me how to feel
We both know this isn't real
If we don't walk away
It becomes more than a game.

Jett was a real wild child, throwing herself down on the stage in a dramatic fashion before getting up and leaping into the cheering audience. She crowd surfed like a pro, eating up all the attention.

I was in the middle of a solo piece that I was particularly proud of when I felt that I was being watched. It was a ridiculous sensation considering that hundreds of people were watching us play. But this wasn't that kind of watchful feeling. It was heavier, almost oppressive, like I was being studied.

Sweat broke out on my brow. My fingers flew over the frets, and the solo poured out of me. It had taken a shitload of practice to master the piece, and I couldn't help the proud grin that lit up my face when it came out flawless.

I glanced up to scan the crowd. Right away my gaze landed on the Molly's Chamber boys. They were gathered around a drink-laden table in the back. All of them were watching us very attentively, though none as intently as Arrow.

It was his studious stare I could feel crawling all over me. I felt something sinister in it. Our eyes met across the distance, but he continued to stare at me. I couldn't shake the feeling that he was trying to make me fuck up our set. Well, fuck him. Some guys just can't handle women that give them a run for their money.

No way in hell was I going to let the competition throw me off my game. Redirecting my focus to the crowd jumping up and down in front of the stage with hands in the air, I let the music sweep me away.

By the time we launched into the last song of our set, I'd pretty much forgotten about Arrow. The crowd was screaming. One guy shouted out, "I love you, Jett." She blew him a kiss.

Unfortunately, that brought out the ugly side of a few audience members. An empty beer bottle flew through the air, hurtling toward me. Using the neck of my guitar, I deflected it like a champ. When a second bottle followed, Jett stopped singing and searched the crowd for the culprit.

"Got a fucking problem, asshole?" Jett spoke clearly into the mike, staring down into the crowd.

The rest of us kept the music going. It was going to take more than a pussy with a beer bottle to chase us away.

"What the fuck did you say to me?" Jett laughed, and the sound was deadly. "I don't see you up here, cocksucker."

Another insult was directed at her. The words "suck" and "trashwhore" could be clearly heard. Jett moved fast. She leaped into the crowd with fists flying. There was a commotion as people closest to the action rushed to get out of the way.

There was no suppressing my laughter. This was not the first time Jett had unraveled on a heckler.

We watched as Jett lay a beating on the loudmouthed idiot. Once she got him down, she straddled the guy and fed shots into his face with an aggression I wouldn't have believed if I wasn't seeing it. Security moved quickly to drag her off. Jett's heckler lay on the floor with blood gushing from his nose.

Jett pulled free of the bouncer's hold and ran back to the stage. The crowd cheered her on, feeding off the excitement of the fast beat down they'd just witnessed. The security guys looked uncertain, but in the end, they gave the heckler the choice to stay or leave. Embarrassed, he headed for the door. It was a safe bet that he wouldn't mess with Jett again.

"Now that that's taken care of, are we done, or does anyone else want to step up?" Despite her words, there was a smile on Jett's face. She'd enjoyed that little incident.

We made it to the end of the song without further interruption. My blood was running hot when we finished. The crowd was all worked up, having enjoyed the display of violent werewolf temper.

I left the stage feeling damn good about our performance overall. Now that our set was over, it was time to party. Heading straight to the bar for a drink, I noticed Rowen nearby talking with a few friends. He glanced about, looking for someone. Me?

Instead of heading to the table that the girls had claimed near the stage, I slinked up behind Rowen. Feeling bold, I said, "Sex on the beach."

"Is that so?" He turned with a laugh, a raised brow, and his flirtatious smile. "Sounds good to me."

I glanced pointedly toward the bar and smirked. "My drink. That's what you can get me. Double vodka."

"You guys really kicked ass up there." Rowen waved over a passing waitress and ordered drinks. "But I'm sure you already know that."

"I certainly do. But thanks for saying so. A lot of guys don't have the balls. I think we intimidate them." With a suddenly serious expression, I leaned in close. "Do I intimidate you, Rowen?"

He studied me for a moment, his smile playful and quirky. "You know... I'm not sure."

I playfully tapped him on the nose. "You're cute. I like you."

We stood side by side, waiting for the last band to play. That strange feeling that I was missing something resurfaced. It was like I should know him from somewhere, but I couldn't figure out where. The waitress returned with our drinks, and I was glad to have a way to busy my hands.

"The singer has no range," I said when the final band kicked off their first song. "It's really not helping the lack of a talented lead guitar." I lifted the cherry from my glass and sucked the alcohol from it before dropping it back into the drink.

Rowen watched with stunned intrigue before shouting, "Right. And the drummer seems too talented to match well with the rest of them. But hey, I guess that works in our favor." Rowen spied Sam approaching and shot him a look to keep on moving. I pretended not to notice.

"I guess we'll know any time now."

I was happy to stand there with him, drinking and waiting for the judges to announce which bands were moving to the next round. The loud music and crowd eased the pressure of making small talk. We leaned back against a small partition wall and waited.

The tension was mounting. It all seemed too much like the results portion of a reality TV show for my liking. When the last band finished, the stage lights came up, and my stomach tightened. The DJ kept the music going, but the tension in the room began to thicken as several eager young musicians waited impatiently.

Minutes felt like hours. I shot Rowen a questioning look and played with the cherry from my drink. "Feeling lucky, sucker?"

Rowen watched me slip the cherry in my mouth, then back out again. "I don't think lucky quite sums it up. But yeah, I'm feeling pretty confident right now."

His friends were still gathered around their table. Catching Arrow's eye, Rowen held his drink up in a gesture of camaraderie. Arrow didn't look too pleased to see us standing there together, so I smiled brightly at him.

The lights dimmed, and everyone grew quiet. The spotlight lit up the emcee when he stepped up with a list of names in hand. My palms grew sweaty, and I held my breath.

Only four bands were going through. Crimson Sin was the first one announced. Relief rushed through me. I could have collapsed in a puddle of happy on the floor. I let out a little whoop and downed the last of my drink.

Rowen waited anxiously with his eyes locked on the emcee. His expression soured when the next band announced wasn't his. Two more to go. When the third band's name still wasn't Molly's Chamber, Rowen's gaze dropped to his drink.

I found myself hoping they would get through despite the fact that I should have been pulling for them to fail.

"Molly's Chamber." The emcee said their name, and Rowen slumped in relief.

"Congrats, cutie." I raised my empty glass to him in cheers before popping the lonely cherry back into my mouth.

"Thanks. Congrats to you too. You really deserve it."

Arrow, Greyson, and Sam were suddenly there, voices raised in excitement.

"Fucking rights!" Sam shouted. "Just one step closer to a record deal."

Rowen looked embarrassed by his buddies and their intrusive yelling. It was time for me to vacate and head back to my girls.

I pulled the cherry from my mouth and dangled it by the stem. Still attached to the cherry, the stem was tied in a perfect knot. Dropping the cherry into Rowen's glass, I grinned slyly. "Congratulations, boys. I guess I'll be seeing you next weekend. I can hardly wait."

Chapter Four

My head pounded. My eyes hurt though I hadn't even opened them yet. Rolling over in bed, I groped around blindly for my cell phone, dragging it off the nightstand and across my pillow.

Through bleary vision I made out the time. Almost noon. The scent of bacon helped me shake off the last remnants of sleep. My stomach growled, and I sat up, blinking until my vision cleared. What a night.

I slipped into a pair of soft, roomy PJ pants with little hearts all over them. Not very rock n' roll but comfy enough that it didn't matter. I peeked around the doorway into the kitchen. As I'd expected, Cinder was in there fixing me one of his amazing hangover breakfasts. Well, he didn't call them that, but I sure did.

I crept through the living room and adjoined kitchen to the bathroom. Hoping Cinder's back would stay turned, I wanted to make it into the shower without a row of questioning. I was just swinging the bathroom door shut when he called after me.

"How was your night?"

I hesitated with the bathroom door cracked just a few inches. "It was good. We got through to the next round."

"That's great. And?"

"And? I'm jumping in the shower. Do you mind putting on a pot of coffee?"

I closed the door and turned gratefully toward the tub. Only after I'd taken a hot shower and brushed my teeth did I start to feel like myself again. I'd gone a little too hard on the celebratory drinks. My stomach rolled, and I promised myself that I'd never do it again. But I knew that was just one of those lies I told myself in a moment of regret.

Crimson Sin

In sweatpants and my Clash t-shirt, I gathered my wet hair into a ponytail and emerged from the bathroom feeling less like the walking dead than I had when I'd gone in. Cinder had a plate sitting on the kitchen table complete with a steaming cup of coffee. I eyed the cheese omelet, bacon, and toast, sighing with contentment.

"You're the best, Cinder," I said around a mouthful of eggs. We both knew that he only made such wake-up calls when he had something important to discuss. Since I wasn't in a hurry to find out what that was, I used eating as a way to avoid conversation.

He slid into the seat across from me with only a coffee in hand. He watched me in silence as I shoveled food into my mouth. His expression was neutral. If he was thinking that I ate like a pig, it didn't show on his face.

"So," he said when I had all but licked the plate clean. "Tell me about your night."

I took my time, sipping the precious life giving fluid that is coffee. Cinder was patient. In fact, I'd only seen him show frustration a few times in all the time I'd known him. He merely regarded me with a raised brow and an expectant quirk to his smile.

"Well, we got through, like I said. It was great." I pondered him, wondering what it was he was trying to get me to spill. "Jett jumped into the crowd and punched a heckler. I don't condone her casual violence, but this time it was justified."

"I'm sure it was." Cinder smiled and waved a hand for me to continue.

"Don't pull that shit with me, Cinder," I said, spooning some extra sugar into my mug. "What's your deal?"

"My deal?" He feigned misunderstanding, which he often did when I used slang or inappropriate language with him.

I sighed, melodramatic and more exasperated than I really was. My spoon clinked too loudly against the mug, and I winced as my head throbbed. "There's obviously something you're waiting for me to say. So why don't you just ask and save me the headache of guessing? I have zombie brain right now."

Cinder grabbed my empty plate and took it to the dishwasher. His tendency to cook and clean for me had once made me feel very uncomfortable. And a little like a child. I'd come to learn over the years that he enjoyed the mundane human tasks. It was like watching a high-up authority figure for the first time joining the commoners in their day-to-day tasks and finding it joyful simply because he'd never had to do it before. I didn't get it, but it was cool with me. I hated housework.

He was dressed like a college kid in baggy jeans and a U of A hoodie though he'd clearly never attended. His shaggy hair was hidden beneath a backwards cap. No white robe or halo, it wasn't how I would have envisioned an angel. Maybe the robe and halo were reserved for special occasions.

Cinder's human look was always changing. It wasn't unlike him to drop in wearing a fedora one day and a turtleneck the next. I liked it best when he looked like an Abercrombie and Fitch ad. I never tired of teasing him.

"You know I don't like to tail you, right? It's just that sometimes I have to. It's my job." He paused, giving me a chance to anticipate where this was going. "Ember, you know I would never give you an order or in any way interfere with your free will."

"Yes," I said slowly, dragging the one word out as if it were several syllables long. "You're super fantabulous with cherries on top. What's your point?"

He held the coffee pot up. "Refill?"

"Hit me." I raised my mug to accept the offering.

I waited with growing impatience as he refilled my mug and then puttered around the kitchen, killing time. Finally, after I'd huffed loudly a few times, he returned to the table and sat down.

"Ember, I dropped by the show last night. You girls were outstanding, by the way. A lot of fun to watch. However, I noticed you were quite friendly with Rowen Cruz."

I sat there staring at him, trying to decide if it was good news that he knew who Rowen was or bad. Most likely bad.

"What can I say? He's a hottie." I shrugged and drank my coffee.

This was the part where Cinder told me something I didn't want to hear. It wouldn't be the first time, nor the last I'm sure. It no longer bothered me that Cinder occasionally dropped in where I was. It had when I was certain he was out to cramp my style like the no-fun police seeking to write me up for enjoying myself. That was never the case though. Cinder had a job to do. Protecting me was part of it.

"It's not advisable for you to become romantically involved with him, Ember. I'm sorry. I hate having to say that."

"It's not advisable?" I repeated. Nothing annoyed me more than being told I should or shouldn't do something, not even Cinder's insistent use of my real name. "I thought we agreed that my personal life is off limits."

"We did." He nodded. "It is. With this exception."

I groaned. The eggs sat heavily in my stomach. Intuition told me he was about to say something I'd rather not hear.

"Why? What's so special about Rowen that makes him off limits? Don't tell me he's some prodigal chosen one or something equally stupid." When Cinder stared at me in thoughtful silence, I sighed. "Of course he is. Well, you might as well tell me."

"I'm not supposed to tell you. Not until you make your decision."

"Can I guess? Does that work?" When he didn't answer right away, I rushed on. "Rowen isn't human, is he? No, of course he's not. That explains the weird feeling that I knew him from somewhere."

Cinder fiddled with the fading Star Wars logo on his mug, scratching a nail over it. "Nobody is supposed to see him as anything other than human. He's under protection right now."

I sat back in my chair, replaying my meeting with Rowen. Nothing had clearly indicated that he was anything other than human. It was a bummer to discover otherwise. This city was crawling with the supernatural, like much of the world, but couldn't I just dig a normal dude?

"He's nephilim, isn't he?" I guessed, certain that he must be if Cinder was in on it. "He must be a big fucking deal to have his identity hidden."

"Ember, you shouldn't swear like that. It's filthy."

"It is. I know. It's a bad habit. Stop avoiding my question. If you can tell me not to get the warm and fuzzies for him, then I'm sure you can tell me why." I chugged back the rest of the coffee. My body cried out for the caffeine rush though my stomach protested.

"I'm not at liberty to discuss the details with you. Rowen doesn't know who he is. Not yet. His talents are contained until it is his time to choose. He is highly sought after by the dark, which is why his identity must remain hidden."

I stared at Cinder, waiting to feel some sense of disbelief. When it never surfaced, I surmised that I was jaded by this shit already. "Well his daddy must be somebody pretty damn special then. Don't tell me he's a Throne or something."

A Throne was just one of the nine classes in the angel hierarchy. The hierarchy was divided into three levels with three classes in each. A Throne was of the first class, a level so high that its angels were often occupied with extremely vital tasks greater than most humans could fathom, according to Cinder anyway. It was unheard of for a level one angel to commit such a sin as bedding a mortal.

The demon hierarchy mirrored that of the angels. When an angel fell from grace, he remained in the same class, forsaking the honorable duty once bestowed upon him and taking up the nasty tasks of his new kin. Despite the various levels and classes of both angels and demons, there was no such thing as a weak or harmless one. They were all exceptionally created, all of them a force to be reckoned with.

Cinder himself was a Dominion, the highest of level two angels. He oversaw the activities of other angels and nephilim. He had great responsibility in seeking out undecided nephilim, like me, and guiding us into the fold, should we be willing.

Cinder shook his head but remained quiet. He looked worried, like he was afraid he'd shared too much. It's not like I was going to tell anyone.

Something occurred to me then. "Does Arrow know? It can't be a coincidence that they're friends."

Cinder's dark-blond brows rose, causing his scar to wrinkle. "No, I'm sure it isn't. I'm sorry. I wish I could tell you what I know, Ember."

"Spike," I growled, grumpy and annoyed. "It's Spike."

"Ember is a lovely name. Your father gave you that name."

"Yeah? And where is he now? Oh, right. He's locked up in a holding cell in hell." I would never have uttered such a phrase in front of my mother. I kept the bitterness I felt about my parentage and the circumstances surrounding it to myself, until it spilled out at moments like this.

Cinder drifted back into the kitchen where he tidied the counter and pretty much invented reasons not to speak. My brain hurt too badly to think this over. I glanced around the living room, and my gaze landed on the empty terrarium in the corner.

"Where's Seth?" I asked, scouring the floor for any sign of the tiny tortoise.

"I saw him heading for the couch. He's probably underneath."

A search beneath the fake leather couch revealed my little, shelled friend. I pulled him out, making kissy faces at him until Cinder laughed. Then I set Seth back down and let him slowly shuffle off toward a throw pillow on the floor near the TV.

I'd made a passing comment to my mother in a pet store about how cute I thought he was. A week later, she brought him over, citing him as a gift. My mother had spent much of my life spoiling me. Not because she thought I deserved it but because she felt guilty. I wasn't normal enough for her, so she fought tooth and nail to make my life as normal as possible.

Our relationship had become strained since my father's heritage had really manifested itself at eighteen. Being around me when I accidentally started a fire was too much for her. The accidents had stopped when I grew into my abilities, but I moved out anyway. Now we spoke on the phone more than we saw one another. It was easier that way for both of us.

I didn't hold any grudges against my mother. She'd done her best with what she had to work with. And now, so must I.

"So what's it going to take for me to get some answers out of you?" I went to stand near the kitchen, blocking Cinder's path when he tried to reach around me to the pantry.

"Not until you make your choice," he said with a shake of his head. "Since it's bothering you so much, I will tell you one thing."

He paused, and I wasn't sure if it was to be dramatic or if he was merely second guessing his decision. I waved a hand for him to spit it out.

Then I reached past him to the cupboard where the painkillers were. My head was absolutely banging. I poured two pills into my hand and filled a glass with water from the cooler. Thinking *Godspeed, little pills,* I swallowed them down and fixed Cinder with a stern stare.

"You could inadvertently draw others to him," Cinder said finally. "Especially while the dark is working so hard to recruit you.

They aren't supposed to know who he is. That is just one reason why you shouldn't become romantic with him."

"And what's the other one?" I dared to prod, my curiosity piqued.

Cinder stared at the checker pattern on the linoleum floor. He seemed to be wrestling with how much he could tell me without breaking his oath of secrecy. He finally stated, "If you join the light, helping with Rowen's protection was to be your first major assignment."

I was surprised. As sharp as my intuition was these days, I hadn't anticipated that one. I stared at Cinder, mouth agape, at a loss for words.

"Oh," I managed. "I see."

Chapter Five

I stared in stupid silence at Cinder while he politely gave me a few minutes to process what I'd heard. Many times I'd let my imagination run wild, concocting all sorts of wild tasks I might be entrusted with if I were to choose a side. Espionage, intel, assassination, all outrageous things straight out of the movies. I hadn't anticipated that guarding someone from my everyday life would be part of it.

"You're not bullshitting me, are you?" I said when the shock wore off.

Cinder frowned at my obscenity and shook his blond head. "Of course not. I would never do that. Not about something so serious."

"So is this a thing then? Assignments are directly related to our regular life? That seems like a good way to really fuck things up." I frowned, and the small act of knitting my eyebrows caused my head to hurt. Or perhaps it was the thinking. Yeah, that. The thinking really hurt.

"Quite the contrary, actually. Giving nephilim assignments that relate to their lives ensures a higher chance of success. It makes sense, really. You have to do what you can wherever you're at in life. Given that you are so fully immersed in the local music scene, as is Rowen, you're naturally our first pick to keep an eye on him."

"Ok." I held up a hand to stop him from continuing. "I've heard enough. My head can't possibly take another word about Rowen or assignments or anything else. It's a hangover day. I just want to crawl back into bed."

"What about training?" Cinder questioned, getting that pinched look that usually meant he was about to scold me. "You skipped out on our last session. You promised not to do that again."

I leaned heavily against the counter, trying to conjure up a valid excuse since hangover obviously wasn't going to cut it. Cinder stared at me, expecting an argument.

I'd grown to enjoy and appreciate our training sessions. Cinder said that learning to fight and to hone my skills was essential whether I joined a side or not. Even if I tried to live a human life, the creatures of the dark would hunt me down. I needed to know how to defend myself.

"I have a show at The Wicked Kiss tonight, and I really need to grab a nap first…" I began, trailing off as his stare became a glower. "Forget it. Just let me get changed. But you better take it easy on me today."

I retrieved Seth, who was attempting to climb over an especially large stuffed elephant that I'd won at last year's summer carnival, and set him back inside the safety of his terrarium. After ensuring he had clean water and some fresh lettuce, I grumbled my way into the bedroom to change into yoga pants and a tank top.

We did most of our training at the gym a few blocks away. They offered room rentals for those in need of a private exercise area.

By the time I dragged my gear to the Nova and then into the facility, I was ready to drop. Cinder, however, seemed especially pleased. He watched me drag the heavy bag of swords, throwing stars, and other various weaponry inside with a wry smile.

"Not feeling so good about the drunken shenanigans now, are you?" He smirked though it lacked true malice.

I pulled a water bottle from my bag and drank half in a few swallows. Dehydration was going to kick my ass. Stifling the urge to complain, I opened the bag and pulled out the two wooden practice swords.

"Can we use these?" I asked. "If we use real metal, you're probably going to cut my head off. I'm not feeling too energetic today."

Cinder picked up one of the blunt wooden swords. "You know, it is possible to have a good time without drinking yourself blind."

"Is it? Maybe I'll give that a try sometime." I cracked a smile, knowing he didn't find it funny. "Really, Cinder, why do you put up with me? How can I possibly be of use? I'm a flawed woman." I said it as if I were joking, but an element of truth colored my statement. I failed to understand how I could assist the light. I was very much equipped to live a life of darkness—not that I wanted to join them, of course. I was just so damn far from perfect.

"The greatest people in God's kingdom were flawed. There are no perfect people, Ember. The greater the flaws, the greater the potential for goodness." He tossed the other wooden sword to me, faster and harder than I'd anticipated. "Now, are you ready to begin?"

The sword slapped my fingertips before clattering to the floor. "Ouch. Son of a bitch."

Needless to say, it wasn't my best training day. Cinder didn't take it easy on me either. He came at me hard and fast, forcing me to block repeatedly, giving me no opportunity for an offensive move. If it had been real combat, I would have been dead several times over.

When he succeeded in knocking the sword from my hand and delivered the fake killing blow, I saw anger in his violet eyes. "I hope you're taking note of how the poisons you joyfully consumed last night have weakened you. It's not a simple matter to be brushed off. If you get yourself killed, it's going to reflect very badly on me."

We'd been through this before. For the most part Cinder was a lot of fun, a good friend and a funny guy. But that Cinder ended where the hard-ass Cinder began. And that side of him was not nearly as pleasant to be around.

Feeling grumpy and tired, I retorted, "But I'll be the one who's dead."

"Yes. You will be. Tell me, why exactly do you want that?"

"I don't."

He snapped, "Then grow up and take responsibility for yourself." Immediately his anger vanished, and he dropped the wooden sword. "I'm sorry, Ember. It worries me that you're so willing to compromise yourself. I don't mean to be a jerk. Let's call it quits for the day."

I felt bad. Guilt was an emotion saved for my mother and for Cinder. It wasn't because they forced it out of me in some unjust manner. It was because they were right, and I knew it. I was letting my guard down too much.

"Cinder, you know I don't mean to be such a pain in the ass," I started. "It's hard to meet the standard you think I should be at. I'm in my twenties. I just want to have a good time before I'm old and senile."

Arms crossed, head cocked studiously, Cinder regarded me with a strange calm. "I understand. Unfortunately, most nephilim don't live long enough to be old and senile. You might want to think about that." When I tried to speak, he stopped me. "I'll talk to you soon. Have fun tonight."

The sound of wings accompanied his departure. He left me standing there alone in the middle of the large training room. I stared at my reflection in the mirrored wall to my right. I hadn't meant to piss him off. With an exaggerated sigh and a few choice words to my reflection, I gathered up my things and dragged the heavy bag back to the car. Maybe I could squeeze in a nap before I had to get ready for the show tonight.

* * * *

A three-hour nap and another pot of coffee later, I was starting to feel like myself again. I stood in front of the full-length mirror in my bedroom, scrutinizing my outfit.

I wore a pair of ripped, skinny jeans and a sheer, black top that hung off one shoulder. My Victoria's Secret, leopard print bra was slightly visible through the mesh, fishnet-like material. A chunky, black onyx bracelet encircled my wrist, and a spiked collar adorned my neck.

After teasing up my hair until it was wild and untamable, I made the black liner framing my eyes even thicker before selecting a deep, wine-red lipstick. Not bad for being hungover. Nobody would even notice.

I ignored my ringing phone, knowing that Jett was calling to bitch at me for not being at the venue yet. I was running on the late side and rushing to get out the door. At least if I answered while I was dragging my guitar down to the car, I could say I was on my way without lying.

The drive to The Wicked Kiss didn't take all that long. Once I crossed the river, it was just a few minutes to the venue. Traffic was busy but manageable. I parked close to the staff door on the side of the building where the other girls were unloading our amps from the back of Tash's mom's minivan.

The Wicked Kiss wasn't your typical bar. In fact, it was so far from typical that even we needed some time to get used to playing there. It was a vampire bar, which is exactly what it sounds like, a place for vampires to feed from willing victims, and there were a hell of a lot of willing victims.

The place had given me the creeps right from the start, but Jett assured us it was worth it to have a regular, paying gig. We'd become somewhat of a featured act at The Wicked Kiss due to our willingness to play surrounded by vampires. The club owner was a nice, if a little shady, vampire-werewolf hybrid who paid us well, which was what really mattered. So far, it had been good for us.

I pulled my guitar case from the backseat of the Nova and turned to go inside. When I sensed movement beside me, I turned to find a demon standing there expectantly. He was a tall, imposing figure who brought with him the stink of sulfur.

"I really don't have time for this right now," I said to Koda, trying to muscle by him with my guitar case.

The demon blocked my path, hands up to stop me should I try to resist. His blood-red eyes were like deep, gaping chasms. "You're always in such a rush. Would it really hurt you to take a few minutes to chat with an old pal?"

Koda smiled as if we were friends when in fact he was nothing more than a distraction. His entire job description, as far as I was concerned, was to be a distraction. Really, it was to persuade me to join the dark. He'd come into my life around the time Cinder had. Where Cinder tried to guide and strengthen me, Koda sought to mislead and weaken me. A manipulative demon brimming with evil, Koda had made my life hell for a time, until Cinder stepped in at my request. Now Koda was limited, able to do only so much to get inside my head. It was very much like having the Freudian angel and demon on each shoulder, each of them fighting to be heard over the other.

"Koda, please. I'm late. And I'm really not in the mood to humor you today." I sidestepped around him, but he stepped to block me. Frustrated, I counted to ten since losing it and getting mad would only encourage him.

"I just wanted to pop by, to touch base with you. It's been a while since we've spoken." He spoke in a friendly lilt, the kind of tone reserved for acquaintances when you bump into them unexpectedly.

"I don't want to talk to you."

"Aww, don't be like that. We used to be friends."

I gawked at him. Demons didn't handle rejection well. I'd discovered that over the years. Their pride just couldn't take it. "We were never friends. I am not your friend. I am your job."

Koda had done a good job of convincing me that maybe he wasn't such a bad guy after all. Young and stupid, I'd fallen for his tricks, his lies and half-truths as they were. Koda had a way of making the most horrific things seem perfectly acceptable. Cinder had helped me to see through his act, but having the demon constantly gunning for me was difficult. Depressing. *And Cinder wonders why I drink.*

"Job? You are much more than that to me. I could love you if you'd let me."

I snorted. This was his latest thing, trying to convince me that he loved me and that, if only I joined the dark, then we could be together. Crappily ever after.

"Oh, my God, Koda that is fucking pathetic." I enjoyed throwing the big G word around when Koda was near. Occasionally I could make him wince. "I'm not a starry-eyed fourteen year old who's going to fall for that shit. It just makes you look like an idiot."

Koda drew himself to his full height and glared down at me. "Well, I must say, you seem to be more suited to our side every time we speak. You've got a nasty mouth on you, girl." He smoothed back his short, black hair before straightening the sleeves of his long jacket. Fussing with his appearance was one of his tells. It meant he was digging for something, trying to find a way to keep me talking.

"You're in my way," I said, glaring up at him. At well over six feet, he towered over me. It had once frightened me. Koda still scared me, but I'd learned how to deal with him over the years.

"Spike," he said my name carefully, as if it were fragile. He liked to make a point of using the name that Cinder refused to use, as if that would win him some points with me. "You can't avoid me forever."

"I'm aware." I readjusted the guitar case on my shoulder. "This thing is getting heavy. So move it or lose it."

Losing his phony, friendly tone, he warned, "You don't want to make the dark your enemy."

"I've got a show to play right now, but I'll try to keep that in mind. Feel free to come inside and enjoy the tunes if you're so inclined. And if not, have a nice night." I smiled as I pushed by him. This time he let me go.

Demons didn't often enter The Wicked Kiss. When I'd asked, Cinder had told me that was because of the club's owner. Something about her made her different from others like her. She had a link to the light that unsettled demons. And that was just fine with me.

Jett was all worked up by the time I joined her. "Where the hell have you been?" she demanded, shaking a fist at me. The silver bangles stacked on her wrist jangled threateningly.

"I got held up. Koda." I didn't have to say anything else. That name was enough.

"Oh, well I hope you told him to fuck off."

"Yep. Like I always do."

We got busy dragging our gear on stage. The place was starting to fill up. The Wicked Kiss had changed over the years, but the crowd was always busy and loud, just the way we liked it.

We were well received. Once we took the stage, the crowd gravitated closer, filling the dance floor in front of us. People sang along, which was a thrill that couldn't be matched by anything else. Watching the lyrics Jett and I had written on the lips of both humans and vampires was enough to make me a little giddy.

It was no surprise when a fight broke out. I couldn't recall a single night we'd been here without some kind of commotion. Two vampires started brawling over a human trophy. Or perhaps there was more to it.

Jett shouted at the crowd, drawing their distracted attention back to her. On her knees, with her purple hair whipping about, she soon had more eyes upon her than on the fight.

Halfway through our set, our friend, a Goth kid named Gabriel, caught my eye. I'd never seen him here before. In fact, as far as I knew, he was adamant about staying as far away from this place as possible. So what the hell was up?

My fingers flew over the frets of my guitar, the riff so deeply ingrained in me that I could have played it in my sleep. My gaze stayed on Gabriel though. Something was up with him. Something was... different.

I wasn't close enough to get a read off him. Far from average, he always felt different than the other humans. He'd been born with abilities that some would imagine a gift though he considered his gift a curse. Not only was he magically inclined, he was precognitive as well. He could see the future of those he touched.

With long, black hair and dark eyes, Gabriel was tall and thin, a little on the lanky side. He was a hottie though. Jett had hooked up with him once, even though I'd given her a hard time about their five-year age difference.

"He's nineteen," she'd said. "Totally legal. Besides I think it takes more than a five-year difference to make me a cougar."

"Definitely the wrong animal," I'd replied.

They had never been more than a drunken hook up though, as far as I knew. Shooting a glance at Jett, she too was watching Gabriel. For a split-second, her expression held more alarm than curiosity. Then it was gone as she threw herself back into her performance.

My curiosity was piqued. By the time we finished our set and exited the stage, I was eager to speak with him.

Jett grabbed my arm before I could wade into the crowd to find him. "Spike, wait. Did you see Gabriel?"

"Yeah, I was going to go find him. He never comes in here."

"That's because he was never a vampire before," she said, her eyes dangerously close to becoming wolf. She was all fired up and anxious.

I nodded slowly. "So that's what's different."

"Better be careful. Don't let him get too close. You know, just in case. I'm going to give the others a heads up."

Tash and Rubi had taken the news about the many creatures of our city surprisingly well. It had never been an option to hide our true natures from them. Those girls were like sisters to Jett and me. Though Jett and I couldn't share everything with them, Tash and Rubi needed to know what kind of world they were walking in.

When Jett and I had told her everything, Rubi had said, "Well, that explains everything. I always knew there was something fucked up about this city. No wonder they call it Deadmonton."

I navigated my way through the crowd, shaking my head at more than one vampire who approached me with a hungry grin. Thankfully most of them weren't total assholes about it, although on occasion they would get out of hand. Security at The Wicked Kiss was serious though, and they quickly dealt with those who didn't want to play by the house rules.

I spied Gabriel speaking with the club owner near the back exit that led into the private area where vampires took their snacks. I had never been back there and fully intended to keep it that way.

I lingered near the bar where he could see me, waiting for a chance to talk to him. Whatever they were talking about, it didn't seem to make him very happy. When he broke away from her, he was muttering beneath his breath.

"Hey," I stepped out in front of him, forcing him to see me. "Where've you been? Or is the answer to that question obvious?"

Gabriel jerked to a halt. He seemed nervous, glancing about as if expecting someone to jump at him. "Spike, hey. Sorry I missed the show last night. I was busy."

"Busy drinking blood?" I asked, unafraid to get to the point. "Is this why you've been so weird lately?"

"It's part of it." He stood at a distance, making it hard to hear him.

I noticed he was wearing leather gloves, something he did only when the precognitive stuff was driving him crazy. I wondered how vampirism affected that.

"So, what happened?" I asked.

I wasn't afraid of Gabriel, but I was afraid of what he was. Up close I easily detected that inhuman vibe he now had. He was also insanely beautiful, the way most vampires were, with smooth, pale skin and eyes that seemed to glow with wretched hunger.

As I looked at him, I began to feel strange. I wanted to climb all over him, just to touch him and maybe even to bleed for him. It was disorienting and entirely fucked up. Some vampires had the kind of allure that would turn the most uptight of prudes into wanton sex slaves. Just one of many reasons to stay the hell away from vampires.

"It's a long story. Let's just say demons always get what they want. So make sure they never have a reason to want anything from you." His dark eyes scanned my face before dropping to my neck, seeking my pulse, which lay hidden beneath my spiked collar.

"Um, do you remember my history? They already want me. So why not tell me the truth? You used to share this shit with me." There had been a time when Gabriel confided in me about the demon he'd gotten himself involved with, but that had come to a stop. Now I saw why. He was in too deep.

"It's too late for me, Spike. Ok? That's all I can tell you. A demon wanted this for me. He wanted me to be hard to kill with a power boost. So here I am, with the blood of the most powerful vampire in the city running through my veins. You know how demons operate. I didn't stand a fucking chance." There was no anguish in his voice. He tossed his long hair out of his face and tried to stare anywhere but at my neck.

"Who is this demon, Gabriel? If you tell me his name, maybe I can help you. I could talk to Cinder—"

"No!" The word exploded out. "You have enough demon problems of your own. I can handle this." He glanced over my shoulder, and I followed his gaze. Jett was weaving her way through the crowd toward us. "I've gotta go."

"Wait." I reached to grab his arm. When he jerked out of reach, his eyes flashed with such monstrosity that I recoiled.

"I don't want to talk to you guys right now," he said. "It's not a good time for me if you catch my drift. I don't want to hurt you. I'll call you, ok?"

"But, but..." I fumbled for words as he tried to make a quick getaway. "I wanted to ask you about Arrow Lynch. You know him, right?"

Gabriel paused a few feet away and glanced back long enough to say, "Stay away from Arrow. In fact, stay away from the dark altogether. I mean it, Spike. Do yourself a favor. Choose the light."

Then he was gone, a black blur moving through the busy nightclub. I stared after him, feeling cold inside.

Chapter Six

"I can't believe he just took off like that. I mean, I know I never called him after our fling, but I didn't think he really expected me to. What's his fucking deal?"

I lay on the couch in our jam space, listening to Jett rant. Once she got into the booze stash in the fridge, she'd gotten all worked up over Gabriel's hasty disappearing act.

"His fucking deal, Jett, is that he's a vampire. A fucking vampire." Tash's voice was shrill, echoing in our rented space. "Cut the guy some slack. You didn't want him anyway."

Jett pouted, twisting a lock of purple hair around a finger. "I know. But I wanted him to want me." Because Jett was her own biggest fan, she launched into an acapella rendition of Cheap Trick's `I Want You To Want Me'.

I rolled my eyes and dragged on a cigarette. It was only my third of the day because I was trying to quit. Cinder was right. I needed to take things more seriously.

After our show at The Wicked Kiss, we'd promptly headed over to the jam space to practice. We never stayed long after a show at the vampire bar. It just wasn't our scene.

"Oh, I'm sure he does want you," I said, remembering the way Gabriel had ogled my neck like I was food. "But I'm pretty sure it's a lot more than a good fuck he's after now."

"I can't even believe that happened to him." Tash shook her head. "It's so sad."

It certainly was. Though considering that he was involved with a demon, it was nothing short of a miracle that it hadn't been worse. I'd seen what demons could do to a person. Hell, I had my very own demon trying to do it to me.

I thought about Arrow and his friendship with Rowen. To Rowen it was a genuine thing, two guys bonding over whatever the hell guys bond over: sex, beer, video games, music. But to Arrow hanging with Rowen was a job, getting inside Rowen's head to ensnare him for the dark. It made me feel ill to think about.

"It's fucked up is what it is. Good ol' Deadmonton. City of evil." Jett tapped a finger against her mike. The sound was loud through the amps.

Rubi twirled a drumstick between her fingers. "Hey, I love this city. You two talk so much shit about it, but for us regular folk, it's still a great place. And there's no way this stuff only goes on here. It's gotta be world wide."

"Muggle," Jett muttered.

Rubi smirked. "Bitch."

After listening to the two of them trade insults until it was clear they had no intention of stopping, I rolled off the couch and picked up my guitar. To show off a little and to shut them up, I cranked up the volume and played the opening riff to 'Sweet Child O' Mine'.

The bass line was next, and Tash came in right on time. Smoke between my lips and black hair hanging in my face, I channeled my inner Slash. The notes danced out of my fingertips as I played one of my favorite songs by one of the greatest rock bands of all time. I was in my element.

Rubi came in with the steady beat of drums, and everything clicked. Music was a deeply ingrained part of me. Would I have to give it up if I joined Cinder and the light? God, I hoped not. When I played, I became the music. And it felt like a gift.

A goofy smile lit Jett's face. She watched us like a proud mother, nodding her head in time to the music. She opened her mouth to sing, but then the door opened.

Arrow stood in the doorway. The music stumbled to a stop as we all took notice of him. I blinked a few times, unable to believe my eyes. What in the ever-loving crap was he doing here?

Jett recovered from the surprise interruption first. "What the fuck are you doing here? You wouldn't happen to be stalking us, would you?"

Her dark eyes became wolf, and I half expected her to bare fangs at him. She didn't. The predatory stare she fixed on Arrow brought a wan smile to his face.

With a half-assed shrug he said, "Sorry. I knocked, but you guys couldn't hear me. It's no big secret that you jam here. My buddy's band jams at the other end of the lot. I came by, saw the cars outside, and thought I'd say hello."

Jett and I exchanged a look. She was the only one who knew what Arrow was. Keeping it from Tash and Rubi had been for their own safety. Knowing of the nephilim was one thing but knowing who they were could get you killed.

"Bullshit," I said, eyeing him with suspicion.

He turned his hazel eyes on me, and they sparkled with mischief. "Ok, it's bullshit. I came to talk to you. But you could humor me, offer me a drink or something." He pointed at the beer in Jett's hand.

"Get out." My tone was harsh with sudden, thinly veiled vehemence. Arrow was a ballsy piece of shit, that was for sure. I despised him, and I barely knew him.

Unfazed by my rude demand, Arrow strode inside and took the seat on the couch I'd just vacated. The chains hanging from his jeans clinked as he sat. Pulling a pack of smokes from a back pocket, he pulled one out, acting surprised when a small bag of white powder fell out with it. Holding the bag up, he shook it as if it were filled with the secrets of the universe. To some people, perhaps it was.

Sticking the cigarette between his lips, he asked, "Anyone interested? I always give free samples to first time buyers."

I glanced at the other girls, finding they all wore similar expressions of distaste. A few years back, when the band had first formed, we'd gone through a rough time that included some heavy drug use that went far beyond the mellow buzz of marijuana. It had left us all feeling less than satisfied with ourselves. Knowing we were better than that, we'd sworn off the hard stuff.

"Not interested," I answered for all of us. "Not today. Not ever."

Arrow looked long and hard at me. He stared so long without saying anything that the tension in the room grew tangibly thick.

It came as no shock that Arrow was peddling hard street drugs. It seemed to be the type of thing his kind would do. He held the bag up a moment longer before stuffing it back into his smoke pack.

"Ok then," he said, his gaze still upon me. "The offer always stands if you change your mind."

"So, I guess you'll just be on your way now." Jett pointed with the mike at the open door.

Arrow rose, but he didn't leave. Instead, he helped himself to a beer from our fridge. I stared at him, aghast. This little voice inside me cried out that he was the enemy. It became undeniably clear in that moment that, should I choose to live as a human, Arrow and others like him would still be creeping around, planting seeds of addiction and suffering and God only knew what else. That wouldn't change.

"Dude, who the fuck do you think you are?" Jett was getting mad now. She spoke around a set of fangs that still looked as menacing as they had the first time I saw them.

Arrow popped the cap off the beer and smirked. "I'm pretty sure you know exactly who I am."

Rubi and Tash watched Jett with trepidation. Her reaction to Arrow was telling, making it obvious that there was more to him than met the eye. Keeping his attention off them was important.

"You said you wanted to talk to me?" I took off my guitar and placed it in a stand. "Then let's talk. Outside."

I stood beside the open door. Arrow, enjoying the awkward tension he was causing, took his time ambling out. He paused to glance back at the girls with a slimy smile before disappearing outside.

Jett dropped her mike. "You are not going out there alone with him."

I gave her a look, or at least I tried to. She was being too obvious. "It's cool. He's just a drug dealing douchebag. I'll be right back."

I followed Arrow out and closed the door behind me before Jett could argue. I heard Rubi say, "What the fuck was that all about?"

I held the doorknob until I was sure Jett wasn't about to burst out behind me in a flurry of fangs and claws. When she didn't, I followed Arrow into the parking lot.

Before he could speak, I said, "Don't ever come here again. In fact, don't ever come near me at all."

"Big words from the undecided angel girl." He dragged on his cigarette and regarded me with both amusement and hostility. "You don't get to make the rules, Spike. Haven't you figured that part out yet?"

"Why?" I asked, having no retort to that. "Why are you here? What do you want?"

Arrow's black hair spilled out from beneath the knit cap that hung off the back of his head. A smudge of eyeliner beneath his eyes gave him a haunted appearance. He was heavily tattooed, his arms a mass of color one would have to study closely to pick apart. A winding vine with a black rose wound its way from beneath his t-shirt up the side of his neck.

He caught me looking at it. "That one is my newest. Turned out pretty good, huh? Nice wings by the way. I bet that took a long time. You could have real wings, you know. One day."

"Yes. I know." I spoke through clenched teeth. "I'm undecided not some ignorant newbie. So if you came to fuck with my head, let me save you some time. Don't bother. I'm on to you." Feeling self-conscious in my sheer top that revealed the wings spanning my back, I angled my body so that he couldn't see even a smidge of them.

"Are you?" He breathed the words, low and menacing, exhaling smoke as he did so. He leaned in close so I could smell the musky scent of his cologne mingled with beer. "If you want to get all over me, baby, there's no resistance here."

I frowned and somehow managed to suppress a shudder. In a cool, calm tone, I said, "Everything about you repulses me."

"You don't know everything about me. Be careful what you say. You may have to eat those words." He laughed then, revealing a tongue stud, his only visible piercing.

"You're dark. That's all I need to know." I crossed my arms so they weren't hanging awkwardly at my sides. I wasn't sure what to do with myself. All I knew was that I wasn't ready to take him on. Cinder's warnings echoed in my head. I was so inexperienced.

"Does that mean you've made your choice?" Arrow studied me with an intensity that made my skin crawl. When I didn't answer, his gaze dropped, taking in all of me. "Women are rare among our kind. It would be a damn shame to lose a fox like you to the light."

"Ew, you're kidding, right?" I sneered. "Me and you? It's never gonna happen, dude."

Standing there while he ogled me wasn't easy. I knew he was just trying to rattle me. Either that or he was a total pervy dick, or maybe both. But I stared in stony silence at him while he looked me over like a used car he was thinking about buying.

"Do you have any idea how amazing a night together would be? Fucking a nephilim is a trip for a human. Ever wonder what it is about us that gets them so hot?" Arrow puffed on his cigarette, blowing a cloud of smoke up toward the sky that stretched black above us.

His sleazy nature did nothing to incite my interest. It did however, bring to mind my last boyfriend's claim that sex with me was so intense that it was like an out of body experience. He'd described it like a drug trip. I had never been with another nephilim. Judging by the lecherous way Arrow was eyeing me, neither had he.

"I am not fucking you," I said, unable to keep the disgust from my tone. Was this going to be a thing? Would male nephilim be constantly seeking me out for a good time? Fuck that shit.

"Because you're into Rowen," he said with a knowing head bob.

I had no idea what Arrow knew about Rowen. If this was some ploy to get me to spill what I knew, then the joke was on Arrow because I didn't really know shit.

"I barely know Rowen. And I sure as hell don't know you, and I don't really want to." A tingle started in my palms, so I clenched my hands into fists.

"Might as well get used to it. We're part of the same world. You're going to get to know me whether you like it or not." Arrow cocked his head to one side and grinned. "Besides, I'm not such a bad guy. Really. You'll see."

A sinking sensation settled in my stomach. I had a horrible feeling that he was right, that this wasn't the last I'd be seeing of Arrow.

"Why did you really come here?" I demanded. "Don't tell me it was just to see if you could bang me. You could've tried that at The Spirit Room."

He wasn't fooling me. I was starting to suspect that he'd been sent to talk to me, or at least, sent to scope me out and gather some dirt. Whatever it was, I didn't like it. Wasn't Koda enough? Did the dark really have to send Arrow of all people?

"I just wanted to chat with you. Remind you that you have options that you need to consider carefully." He reached out to run a finger along my side, around to my lower back, over the edge of a tattooed feather.

Adrenaline pounded through my veins, and I jumped back out of reach. A streak of fire shot through the sky overhead. A moment later sparks began to rain down around us. Over the years I'd had a lot of practice controlling my fire, but nothing could set it off like an emotional outburst. Like most times I'd unintentionally caused something to happen, I felt both embarrassed and afraid.

Arrow glanced up at the falling fire before dropping his smoke and squishing it with a Converse-clad foot. "So the girl can make fire," he commented casually. "You and I would make a great team. Just wait until you see what I can do."

"You're assuming I'll choose a side," I countered, clenching my fists tight. "Maybe I'll just say fuck the whole thing and play human for the rest of my life."

Arrow laughed bitterly, and something like anger flashed in his eyes. Then he was his sardonic self again. "You can try, but you'll be a sitting duck, just waiting to be picked off. Might as well join a side and have a fighting chance."

"You've made your choice." I shivered from the chill of the fall night or perhaps from my growing unease. "I'll make mine. Nothing you say or do is going to sway my decision."

He held up a hand in surrender. In the other hand he held the beer he'd swiped. "Not here to sway. Just to invite."

"Yeah, well you can take your invitation and shove it up your ass." Goosebumps prickled on my arms. I rubbed them briskly and squinted up into the night sky. I should've set Arrow on fire instead.

"Up the ass, huh? I'll keep that in mind." Arrow finished the beer and tossed the empty bottle at the large garbage bin near the edge of the parking lot. It smashed against the open lid.

My temper was normally relatively stable. It took a lot to really piss me off. Something about Arrow, however, threw my mental calm out the window. Just looking at his smug face made me livid.

The tingle in my palms returned, growing quickly into an itch. Though I feared starting one hell of a fire, I wanted to drive Arrow off. He watched with something that looked a little like gleeful anticipation, like he wanted me to take a shot at him.

Neither of us got the chance to find out what kind of damage I could do, if any at all. The air moved unnaturally with the telltale current of either an angel or demon. We were no longer alone.

My heart tripped in an unsteady beat as I feared the worst. If Arrow hadn't come alone, I was screwed. But he appeared just as wary as I was at the sensation.

"Your guardian came to chase me off," Arrow said, glancing about expectantly, waiting for our unseen visitor to appear. "Must be nice to have a white lighter come riding to your rescue."

When Cinder appeared next to me, I was relieved at first but then mortified. He never stood in front of me nor behind, instead showing that he regarded me as an equal by standing beside me. Still, the damage was done. His arrival effectively ended the conversation with Arrow while making it seem like I couldn't handle things on my own.

Arrow was already stalking across the parking lot to the metallic-black BMW parked next to Jett's convertible. Selling drugs was apparently quite the moneymaker for him.

He swung the door open and paused long enough to say, "See ya on Saturday, Spike."

"What's on Saturday?" Cinder asked, his voice low and his gaze fixed on the black car as it sped out of the parking lot with a squeal of tires.

I watched the taillights of Arrow's car until they could no longer be seen. "Round two of the Battle of the Bands at The Spirit Room."

"You shouldn't go," Cinder stated, short, clipped, and matter of fact.

"Oh, I'm going. We have a real chance to win this thing. There's no way I'm going to cower at home and let Arrow have it."

"I don't trust him. He's up to something."

I snapped, "No shit, Sherlock. What was your first clue?" At Cinder's wide-eyed expression, I added, "I'm sorry. You don't deserve that. I'm just pissed off and taking it out on the wrong person. But I am playing that show. You can't stop me."

Cinder was silent for so long that I began to grow uneasy. His demeanor was so aggressive that he looked more street thug than Abercrombie model.

"No," he finally said. "I can't stop you. I don't even want to. I want only to keep you safe as long as it's within my power to do so."

"It isn't anymore though, is it?" Years ago, when I first discovered what I was, the moment of choice had seemed so far off. It had been easy to shove it aside, promising myself I'd think about it later. The luxury of later was an illusion.

Cinder sighed, a deep, tired sound. It worried me. He asked, "We train tomorrow?"

"Yes. I'll be there. I promise."

The door opened, and Jett poked her head out. The fierce expression on her face changed to one of subdued calm at the sight of Cinder. She nodded and closed the door.

When I looked back to Cinder, he was gone. I stood out there, alone in the dimly lit parking lot, shivering. The countdown was on.

Chapter Seven

The week passed quickly. Too quickly. Between evening jam sessions with the girls and squeezing in work and training with Cinder during the day, I kept busy. As a freelance graphic designer, I could pay my bills and set my own schedule. It was a good job. It kept me busy. I enjoyed the art though it didn't inspire the passion I felt with music. Unfortunately, busy made the time fly by.

When I woke up on Saturday morning, my stomach was a mess of butterflies that even Cinder's delicious strawberry and whipped cream waffles couldn't settle. I ignored Jett's repeated demands that we get together for one more jam before our set that evening. Instead I paced the length of my small apartment, pausing to talk to Seth only to hear the sound of a human voice.

Cinder had left after breakfast but not without making me promise not to let Arrow, or anyone dark, get me alone. Knowing we would have to share a dressing room with the other bands, I opted to get ready at home. The thought of being in that small dressing area with Rowen and Arrow was suffocating.

As I rolled a thigh-high, fishnet stocking up my leg, I replayed the conversation with Arrow outside the jam space in my mind. He was up to something, and I suspected it had to do with more than merely screwing another nephilim. My instincts had been right about him. As soon as I saw him, I had known he was trouble. The conceited dick had tried to add me on Facebook. I had promptly denied the request.

Feeling feminine, I chose a fluffy, black, tulle tutu that ended at the top of my stockings. A black bustier gave me more cleavage than I really had, a handy little illusion. My only accessory was an angel wing pendant made of amethyst. It had been a gift from my mother.

I curled my hair, finding comfort in the slow, meticulous repetition of the act. When my eyes were lined with thick liner and silver shadow and my lips painted as red as possible, I was ready. And then the nerves struck hard.

Deep, calming breaths didn't do a damn thing. So I gathered my things, stuck an unlit cigarette between my lips, and headed out the door to meet my cab. It was almost show time.

Smoking and talking, people mingled outside The Spirit Room when I arrived. The strains of a guitar being tuned made its way out onto the street as the first band prepared to play. I peered intently at the leather-clad rockers who arrived in droves to see the four bands face off. One of which wouldn't be going to next week's semi-finals, but it wouldn't be Crimson Sin getting the boot. I refused to believe otherwise.

The sound of my name drew my attention to a couple of young guys standing near the door. One of them held a Crimson Sin CD out with a hopeful expression. I didn't even know people bought our CDs anymore now that our music was online.

"Sorry to bother you, Spike. I was hoping you'd sign this for me."

He even had a Sharpie ready. People didn't ask for my autograph often. How could I possibly refuse? It was always humbling to have someone approach and show an interest in our music.

"It's no bother at all." With a wink, I took the marker and scrawled my name on the cover jacket. I saw that Jett had already done the same. "If you want to grab the other girls for an autograph, don't hesitate. It's cool. We love to hear from you guys."

"Wicked, thanks. You guys kick ass. If you don't win this, it will be fucking robbery."

I smiled to myself, watching them walk away. Funny how something so simple and brief could make my whole night brighter. It pumped me up, and suddenly I was impatient and eager to be on stage.

The first band was doing sound check. The ladies running the beer tubs and handing out shooters were already busy. People kept streaming into the building. Perfect.

Arrow was just leaving the dressing room when I entered. He was wearing a Nine Inch Nails t-shirt and a sneer to go with it. I smirked but didn't waste a breath on him.

The girls sat chatting with one of the Sacred Stone guys. I was annoyed with the small space that all four bands were expected to share, but of course the girls wanted to hang there.

"I hate this fucking dressing room." I couldn't resist a peek in the mirror though I'd just done my makeup less than an hour ago. "I already feel like you're all sucking up the air."

Tash laughed and swigged from a beer. "Yeah it's definitely not for the claustrophobic."

"Are you guys coming to the party at Arrow's after?" This from Jett, who rolled a joint on the small coffee table in front of the couch.

"Yes," Rubi spoke quickly, looking at Tash as if expecting an argument. "We are. Right, girls?"

Tash shrugged her agreement. When I didn't respond, they all looked to me.

"Really?" I asked. "A party at Arrow's? But he's such a dick."

"Right. So let's go to his place and drink his beer." Jett was flippant, like it just made sense.

A party at Arrow's might not be such a bad idea. There would be enough people there to avoid having him catch me alone. And Rowen would be there. Now *his* Facebook friend request I *had* accepted. A chance to speak with him again would be nice.

"Sure, whatever," I said with a nod. "I'm up for an after party."

"Ok, bitches. I'm going to go start drinking. You coming?" Jett waited for a response.

I set my guitar down in the corner next to Tash's bass. We still had to unload our amps from her van, but there was always time for a drink first. "Right behind you."

"We'll meet you down there," Rubi said to our retreating forms though her gaze was on the Sacred Stone drummer.

Jett started the night off with a round of shots, her usual. We each had two Alabama Slammers, a yummy shot that left me feeling warm and tingly. We moved through the bar, mingling with friends and acquaintances.

The emcee stepped up to the mike to announce the first band, and the crowd cheered.

"Isn't that your boy over there?" Jett nudged me and pointed through the mass of people.

Rowen sat at a table with the rest of his band mates. I allowed myself a moment to enjoy the view. His mohawk was perfect; that long piece falling in his eyes was so damn sexy. Then my gaze settled on the perky blonde chatting him up, and my bubble popped.

Disappointed, I said, "Looks like he's busy." Maybe it was for the best. I wasn't supposed to be interested in him anyway.

"Screw that. They're just talking. You can go talk to him too." Jett smiled, her glossy lips curving mischievously. "Tequila him."

I eyed Rowen thoughtfully and chuckled. "Oh, Jett, that's so bad."

"And it'll work like a charm. Go on. Work it, bitch." She gave me a shove toward the bar. It was all the encouragement I needed.

As I waited in line at the bar, I glanced back at Rowen again. He was shaking his head at the blonde, who didn't appear to be too steady on her feet. She reached for his arm, but he shook her off, frowning in annoyance. Perhaps he wasn't busy after all. Watching them interact I became certain that she was an ex.

I ordered two tequila shots, grabbed two slices of lime and a saltshaker, and made my way toward the Molly's Chamber table. My pulse sped up as I neared. Ignoring Arrow was going to be difficult, but I wasn't interested in him, which was about to become very clear.

I sidled up to Rowen, coming up on his other side, opposite the nagging ex-girlfriend. I nodded a quick hello to his friends, refusing to meet Arrow's eyes.

"Dude, you're totally missing out on tequila shots." Holding a shot glass out to him, I turned a phony smile on the girl clinging to his arm.

"Hey, Spike." Rowen brightened at my arrival. He glanced at the drinks I held. "Thanks but I don't really drink tequila."

Without missing a beat, I tilted my head and sprinkled salt on the side of my exposed neck. I shot Rowen a daring look. "You do now."

I sensed his intrigue, which turned to discomfort, and took joy in knowing it was a game and that he would play. The blonde gaped at me. Rowen glanced between the two of us before he took the shot glass and stood up, leaning in to lick the salt from my neck.

The warmth and heat of his tongue on my sensitive flesh caused me to quiver. Did he feel it? I hoped so. Rowen lingered for just a moment, his tongue sweeping across my skin a second time.

That's when I met Arrow's watchful gaze. I raised a brow and smirked. He stared, his expression unreadable.

Rowen tossed back the shot and accepted the lime I offered. He sucked it into his mouth, and my gaze dropped to his lips. Damn I wanted to kiss him. My face felt flushed, and I knew my cheeks were pink. The sensation of his mouth on my neck had lit a fire inside me.

The blonde made a noise of disgust before spinning on a heel and drunkenly storming off.

I asked, "Ex-girlfriend?"

"Was it that obvious?"

"Yeah. Most guys don't look like they're in that much pain when talking to a chick in a skirt that short."

Rowen ran a hand over his hair and grinned. A faint blush colored his cheeks. "Thanks for the save. And the shot."

"Anytime." Heat flooded me, leaving me slightly breathless. The fire he'd started could only be extinguished one way. Our moment had been too brief, and I craved more.

Rowen offered me his seat and swiped another for himself from the next table. I settled in with the Molly's Chamber boys, beaming brightly when I caught Arrow scowling in my direction.

For the next hour I sat there, talking and joking, getting to know Rowen. We exchanged our craziest show stories and shared our experiences in the rock scene so far. When we compared our favorite bands, we learned that we had both been raised on '70s rock like Black Sabbath and KISS.

Sam, seated on my other side, joined in our conversation, but due to the noise Arrow and Greyson talked among themselves. For the most part Arrow did a good job pretending there was no reason for tension between us. Just twice I caught him looking at me with thinly veiled contempt.

The first band wrapped up their set, my cue to leave. "Thanks for the seat," I said, gesturing to my chair as I stood, smoothing my skirt into place. "We're up next so I'm out of here."

Rowen stopped me with a hand on mine. His palm was warm, kick starting my libido. "You're coming to the party after, right?" He turned his hopeful amber eyes on me.

I melted under that gaze. I could feel Arrow's sudden interest as he awaited my response. Resisting the urge to laugh in his stupid face, I said, "I'll be there."

"Break a leg," Rowen added as I turned to go.

"Break both legs," Arrow muttered loud enough to be heard over the noise. Then he laughed as if it had been a joke.

I laughed it off, which wasn't easy. If I fell off the stage and broke my damn legs or something equally screwed up, I'd know who cursed me. And he would pay.

I fetched my guitar from upstairs before rushing outside to help the girls unload the van. We hauled our stuff on stage and plugged in. As usual Jett was off schmoozing and drinking while we did the work. The stage lights were dim, leaving us in shadows as we did a sound check.

I could feel the weight of a gaze upon me, but this time I knew it was Arrow. Nothing he could say or do was going to bring me down from this high. The rush of Rowen's gaze and the memory of his tongue on my skin elevated me to a level of giddy that no drug could replicate.

I kept reminding myself that I wasn't interested in dating. Relationships were for suckers, and I was done being a sucker.

By the time Jett joined us, she was tipsy and overflowing with enough excited energy to keep us all going. She rambled on about the hottie guitarist from Sacred Stone who chatted her up while I was with Rowen. She used the word delicious so many times, I had to laugh.

Turning one of the tuning pegs on my guitar until it was just right, I said, "I can't tell if you want to fuck him or eat him."

Jett flashed a secretive smile. "I haven't decided yet."

"It's about time you found yourself a new toy." And it was. Jett had been steering clear of guys since her breakup, which made her a nagging pain in the ass when any of the rest of us showed interest in a guy, especially poor Tash.

"True enough." Jett shrugged and checked that her mike was hooked up. "He's a fox. He'll make a good way to kill some time. I think it'll be fun."

"What if they kick our ass? Will you still fuck him then?"

"If they win... then I might have to eat him."

We shared a laugh.

Moments later the emcee announced us. The crowd settled down until the moment we began to play. Then they erupted in shouts and cheers so loud I thought they might blow the roof off the place.

The notes poured out of my fingers, coming from deep within me, projected out through my guitar, becoming something to be shared with the rowdy audience. I forgot all about Arrow and even Rowen. In that moment I was caught up in something greater. And it was amazing.

* * * *

Arrow's house wasn't as big as I'd anticipated. It wasn't small either though. A two-level house in a nice neighborhood with a finished basement, it seemed like more of a family home than a bachelor pad... until we got inside.

The heavy masculine aroma was instant and strong. The place wasn't a mess, but it did border on untidy. It was bare of any real sense of décor. The mismatched furniture appeared comfortable at least. Posters adorned the walls, everything from The Beatles to a Playboy Playmate.

The lively sound of celebration filled Arrow's house. After another night of fighting for a dream, three bands were going to the semi-finals: Molly's Chamber, Sacred Stone, and Crimson Sin. I could have fainted with relief when the emcee called our name.

The drugs and alcohol flowed freely, accompanied by a steady stream of live music. People littered the house from top to bottom. The majority congregated in the basement, which Arrow had turned into a jam space.

On our way down the stairs to join in on the music, we passed Rowen on his way up with an armful of empty bottles and cans. He gestured with a head tilt for me to join him, so I promptly abandoned the girls.

I followed him into the kitchen where he opened a back door and tossed the empties into a large, plastic bin.

Teasing, I asked, "Do you usually clean up while the party is still going on? Seems like an exercise in futility."

He laughed, a soothing sound that made me want to hear more. "Well, you're not wrong there. But if I don't at least try to keep up on it, then it's going to be so much worse tomorrow. Arrow sucks for cleaning. He'll let it pile up until I just do it."

It dawned on me then that the two of them were roommates. Oh how very unfortunate. I hid my dismay behind a neutral smile.

The floor vibrated beneath our feet from the high volume in the basement. Several voices blended in to make a cacophony of noise.

"Sounds like we showed up at a good time. Congratulations, by the way, on your big win."

"Thanks." His grin couldn't possibly be any brighter. "You too. Don't tell Arrow I said this, but I think you guys are going to be the last band standing."

"Aww." A blush warmed my face. It had been a long time since I'd had butterflies like this. The infatuated rush of attraction left me dizzy. "That's so nice of you to say."

"I mean it." Back inside the kitchen, Rowen dug around in a cupboard before producing a bottle of Jack Daniels. He held it up for my appraisal. "Are you a whiskey girl?"

Though my drink of choice tended to involve clear spirits, I was up for anything. "I can be."

"Great. Do you want it mixed or anything?"

"Surprise me."

With a shrug Rowen closed the cupboard, unscrewed the lid, and swigged straight out of the bottle. I accepted the bottle when he offered it and took a burning swallow.

"I'd take you downstairs, but honestly, I'd rather keep you to myself." His laugh was a caress on my skin.

"No complaints here." I followed him into the living room, delighted at the chance to speak to him one on one away from the noisy bar scene. Cinder's warning resurfaced in my thoughts, reminding me that this wasn't supposed to be happening.

But I haven't done anything wrong, I thought. *We're just hanging out.* Besides, the last thing I wanted was something serious. Relationships and I didn't go together so well.

Rowen fetched a guitar from the many littering the house, and we sat alone in the living room. The noise from downstairs was tremendous, and the poker game in the dining room was filled with loud chatter and cursing. I was oblivious, happy to drink whiskey and watch Rowen play guitar.

"I think you look better with the bass," I said with a coy smile. "But I like this too. What else can you play?"

He hung his head so that the long piece of his mohawk fell into his eyes. It was so damn irresistible that I had to fight the urge to brush it back.

"I've been known to sing on occasion. I kind of prefer not to be the front man though. Bass is my favorite. It's where all the soul is."

Rowen strummed the guitar with the touch of a lover, making me envious of the instrument. I could have watched endlessly. It seemed to come so naturally to him.

"What about you?" he asked. "How long have you been playing?"

We passed both the bottle and the guitar back and forth. While one of us drank, the other strummed. We talked and we played, and it was fantastic. I learned that Rowen was a mechanic by day. His love of cars and rock music showed through his infectious enthusiasm. For a while I even forgot that we weren't really two regular people who happened to share a love of music. What we shared went beyond this world. And Rowen didn't even know it yet.

The spell was broken when Arrow pounded his way drunkenly up the stairs. He stumbled his way over to us with an unlit cigarette in one hand. He sat heavily on the floor next to me, snapping the cigarette in the process.

"Son of a bitch." Tossing the smoke aside, he grabbed the bottle from me and took a large drink. "You've got a smoke I can get off you, right?"

"Seriously?" I sat up straighter, wary now, and gave him an appraising glance. "Maybe. But don't jack the last of the whiskey, bitch."

Holding a finger up, Arrow dug around in his jeans pocket until he pulled out a joint. "Peace offering?"

As Rowen played a song, I lit the joint and began to pass it around our small group of three. The Jack Daniels bottle followed. The tune he played was good. I wasn't sure I'd heard it before.

"Is that a Molly's Chamber song?" I asked. "It's really good."

"No." Rowen shook his head and blushed. "Just something new I've been working on."

Arrow made a show of gagging. "Did you write a song for your new crush here? How fucking sweet."

Rowen grumbled, "Shut up. You heard it already, and you said it was good, so eat ass."

New crush? That gave me pause. Surely Arrow was joking. Rowen and I had just met a week ago. Letting my hair fall forward, I studied him from behind a veil of black. Turning his attention back to the guitar, Rowen continued to play.

"I think it's beautiful, Rowen." My words sparked a light in his eyes, and I smiled. I was starting to really adore this guy. That could get dangerous.

Arrow studied us, looking from me to Rowen. "You guys do realize that there's an extremely good chance our bands will go head to head in the finals. Right?"

I shot him a daring look. "And your point is?"

"That this little fling you two are working up to may not be so fun when that happens." With an indifferent shrug, Arrow blew out a puff of smoke and eyed us knowingly. He was such a dick.

"Who says it has to just be a fling?" Rowen challenged, and I looked at him sharply.

"Oh no." Arrow lay back on the floor, stretching languorously. "Not this again. You've got to give up on this ridiculous pursuit of love, Rowen. It's not good for you." To me he added, "No offense."

We stared in tense silence at one another. I didn't want Rowen to pick up on the unspoken animosity simmering between Arrow and I, so I said, "None taken." I smiled, a brittle twist of my lips that made my face ache. "I wouldn't expect you to know the first thing about love."

"Whatever, Spike. That battle is ours. Love be damned."

Rowen strummed a little louder, as if trying to drown out the awkward conversation. I sat back, leaning on one hand while puffing slowly on the joint with the other. My head swam, and I handed it off to Arrow, feeling like I'd had enough.

He tried to pass me the whiskey bottle, but I held up a hand and shook my head. My tongue felt heavy and thick. It was hard to form a thought. I knew I was drunk, but I didn't think I was that drunk yet. Still a thick fog cloaked my brain.

Arrow watched me closely, and I knew then that he'd done something. He'd added something sketchy to the joint or the whiskey. Rowen set the guitar aside and leaned back against the wall. He said something, but it didn't compute. Whatever it was, Arrow replied, his tone smooth and even. What the hell was going on?

My mouth was dry. I needed some water. Unable to put my need into words, I tried to get up. The world turned. The room shifted suddenly, and like a dropped camera, I was looking at everything from the wrong angle.

    Deep inside me, where a sober thought still dwelled, I knew this was wrong. I knew I needed to fight, but that coherent certainty couldn't surface from the depths. Hazy and out of focus, each slow blink made my vision darken a bit more until there was only black.

Chapter Eight

I blacked out. Not the unconscious, snoring, passed out kind of black out, but the still functioning with no idea what the hell was going on kind of black out. The dangerous kind.

Everything was a blur, a jumble of random images and sensations that made no sense: Rowen slumped against the wall. The overpowering stench of whiskey. Someone whispering in my ear.

The scent of cologne filled my nostrils at one point. The heat of a mouth on mine followed. It was all very disorienting. I knew I didn't want my first kiss with Rowen to be like this. It was all wrong. When I felt the smooth touch of a steel tongue stud against my bottom lip, I panicked.

These things came rushing back to me when I woke up several hours later.

Worst. Hangover. Ever.

My head felt heavy, and when I felt a pillow beneath my cheek, I was afraid to open my eyes. Then I was afraid not to.

Shame slithered through me before I had even assessed the situation. I was in a bed, that much was clear. Beside me I felt the weight and warmth of another person. It had been a long time since I'd woken up beside someone with no recollection of the previous night. It wasn't something I made a habit of. As far as one night stands go, I'd only had one, and I had hoped to keep it that way.

My pulse pounded as I lifted my head and prepared to face my poor choices. The sheets slid against my skin. I was dressed in only my bra and underwear. Still, that was promising.

Holding my breath, I turned to my companion, and my heart sank. Arrow was passed out beside me. Arm flung up over his face, sheets bunched around his waist, he slumbered. He was very obviously naked, and I swallowed hard at the sight of what the sheets barely hid.

"This can't be happening," I whispered. Unable to look away, I stared at him.

The collage of skulls, roses, and winged creatures tattooed on his arms was not the end of his ink. Song lyrics were written on his side in script. Low on his hip sat a raven, it's wings spread as if about to take flight. He was well built for his frame. Not bulky but hard in all the right places.

I realized I was gawking at him and suddenly worried that he would feel it and wake up. Casting a frantic glance about the room, I spied my clothes on the floor near the door. Now if I could just get to them without waking Arrow... I slid off the bed, slowly, inch by inch. Only when I was on my feet did I breathe again.

My head spun, and I needed a moment to get my balance. Each step I took was carefully calculated. I kept glancing back at Arrow, afraid to take my eyes off him. I could puzzle out what the hell happened later. I just needed to get out of there.

I bent to pick my clothes up. Sliding my skirt up my legs, I heard motion in the bed behind me and froze.

With his voice husky with sleep, Arrow asked, "Leaving already?" I turned to find him lying there facing me, his head propped up on one hand. Hair disheveled and cocky grin in place, he raised an inquisitive brow.

Confused and horrified, I stammered my reply. "I did not—We didn't—Don't even try to tell me that we—?"

"Fucked? No. We didn't. You passed out. But you wanted it."

I shook my head in disbelief, and the simple action sent a jolt of pain slamming through my skull. "Bullshit. You drugged me. There's no way I would willingly get into bed with you otherwise."

"I'm sure you really want to believe that." As I hurriedly finished dressing, he watched me with the intensity of a predator about to pounce.

"I knew you were dark, but I didn't think you were such a pig." I searched the room until I found my purse, then double-checked that my things were still safely inside.

"That's right," he said, sitting up in the bed. "I'm dark. Which means I'm committed to my agenda. I'll do whatever it takes to fulfill that commitment." He reached out, caught hold of my arm, and dragged me onto the bed beside him.

I shoved him away with both hands on his warm, firm chest and jumped off the bed before he could grab for me again. "Keep your hands off me, Arrow. I can only imagine what kind of sick shit you did to me last night."

He regarded me from his place in the bed, an evil light in his hazel eyes. "I told you. Nothing happened. We made out a little. That's about it. It's not too late to change that though." When I continued to stare at him with contempt, he shrugged and added, "Seriously. I'm not a rapist. Besides, you have to be willing. You're nephilim. I can't take you against your will. Not without punishment."

I had no way of knowing if that was true, but I didn't get the feeling that he was lying. "Yeah? Well, good. I am very much not willing."

My hand was on the doorknob when his next words froze me in my tracks. "Sure. But it doesn't look that way in this photo I took. A photo that might accidentally get sent to Rowen." Arrow waved his phone around, jerking it back out of my grasp when I reached for it. He held it close enough for me to see the picture he'd taken of me asleep in his bed in my underwear.

It was bad. Just one look gave the impression that more had gone on in that bed between us than what actually had. If Rowen saw it, he would believe I'd screwed his best friend.

"Why did you take that?" I asked, trying to act like it didn't bother me. "What are you trying to achieve?"

"At the moment, I'm trying to achieve some blackmail." Arrow tucked the phone under his pillow. "Stay away from Rowen, and I won't show it to him."

I was flabbergasted. "Why do you care if I'm interested in Rowen? Don't tell me this is about who fucks a nephilim first."

Arrow rolled his eyes and gave me a look that implied I was an idiot. "As much as I'd enjoy tapping that fine, angelic ass of yours, this is about something bigger. I have a job to do. Right now it includes keeping you away from Rowen."

"Why?" Between Cinder and Arrow, I was getting fed up with people trying to stop me from getting closer to Rowen. I barely knew him, but I wanted to. Why was that so wrong?

"That's for me to know. Unless you want to tell me everything you already know about him?" Brow raised, Arrow leaned back against the headboard and crossed his arms. There was no telling what he was capable of. Though he looked like any other rock n' roller in the scene, he likely had skills that reached into another world, skills far greater than my undecided abilities.

Either Arrow knew everything I knew about Rowen, or he was trying to trick me into spilling something. He'd already made enough of an idiot out of me. I wasn't telling him shit.

"What's there to know?" I cringed at the sound of my phone, a shrill blast of electric guitars that disturbed the relative quiet. Silencing it with a finger, I kept my gaze on Arrow, studying him for a sign that he knew Rowen was nephilim.

Arrow's expression was a neutral mask, revealing nothing. "Here's what I do know about Rowen. He would never get involved with a chick who got so loaded at a party that she went to bed with his buddy."

The blood drained from my face. My head pounded, but whether from the hangover or from sudden rage, I didn't know. Raw hatred had me seeing red. My palms tingled, the sensation creeping up my arms.

He taunted, "What are you gonna do, Spike? Light a candle? I've got years of experience on you, and you're still undecided. Don't embarrass yourself."

The pressure inside my head increased. I wanted to kill him. He was such a vile, nasty piece of crap. Dark. He was so dark that he reeked of it. Staring at Arrow, seeing his evil for what it was, I was downright disgusted.

In response to my utter vehemence, the pillow I'd slept on burst into flames. He quickly vacated the bed and grabbed a glass of water from the nightstand. It was just enough to kill the small fire.

Arrow turned to me, naked and angry. "You crazy bitch. Are you trying to burn my house down?"

That was why my father had named me Ember. Even before I was born, he had known that one of my greatest weapons would be fire. I'd gotten it from him.

I stared steadily at Arrow's face until circumstance demanded that I check out his package. It was right there. How could I not? So I did. And I did it slowly, appraisingly, hoping that he hated it. It wasn't bad, in all honesty. Nothing to brag about but nothing to be ashamed of either. Still, I twisted my lips into a judgmental smirk, as if I found it lacking.

"You're going to be sorry that you underestimated me, Arrow." It was a threat that I had no idea of how to fulfill. But I would.

I made the safest decision, leaving before things could escalate. Except I really headed for the door because I feared Rowen would discover me there in Arrow's bedroom. Hastily, I made my way out of the house, moving swift and light on my feet.

A couple of guys I didn't know were passed out in the living room. I didn't see Rowen but assumed him to be in his bedroom. I didn't stop moving until I was a full block away and out of sight of the house. Then I called a cab and waited. I felt very much like I'd just done a walk of shame though I had nothing to be ashamed of.

As I waited for the cab, I began to plot. Arrow had crossed a line I didn't know I had when he opted for blackmail. It was just so low and underhanded, so devious.

My phone rang again, reminding me that I had missed a call. It was Jett.

"Hey, bitch!" she shouted, sounding far better than I felt. "What the hell happened to you last night? I came upstairs looking for you, but someone said you left with a guy. Did you hook up with somebody? Please tell me it was Rowen."

"I didn't hook up with anyone. Except that I kind of did." I explained what had happened and how I was sure that Arrow had drugged me. "I think he did it to Rowen too, maybe to get him out of the way for the night. Anyway, he's holding a photo of me in his bed hostage. He said he'd show it to Rowen and tell him we slept together unless I back off from Rowen."

Jett let loose a steady stream of curse words. Her description of Arrow went on so long I almost laughed. Except I was too mad to laugh.

All too seriously, she asked, "Do you want me to kill him? I'll fucking kill him for you, Spike. Nobody threatens my bestie and gets away with it." She wasn't joking. Maybe she wasn't as violent as she liked to pretend to be, but Jett was dangerously protective of those she loved.

"No killing. He's not worth it. I'll find another way to deal with him." Now if only I knew what that would be.

"Where are you? Do you want me to come over and hang out for a bit? We can scheme together."

Her hopeful tone brought a smile to my face. I spied my yellow taxi in the distance and sighed with relief. "I'm heading home to shower and change before Cinder pops in. I'll catch up with you later."

"Ok, but don't forget that we have plans tonight. We have to celebrate how far we've come." She paused, the flick of a lighter audible in the background.

The cab pulled to a stop beside me. I opened the door and sank into the backseat. "I'll be there."

* * * *

Whatever Arrow had slipped us, it was lingering. I popped a painkiller for my headache before grabbing a shower. Dressed in sweats, I threw a sandwich together and quickly scarfed it down before gathering my gym bag. I paused long enough to give Seth some love, fresh food and water.

What I really wanted to do was head for my bed and sleep the day away. Until today I hadn't had any idea what my choice would be. I still wasn't ready to make my decision, but I was a step closer. *Thanks, Arrow.*

I headed for the gym. It didn't take me long to work up a sweat. I did some yoga, ran on the treadmill, and then ran through some sword practice moves. With every swing of my blade, I pictured Arrow on the receiving end. Instead of tiring, I grew more energized, more aggressive. I muttered every bad word I knew, even combining a few to make whole new swear words. It had been some time since I'd been this pissed off.

I sensed Cinder seconds before he materialized. Whirling to face him, I swung my wooden practice sword, aiming for his neck. He met my swing with his own sword held ready. Since it was real, it sliced through my wooden one, leaving me holding a stub.

"That was impressive," he commented with an admiring nod. "I must admit, I wasn't expecting to find you here."

I tossed the remains of my sword aside. Bouncing off the bench against the wall, it clattered loudly in the relative quiet. "Yeah, well, that makes two of us."

"Are you ok, Ember?" He laid a hand on my shoulder and squeezed. "Tell me what happened to get you so worked up."

Breathing hard, I pushed my messy ponytail off my shoulder and sighed. "Arrow happened."

Cinder sat down on the bench, patting the spot beside him. "I take it last night didn't go so well."

"It started great. We kicked ass. Made it through to the next round." I sat heavily beside him and leaned my head on his shoulder. "We went to an after party at Arrow's. What a fucking mistake that was."

Cinder didn't even lecture me about swearing or give me a look. He sat there and listened while I told him everything. Every time I told someone, I relived the parts that I remembered, which fed my seething rage.

"Arrow is doing what he feels he must. As we all do. I'm sorry he did that to you." Cinder's arm slipped around me, warm and comforting.

I angled myself on the bench so I could meet his gaze. "It's ok. I've had years to get used to this, but I didn't actually think I knew what I wanted until this morning."

Cinder blinked a few times, as if he'd expected me to say something else. He clasped one of my hands in both of his. His emotional reaction was not entirely unexpected. If I chose a human life or, God forbid, the dark, my journey with Cinder would end. His deep concern meant so much to me. He was the kind of friend I only hoped to be.

He asked, "What does that mean?"

"It means that I'm not ready to choose, but I'm ready to get serious about choosing. If that makes any sense. I can't pretend to be human knowing everything I know. Being a nephilim is who I am. And if Arrow is any indication of what being dark is like, then I know I don't want to be part of that."

He hugged me so tightly to him that he squeezed the breath from me. Cinder kissed my forehead. "It overjoys me to hear that. I understand your fears, but please know that the reward will be greater than the risk." He pulled back and studied me, smoothing back a strand of hair that had escaped my ponytail.

His kind words delivered such comfort that I didn't mind the inability to breathe. Something small and special blossomed into something vast and strong. I hugged Cinder, holding him as if he would disappear if I didn't. "Thank you for always being so patient with me. For letting me make this decision in my own time."

He brushed a gentle hand down the side of my face. "I just want you to embrace who you were meant to be."

Chapter Nine

Strobe lights lit up the stage. The incessant shrieks of hundreds of women drowned out the music. A smoke machine generated a cloud of dramatic fog. The silhouette of a man in fire fighting gear sent the shrieks to a deafening decibel.

Our ladies' night out had been Jett's idea. We sat around a table near the stage with Tash and Rubi, eagerly awaiting some sexy male entertainment. It had been ages since we'd done this. It wasn't a bad way to celebrate our most recent Battle of the Bands achievement.

After my talk with Cinder, I'd been so concerned with training that I'd begged him to spend the day with me. He had lovingly refused, insisting that I spend some time with my friends. At first, when Jett announced her plan to take us to the male strippers, I'd been reluctant. Now that I was here, watching a hard-bodied dancer move in ways I never dreamed a man could move, I was happy for the escape.

As each man came out and gyrated for us, the screams seemed to get louder. Perhaps loudest of them all was Jett. She waved a five-dollar bill overhead, whooping in glee when the fireman danced over to our table. She stuffed the cash in his tiny g-string, taking the opportunity to run her hands over his chest. Then she plucked another bill from her purse and waved it over my head, shouting, "Over here, big boy."

Before I knew what was happening, he lifted me out of my seat and wrapped my legs around his waist. While the crowd of ecstatic women watched, he ground his groin against me in a dirty dance that made me both mortified and hysterical with giggles.

By the time he put me down, my face was hot with embarrassment. I didn't know how I was going to get Jett back for that one, but her day would come.

"Oh, I'm jealous," Rubi gushed. "He's sexy. Did he smell good? I bet he smelled good."

I'd been so horrified by what was happening that I hadn't taken note of his smell.

Laughing along with the girls was exactly what I needed after the previous night. I wasn't sure today could get any better.

But then it did.

My phone vibrated in my purse. Since I was already with my closest friends, I assumed it was my mother, even though we'd spoken earlier. When I saw that it was a text from Rowen, my heart stuttered.

I'm sure you're busy but what are the odds that I could see you tonight?

I didn't know what to say, so I stared stupidly at the screen feeling both delighted and disappointed. Though I had yet to make a commitment to the light, I was sure that Cinder would frown upon me spending time with Rowen. Then again, if he was to be my first task, wouldn't spending time with him be beneficial? It could be a good way to get to know him, to build trust.

With a glance at my crazy friends, who were completely losing their minds over a choreographed routine featuring three men dressed as cowboys, I replied to Rowen that I was occupied at the moment but possibly later we could meet up.

Nervously I awaited a response, toying with the silver cross pendant hanging from my neck. Cinder had given it to me with the instruction to wear it after dark, when demons were at their strongest. I kept checking my phone even though the vibration would alert me to a new message. It felt like forever before he replied with a simple: *Let me know when you're free.*

After a few cocktails and a few more wildly entertaining dances, the four of us had lost any sense of what was proper, not that we'd had it to begin with. Even so we still had nothing on the group of middle-aged soccer moms over at the next table. They screamed their hearts out like they were fifteen-year-olds at a boy band concert. Their antics were every bit as entertaining as the men.

I eased off the drinks early. Still recovering from last night, I knew I'd have time for more drunken shenanigans later.

The host announced a small intermission, encouraging us all to flock to the bar. In tandem, we pulled out our phones, checking for messages and posting goofball selfies to Twitter.

"Shit," Jett said, frowning at her phone. "Ladies, I'm sorry. I have to go."

"What's up?"

"It's pack stuff. I'm not sure what's going on, but they want me at the clubhouse." She vacated her seat and gathered her things in a rush. "Sorry, girls. I owe you one."

"No worries. I'm kind of tired anyway." I waved her away, unable to believe my luck. The Doghead pack seldom demanded Jett's full attention, but when it did, she never hesitated. Seeing an opportunity, I told Rubi and Tash, "If you guys want to call it a night, that's totally cool with me."

They exchanged a look. Rubi shrugged. "I have a psych assignment due. I don't mind heading home early."

Tash said, "Riley wanted to hang out tonight, but I told him I had plans. I'll just give him a call and tell him to pick me up."

That was easy enough. Ditching my friends hadn't been the plan, but I was ridiculously eager to see Rowen one on one, away from the bar and Arrow. Rubi's university studies and Tash's country music-loving boyfriend gave me the perfect escape.

"Sounds good." I tried to keep my hands still so I wouldn't send a rushed text to Rowen. "I'll see you guys tomorrow at the jam space then."

I laughed when Jett leaned in to press a giant kiss to my cheek. "I know that look," she purred in my ear. "You're going to see that boy. I expect to hear all about it tomorrow. Don't do anything I would do."

"That's kind of my personal motto." I grinned and wiped her red lipstick mark from my cheek with a napkin.

I waited patiently for my friends to vanish through the exit before I followed. My fingers flew over the screen as I texted Rowen. He responded fast, as if he'd been waiting on me. We agreed to meet at the coffee shop across the street, giving me ample time to touch up my hair and makeup in the ladies room.

The tickle of butterfly wings had me stifling a nervous giggle as I scrutinized my stay-put, red lipstick that was really staying put. Nice. It wasn't often that a product did what it claimed. I would be putting that brand in my regular rotation.

I ran my fingers through my black hair, satisfied that it looked shiny and sleek. It wasn't my original color, not by a long shot. It had been years since I'd seen my natural hair color. From what I could recall, it was some kind of dirty blond or light brown. After going through the rainbow in my late teen years, I'd gone black during a Goth phase, and it had stuck.

My dress was simple, black with a cinched waist and skirt that moved freely just above my knees. Steel-toed boots with four-inch heels took the dress from modest to badass. Just the way I liked it.

I left behind the gyrating men and the screaming housewives. Crossing the street to the coffee shop, each step brought me closer and made my heart race faster. Geez, it was just a coffee date with a guy. What was with me?

Whatever it was, it likely had something to do with the fact that the one and only guy I'd ever loved had dumped me for my ex-best friend when I was twenty. Since then I'd been avoiding anything serious with the opposite sex. It just wasn't worth the risk. And really, nobody had caused my pulse to jump in ages. Until now.

Of course, several months had passed since I'd seen any action. I had the occasional hook up, but they were few and far between. Not one to sleep around, I was picky in that area. Since my one and only one-night stand a year ago, I had decided that nameless sex wasn't what I wanted. And since love wasn't what I wanted either, I'd been on a self-imposed celibacy. But Rowen, he sure did tempt me to break that unspoken vow.

Waiting for him to walk in was unbearable. I fidgeted with my hair, my mocha latte, and especially with my phone. Anticipating the first glimpse of him, I also prayed that he hadn't seen Arrow's picture of me. If he had... No, I couldn't entertain that thought.

I was scrolling through tweets when he walked in. I knew it was him even before I looked up. My heart flip-flopped awkwardly, choking off my breath.

A lazy smile lifted the corner of his mouth. It was crazy sexy. His striking blue mohawk contrasted with his amber gold eyes, making them almost glow.

He raised a hand in a small wave before angling toward the barista. The next few minutes were agony. I continued to sneak peeks at him while he waited for his drink to be prepared. Damn, why did he have to look so good?

"How's it going?" Rowen asked as he plopped down on the chair opposite me. "I'm not late am I?" He fished his phone out of his jeans and checked the time. "Here, this is for you."

He tossed a thumb drive on the table between us. I stared at it, blinking in surprise before I picked it up.

"What is it?"

"It's a song." His smile turned sheepish. "It's the one I played for you. Watching you play kind of inspired it."

This guy just got better and better. I was quiet for a moment, processing this little nugget of information. I tucked the thumb drive away into my bat-winged heart purse.

"That is the sweetest thing ever," I said, unable to contain the goofy joy of receiving such an item. "Thank you, Rowen. That's so thoughtful of you."

"Don't tell Arrow I gave it to you. He'd shit a brick."

I grimaced. Just thinking about Arrow made my blood boil. "Trust me. I have no intention of talking to that douchebag if I can help it."

Rowen's smile faded. A strange tension settled. "I'm sorry I didn't get a chance to say goodbye to you last night. I don't remember much of it."

My lungs burned, and I realized I was holding my breath. He didn't seem to have seen the photo. What a relief.

"Me neither. Funny how things got foggy after Arrow came upstairs." I pursed my lips in silent judgment. "I don't understand why you'd want to live with someone like that. But he's your buddy, so what do I know?"

"He's crossed the line a few times," Rowen admitted, his face expressionless. "I'm sorry about that. Honestly, I don't know why I still put up with his shit. We've been friends since junior high. More like brothers really. I guess I feel like I have to look out for him. Make sure he doesn't get himself into some serious trouble. You know?"

My bubble of joy popped with those words. The two of them had a full-on bromance going. That didn't sound promising for my crush on Rowen.

He seemed uneasy as an awkward silence settled. For a moment I thought he was going to bail.

He asked, "So is it too late or can I take you to a movie? If we hurry we can catch a midnight showing. You can pick the movie." I certainly wasn't expecting him to ask me out.

Those soulful eyes captured me, and I swooned. This was some seriously cheesy rom-com territory here. But I didn't care; I was walking on clouds.

"Ok, let's go."

We walked down the street, coffee in hand, chatting amiably on the way to his car. He asked me how my day went, and I entertained him with tales of the rowdy ladies at the male strip club. I hated that I couldn't tell him the rest, the parts that really mattered.

Taillights flashed as Rowen pressed the key fob. A black Dodge Charger awaited us. He reached for the passenger door, holding it open for me. I slid into the car with a shy, "Thank you." I'd never had such a simple but gentlemanly act performed for me before. It felt nice.

I took a moment to check out the car. The interior was vast and clean. Matte black rally stripes on the hood shone silver in the streetlight. It made me cringe at the thought of my old junker.

"What year is this?" I asked as Rowen pulled the big car into traffic.

"2007," he said, turning the radio down so we didn't have to shout over it. "I bought it used a few months ago. Traded in my Focus for something with a little more power."

"Does it have a Hemi?" I listened to the engine's purr, wishing my old monster of a car sounded half as smooth.

"Damn rights it does." Rowen chuckled. "Are you into cars? What do you drive?"

The small talk was pointless really, doing little more than filling the space, but it was the highlight of my entire day so far. "I'm into muscle cars. That's about it. I have an old Nova, but it's a real piece of shit at the moment. I'm hoping to be able to restore it one day. But it runs, and that's something."

Talking cars gave us a common interest other than music. We bantered back and forth about which was better, Dodge or Chevy. By the time we arrived at the movie theatre, I was laughing harder than I had in ages.

The theatre didn't offer a lot of selection. Only two movies remained that hadn't yet started. My choices were some superhero action movie or an exorcism horror flick. Since I'd already reached my demon quota for one lifetime, or so I liked to think, I chose the superhero movie.

Comic book heroes had never really been my thing. That didn't matter though. Sitting in the dark with Rowen so unbearably close made it the best movie ever. The scent of his cologne teased me. It was masculine but not overpowering, a subtle and sexy aroma that made me want to bury my face in his neck and inhale.

We shared a bag of popcorn, and I did my best to enjoy it even though I was paranoid about having kernels stuck in my teeth. That wasn't exactly the look I was going for tonight.

I kept wondering if he was going to try anything, like a cheesy, stretch-and-yawn move. He was too smooth for that. Rowen didn't mess around with a lame move. He reached for my hand and slipped his fingers through mine. Adrenaline gave me a warming jolt, and I smiled, glad the darkened theatre hid my blush.

"I saw that coming a mile away," Rowen leaned in close to whisper with a head nod toward the screen. The warmth of his breath tickled my ear in a spine-tingling way. I nodded in agreement though I'd missed whatever he was referring to.

The theatre was almost empty. A group of teenage boys down in front laughed and chattered amongst themselves. Another couple sat in the very back row, making out like it was an Olympic sport. Rowen's amber gaze strayed to them, and his upper lip lifted in a quirky grin. I was both relieved and disappointed when he didn't try to kiss me.

By the time the movie ended, I was convinced that Cinder would discover this date and that he would be terribly unhappy about it. I was also that much more determined to enjoy it simply because of that. This might be my only date with Rowen.

"Can I give you a lift home?" he asked as we crossed through the lobby on our way out.

Since Rubi had picked me up tonight, I was conveniently without wheels. "You sure can. Thanks."

At two in the morning, the streets were quiet. People filtered out of the movie theatre, making the only sound other than the occasional car passing by. We held hands as we walked. My day hadn't gotten off to such a hot start, but it had ended on a high note.

My cheeks were starting to hurt. My smile had been non-stop, genuine though. Rowen's quips and jokes revealed the fun personality inside his sexy exterior, which made me fall so much more in like with him than I already had. Damn.

We had almost reached Rowen's car. The attack was sudden. Vicious. I was flung to the ground, torn away from Rowen. The stench of sulfur was sudden and strong. A sneeze exploded forth as I got to my feet. My knees stung from where they'd skidded on the sidewalk. I shoved my black tresses out of my eyes in time to see the demon target Rowen.

It was Koda. He flung Rowen against the car and pinned him tight with an arm across his throat. Rowen flailed against the demon.

"Koda, what the hell are you doing?" I grabbed his arm and pulled, but he wouldn't be budged.

"Just making a point," he said, shoving me aside with his free hand.

I fell with arms flailing but got right back up. A side of me that I didn't know I had took over, and the training I'd done with Cinder surfaced. I kicked the back of Koda's knee with my steel-toed boots. His leg buckled, giving me the second I needed to punch him in the neck.

Lacking a weapon put me at an even greater disadvantage. I hadn't taken Cinder seriously enough when he told me to carry one. Lesson learned.

"Don't make me hurt you, Spike," Koda snarled. "That's not what this is about."

"So what's it about then?" I grabbed hold of his arm and fought to break his hold on Rowen, who was turning red in the face. I still couldn't budge the demon.

Frustrated and afraid, my fingers tingled seconds before the flames burst forth. They crawled up Koda's arm to engulf him in supernatural fire. He let out a shout and stumbled back, releasing Rowen. I put myself between them, guarding Rowen as he gasped for air.

"You're making the wrong choice, girl," Koda said, giving himself a shake like a dog getting out of water. The flames quickly burned out. Other than a few scorch marks, which promptly healed, he was unharmed. "Being seen with this guy will get you killed."

"You know this dude?" Rowen coughed out. His eyes were wide, his chest heaving. I sure hoped there was no rule about using my gifts in front of him. Too late now.

I held up a hand to keep Koda at a distance. There wasn't a lot I could do, but I'd fight as hard as I had to. "I'll spend time with whomever I damn well please, thank you."

Koda's dark brows knit together as he studied me. "You don't know what you're getting involved in. Being anywhere near him is dangerous." He nodded his dark head toward Rowen.

"Dangerous?" Rowen spat. "Me? Are you fucking crazy?"

"He'll get you killed, Spike. Walk away right now, and I'll take it from here." Koda must have thought I was delusional. He stepped forward, large and intimidating.

My hand flew to the cross hanging from my neck. I pulled it free and thrust it toward him. "Back off."

Koda stopped. His red gaze flicked to the pendant in my grasp. "Oh, come on now. Really?"

I sure hoped I didn't look as pitiful as I felt. Like a scream queen in an old vampire movie, I held the cross up as if it would save me when, in fact, it did little more than piss off the demon staring down at me.

Anticipating Koda's grab for the pendant, I lunged forward and slapped it against his forehead. Smoke rose up from the demon's skin. It stank of sulfur. I yanked the cross away, and some flesh came with it. Bile rose in my throat, but I choked it back and held tight.

Koda gave an anguished cry, fury written all over his face. "Bitch."

"Leave here," I commanded, my voice starting to shake. "Now."

Pointing a finger at me, Koda hissed, "I warned you."

Then he was gone, vanishing from sight with the sound of wings. My shoulders sagged, and my breath came fast. Adrenaline created a roar of white noise in my ears. That had been absolutely terrifying.

"What the fuck was that all about?" Rowen demanded, incredulous. "That motherfucker had red eyes. And the flames? Why do I feel like I've seen that kind of thing somewhere before?"

"You most likely have." I didn't know what to say. What I couldn't do was tell a lie. Since Cinder hadn't coached me on this, I decided honesty was best. "Let's go back to my place. I'll tell you as much as I can."

Chapter Ten

I stared at the coffee maker on the counter before opting for the bottle of vodka in the freezer. Half a pitcher of raspberry lemonade accompanied it when I returned to the kitchen table.

Rowen accepted his empty glass with a nod.

I smiled apologetically. "Sorry about the girly drink. You can drink it straight if you prefer."

"No, this is good. Thanks." He poured twice as much vodka as juice and promptly took a large gulp.

I mixed my drink, my hands shaking even though we were now safely inside my apartment. Cinder had blessed it with protective wards when I moved in, ensuring nothing demonic could freely enter. My safe haven was a relief but also somewhat nerve racking, as I had to go out again sometime.

"I'm sorry about Koda. He's a dick." It was the lamest thing I could muster, but I was afraid. Could having Rowen here get me in seriously deep shit? Or even worse, could it put him in danger?

My pulse raced as I tried to decide how much I could safely share. Rowen was one of us. Why couldn't he know?

"And a demon." Rowen shook his head in wonder and shoved the long piece of blue mohawk out of his eyes. "I feel like I should be more shocked than I am. Is that weird? Never mind, none of this is weird to you, is it? Why is that?"

"Trust me, it's all weird to me," I said, drinking down more of the vodka lemonade. "I wish I had more answers for you. Unfortunately, I have a lot of questions myself."

Rowen finished his drink and poured another one. He peered at me from behind that blue fringe. "Are you a demon? I mean, what's with the fire?"

"I'm a nephilim," I heard myself say. Considering what he'd just seen, I knew I had to be honest. A lie wouldn't protect anyone. "Half-human, half-angel. It sounds crazy, I know."

I waited for him to laugh or sneer, but he was quiet, watching me in thoughtful silence. We sat there drinking as the minutes passed. I didn't want to say anything more until I saw how he processed that information.

When we were on our third drink, Rowen said, "Ok. I can accept that. But what about me? Why would the demon say that I was dangerous?"

Inwardly I groaned. Cinder was going to be so mad. "I don't know. Not really. I wish I did." I shrugged, feeling awkward. Rowen was going to think I was such a sketch case.

So I was surprised when he said, "Can I show you something?" At my nod, he continued. "I can do something too."

Rowen held his hand out, palm up. A small light began to glow in the center. It started as a tiny orb that grew into a perfectly formed ball of white light. So Rowen was a light bearer? A lovely gift. I stared in awe, wondering how it was possible that he could do this if his talents were contained like Cinder had said. The light orb hovered over his palm as if awaiting instruction. I reached out then hesitated.

Our eyes met, and I searched him for a sign that he knew more than he was letting on. I saw only a flicker of confusion there.

Tentatively I touched the orb. It was warm and seemed to brighten at my touch. Then slowly it began to fade.

He took my hand and held tight. "That's been happening for a while now," Rowen said, looking perplexed. "I've never shown this to anyone before. Not even Arrow."

Keeping a neutral expression was tough. It was almost painful to keep from blurting out a warning about Arrow.

Rowen's gaze fell to our joined hands. He shoulders slumped as if he breathed a silent sigh of relief. "So what does this mean? That I'm a nephilim too? I never knew either of my biological parents. I was adopted."

I groaned and ran my free hand through my hair. "It means that I'm going to tell you something that I'm probably going to get in shit for."

He waited patiently for me to choose my words. The liquor in his glass disappeared while I stared at the table, wondering if I was making a mistake. It was too late for that. Rowen knew enough on his own. If keeping him safe was my goal, then he needed to know. Simple as that.

I needed a cigarette something fierce. After finishing my drink, I rose and gave his hand a gentle tug. "Let's go out on the balcony. I'm supposed to be quitting, but I really need a smoke right now."

The balcony gave me a great view of the city at night. All was quiet at this late hour. Far enough away from the high traffic areas, my neighborhood was calm. We leaned on the metal railing, staring out at nothing while we shared a cigarette.

"You are a nephilim, Rowen," I began, hoping like hell my mouth wasn't writing a check my ass couldn't cash. "The gifts start to manifest after the age of eighteen. At some point, you will have to make a choice. Live as human and give up the gifts, or embrace them and choose a side to serve. It's not an easy decision to make."

He mulled this over, taking deep drags off the cigarette. Tension held him tight. His knuckles were white where he gripped the railing.

"Are you telling me that you haven't made your choice yet?" Curiosity flickered through his amber eyes at this realization.

"I've made choices. I know I don't want to give up my gifts, but, no I haven't made *the* choice. Not yet." There was a great sense of freedom in sharing this with someone who was like me. Jett understood what it was to be different, but she and I were worlds apart.

"Well, that kind of explains some of what Koda said and did." Rowen passed me the cigarette, his gaze lingering as I placed it between my lips. "I knew there was something about you, something different that I connected with right away."

I was puzzled. How could he have known about me when he seemingly had no clue about Arrow? They lived together. Surely at some point Arrow would have slipped up.

"Oh? Just me?"

"Just you." He grinned, and it lit up his face in a way that made my knees weak. "Why do you think that is?"

Good question. Considering he lived with a nephilim and clearly had no idea, I couldn't imagine what it was about me that triggered his awareness. Maybe it was because we were both undecided.

"I have no idea. Look, Rowen, I have to be honest. I was told that your gifts were being contained until the time was right to tell you who you are. I don't know what that means. All I know is that you could be in danger if the wrong person finds out. You have to keep this secret."

We faced each other, the view beyond the balcony forgotten. I dropped the cigarette butt into the ashtray on the small patio table. It had left a bad taste in my mouth. I really did need to quit.

"Who told you this?" He reached to brush a lock of hair out of my face, and his hand lingered.

My insides grew warm and fuzzy. Heat crept over my face. Damn, it had been a long time since someone so easily gave me the tingles. "An angel. Cinder. He's a friend."

Rowen lightly ran a finger down the side of my face. "It's kind of a relief. To know I'm not a freak. It's surreal though."

"I know."

His lips were on mine before I could anticipate the kiss. A pleasant surprise, it sent a rush of white noise roaring through my ears along with an exciting jolt of adrenaline. The touch of his tongue was delicate, almost hesitant. Slow and gentle, Rowen kissed me as if he'd been waiting all night to do so. I slid my arms around his neck and reveled in the way it felt to be pressed against him. I would be replaying the memory of this moment for the next week.

We stood there for several blissfully long, silent moments once the kiss ended. I lay my head on his shoulder and hoped so hard that this wouldn't blow up in my face. I kept seeing that photo of me scantily clad in Arrow's bed.

The chill in the air finally got to me. I pulled back and rubbed my arms briskly. "I don't know about you, but I could go for another drink."

Rowen consulted his phone for the time, and I noticed a missed call from Arrow. "I'd love one. But maybe I should get going. It's late."

"You can't drive. You've already had too much. I guess you'll have to stay." It was terrible of me to want to keep him from going home to Arrow, from seeing that photo. But I wasn't wrong. He couldn't safely drive.

We went back inside, fetched the booze from the kitchen, and got comfy on the couch. I dragged my old acoustic guitar out of the corner and strummed a few chords. We didn't bother with mix, drinking straight from the bottle instead. There wasn't much left, so we might as well finish it off.

Rowen's fingers flew over his phone as he texted Arrow. I couldn't help but sneak a peek. Inwardly I cringed when I saw my name. This was going to end so horribly. I'd have to enjoy every second of this night before Arrow destroyed it all for me.

Taking a deep breath, I shoved all thoughts of the dark nephilim aside and began to sing. Being a frontwoman was definitely more Jett's thing, but I enjoyed singing at home, particularly while working out a new song. The liquor encouraged me, giving me a fearlessness that I wouldn't have had sober.

"That's a good riff," Rowen said, setting his phone on the coffee table. "You have a killer voice. You should sing more often."

"Naw. I'm not really the type to handle the crowd. That's more of Jett's domain." I blushed, cursing my cheeks for betraying me. "But thank you."

Rowen studied me, his amber eyes searching me intently. "Let's write something together. Right now. I'll play. You sing."

Before I could protest or laugh him off, he took the guitar from me. He tuned it down a step, twisting the pegs and strumming until the tone reached perfection for him.

"Won't we be committing some kind of band adultery?" I joked. "I'm not sure our friends would be too keen on that."

Rowen grinned, a spine-tingling smile that gave me jitters. "They don't have to know."

Never had I laughed as much as I did while Rowen and I were writing our song. Each time I clammed up, he got me laughing again. At first the lyrics were cheesy, silly shit I'd never really write. Then we got serious along the way, and something started to come together.

Making music with Rowen felt natural, like we were meant to create together. When we had finished off the last of the booze in my apartment, the sun was just beginning to rise. I was exhausted both mentally and physically.

Taking the guitar from him, I rose from the couch and took his hand. "Come on. You can crash in my room."

Entering my bedroom with Rowen in tow gave me pause. This was too special to fuck up. And if anyone was going to fuck it up for me, it was better to let it be Arrow. So when we climbed into the bed, we were fully clothed. I kept expecting to feel awkward with Rowen in my bed but never did.

I couldn't deny that I wanted him, but too many times I'd given my body to a man only to discover that he didn't want the heart that went with it. That was not a chance I was willing to take now. If we ever got that far, I wanted it to mean something.

The blinds were closed against the morning light, which still peeked through the slats in tiny shards of beams that didn't quite reach us.

"Spike?" My name was a whisper on Rowen's lips. "What's your real name?"

We were each on our own half of the double bed. I stared at the closed closet door. The mirrored surface reflected our image back at me.

"Ember. I don't go by it much. Only Cinder calls me that."

"I like it. But I like Spike too. I think you'll always be Spike to me."

He moved closer to me, closing the space between us. The blue of his mohawk looked especially bright against my zebra-print pillow case. When he kissed me, I feared I might have to tell him I wasn't down for a hook up. But he surprised me by cuddling close without making a further move.

Trivial worries flitted through my mind. What if I snored? Or drooled? Or something even more horrifying? My concerns were ridiculous and completely unfounded.

Rowen drifted off before I did. His breathing slowed as sleep claimed him. However, his embrace remained tight, and I did my best to file every sensation away in my memory. He smelled so damn good. His cologne mingled with his own masculine smell, which seemed to reach right into the most feminine part of me. I could practically feel my hormones bursting with glee. Closing my eyes, I savored the way his body felt beside me. It felt like he belonged there. I would have rolled my eyes at myself if I wasn't having such a joyful moment.

I must have slept with a goofy smile plastered on my face because I felt it fade when I awoke several hours later to find an unhappy Cinder standing over us. With arms crossed, he frowned down at me. I opened and closed my mouth a few times in an attempt to find my voice.

Rowen stirred beside me. I felt him jump when he realized there was a man standing beside the bed.

"Get up." Cinder's command was gentler than the fierceness in his violet eyes. "I'll make coffee. We all need to have a talk."

* * * *

Fifteen minutes later Rowen and I sat across the table from Cinder. I felt like crap, certain I looked it as well. A very brief trip to the washroom had given me a chance to wipe last night's eyeliner from my face. Otherwise, I remained pretty ragged.

I went through the motions of adding cream and sugar to my coffee. Rowen did the same, occasionally casting a glance my way. I waited for Cinder to break the tension.

"You told him." It was not a question. Cinder eyed me over his tea before taking a sip.

Pushing a hand through my disheveled black mane, I leaned heavily on one elbow and sighed. "Yeah. I told him about me. But he knows, Cinder. He has gifts."

Cinder studied Rowen who met his gaze evenly. "Tell me what you know. What you can do."

I listened as Rowen told him about growing up adopted, getting into music, and developing strange abilities. Cinder nodded, slipping me a sideways look. Hearing Rowen talk, it was abundantly clear that he was in the dark about Arrow. That jackhole couldn't be underestimated.

I raised a brow, asking Cinder a silent question. He averted his gaze, and I had my answer. We were not going to tell Rowen about Arrow.

That didn't feel right, and yet I trusted Cinder. Maybe it wasn't my place to tell him. If anything, it should be Arrow's. And he clearly had his own reasons for keeping quiet.

"Do you know who my father is?" Rowen asked. There was a strained set to his shoulders, like he was fighting to keep the emotion from showing on his face.

"Yes," said Cinder with a slight head bob. "I don't know him personally though, and I'm not at liberty to tell you his name. However, you must know that being his son makes you a person of interest to many."

Rowen gripped his coffee mug tightly but didn't drink from it. "Is that why this was all hidden from me? Shouldn't I have been told?"

"Under normal circumstances you would have been. Evidently your gifts are too strong to be contained, which means that your human identity may also be dissolving. Is there anyone in your life you can think of who may know that there is more to you than meets the eye?" Cinder was calm, exuding a friendliness that made Rowen relax. I on the other hand was tense.

Giving his head a slow shake, Rowen shrugged. "No. My friends wouldn't even notice if I sprouted wings. They're all a bunch of rowdy drunks."

Yeah, except for the one that was a drug-dealing nephilim. Keeping this to myself was painful. Arrow was already betraying him. How could I do the same?

"Might I suggest that you keep an eye out for anything unusual? I don't want you to be paranoid, but this is serious. Unfortunately, not everyone can be trusted, sometimes even those we trust the most." A small storm passed through Cinder's eyes, and I wondered who had betrayed him in the past.

My stomach hurt. I suspected it might be from hunger and too much late night alcohol but thought it was more likely linked to the secrets I was being forced to keep from Rowen.

Rowen asked, "Do you think someone close to me is lying about who they are?" He hit so close to the truth that I had to vacate the table. "Would I know if they were anything other than human? I kind of knew with Spike. I felt something."

I went to the kitchen under the guise of grabbing a few bananas and a box of chocolate chip cookies. It gave me a minute to compose myself.

Cinder, elegant and smooth, answered the question with ease. "There are ways of hiding one's identity. Underestimate nobody."

Rowen's brow was furrowed in deep thought when I returned. I set the bananas in the center of the table along with the cookie box after I'd taken a handful. Feeling guilty and responsible for the anguish on Rowen's face, I touched the back of his hand, wishing I could do more.

He met my eyes and took my hand as well as the cookie I offered. The small smile he wore was crushing in its simple ability to strike me speechless.

"So what do I do now?" he asked Cinder before dipping the cookie into his coffee. "Keep going about my daily life as if nothing has changed?"

"That's exactly what you do. Pay attention to everyone and everything. Trust your instincts. Your identity was hidden to keep the dark from coming for you. But they will know, and they will come."

Helping himself to a banana, Cinder peeled it without once taking his gaze off Rowen. For someone who didn't really need to eat and drink, he sure did enjoy it. Cinder ate his banana, looking thoughtfully from Rowen to me. It was impossible to tell what he was thinking.

Cinder added, "I must be honest, Rowen. There are things that Ember and I are not able to tell you. But you can trust us, and I hope you remember that."

I offered a smile that I hoped appeared genuine. So far I really liked Rowen. I wasn't sure what would be required of me in the coming weeks, but I knew I didn't want to let him down.

I listened attentively as Cinder answered a few more questions. He was kind to Rowen, giving him enough information to help him understand what we were without being overwhelming. It gave me some comfort to have Cinder here, freeing me of the burden of enlightening Rowen.

"Well, Rowen, I think it's time for you to be going. Ember and I have a few things to discuss." Extending a hand across the table, Cinder wore an expression of reassurance and compassion. "I do hope to see you again."

"I'll walk you out." I got up too quickly, almost upsetting my coffee. The mild embarrassment was nothing compared to the mortification of having been caught with him in my bed.

Closing the apartment door behind us on the way out wasn't enough. I went so far as to walk him to the elevator. "I'm sorry about all that. I love Cinder, but his timing could have been better."

"No, it's cool. I'm glad I got to meet him. He made me feel less crazy and a little more prepared to deal with this." The boyish grin that

Rowen flashed me then was just too adorable, and I gave him an impulsive hug.

He kissed me. Soft and warm, it was affectionate and possibly even needful. When I concentrated hard, I could feel it there in him, the part of him that was more than human. It was a comfort, but it also worried me.

"Can I see you again?" he asked. "Soon?"

The chances of this all ending badly were high. I knew that. Still, I had to see this through. "You can count on it." I kissed him again, stifling a girlish sigh. Then he stepped into the elevator and was gone.

As I padded back down the hall in my bare feet, I let my happy sigh escape. I hated that this moment of giddy excitement was so heavily plagued by the harsh aspect of danger and the threat of Arrow.

When I opened the apartment door, Cinder was in the kitchen tidying up the counter around the coffee maker. He looked up at my return, and his brows knit together in a worried frown.

"This is not good, Ember. It's dangerous for the two of you to be seen together. I hope last night with Koda has proven that. But you both have free will, and that is your choice to make. However, you must know that it could complicate much more than your band contest." He meant well. I knew that my wellbeing meant much to Cinder. Still, I agreed that it was our choice to make. I wouldn't be told who I could or could not fall for.

"What's going on, Cinder?" I asked, an edge of fear causing my voice to crack. "I get the feeling that there's something you're not sharing. Who is Rowen's father?"

He used the dishcloth to sweep a small pile of coffee grounds into the sink. "Some information could get you killed. Or worse. I won't have you tortured by demons for something I shouldn't have told you."

I leaned against the counter, watching him tidy. There wasn't much to clean. He was just going through the motions.

"But they already know, don't they? That's why they've put Arrow so close to him, why they've hidden that asshole's true identity from Rowen. You've got to give me something here, Cinder. I know I'm still a real rookie here—trust me, I feel like one—but damn, this is tough."

Draping the dishcloth over the faucet, he mirrored my pose, leaning against the opposite counter. Today he was dressed in jeans and a Halestorm t-shirt. Maybe I was starting to rub off on him.

"I'll give you something. A task. Keep an eye on Arrow. I want you to follow him tonight. See what he's up to, but don't let him see you. Take a weapon."

I thought about the blunder with Koda. A silver-plated blade would have been handy. A demon could withstand many things. They were unkillable, but silver was one of their few weaknesses.

"You want me to spy on Arrow?" I had a Homer Simpson moment where I wanted to whine *Can't someone else do it?* but I somehow managed to resist.

"We all have our jobs to do, Ember. You want to know how involved he is, so find out. I know you can handle him."

"What about Rowen? Is he safe?"

"For now."

I considered the situation or what I knew of it anyway. "Why doesn't he have someone? Like how I have you."

Cinder smiled then. It was worthy of a toothpaste commercial. "You have to trust that all of you have what you need when you need it. Besides, he has you now. You have a calling, Ember. One that is as precious and rare as you are."

Even though I'd had years to prepare for this, I still wasn't ready. I'd heard this claim before. It reminded me of Arrow's comment about how rare female nephilim are.

"What if I can't do it? How do I even know what I'm here to do?" A headache began to throb behind my eyes, which I attributed to too much liquor and not enough sleep.

Cinder was quiet for so long that I grew concerned. Then he snapped into action. He poured me a glass of water and gave me a gentle shove. "Maybe you should go back to bed for a while."

I resisted, grabbing onto the counter. "Since Arrow has obviously been planted in Rowen's life, does that mean he knows who Rowen's father is?"

Cinder gave me a look that said he wished I would stop asking so many questions and simply have some faith in what I already knew. It was hard to accept only part of a story. I needed the whole thing.

With a hand on my arm, he gently steered me toward the bedroom. He took a seat on the edge of the bed, patting the spot beside him. "I'm going to tell you something, but you must be certain that you want to know it."

I stared at him in exasperation. "You do realize that by saying shit like that you make it impossible for me to not want to know."

"Arrow and Rowen are brothers." Cinder paused, assessing my dropped jaw. "They are the only known set of nephilim siblings in existence. It's unheard of for an angel or demon to manage to commit such a sin twice before being caught, but Arrow and Rowen are living proof. Arrow may or may not know this. Which is one of many reasons to watch him."

I gaped at him, mouth open with no sound coming out. Brothers. Angelic and demonic parents of the nephilim were locked away to await judgment for the crime of tampering with the human bloodline. Whoever their father was, he had to be amazingly clever to create two illicit offspring.

My poor, alcohol-abused brain raced. Only one person had the full answer to this riddle, but I was pretty sure that God wasn't giving out that kind of info. Which was just as well. This was where faith came in, something I sorely lacked when I needed it most.

"I don't understand where I come into this," I finally said. "I'm nobody compared to the two of them. How can I possibly help?"

Cinder pulled me into a squishy hug and ruffled my hair. "Oh, but you are certainly somebody. You don't realize it yet, but inside you exists the power to save them both."

Chapter Eleven

I gave my cheek a slap. "I'm not dreaming, am I? Have I already fallen asleep? Because I could swear I just heard the craziest thing that's ever come out of your mouth."

Cinder's soft chuckle didn't make me feel better like it usually did. Stunned, I sat there, hoping he was about to yell, "Psych!" But he didn't.

"You're destined for great things, kiddo. What can I say? I can't wait to see how amazing you are." Tiny laugh lines crinkled the corners of his eyes. He showed no hint of worry or concern. Cinder really believed what he'd said.

"Yeah, no pressure or anything." I let my breath out in a whoosh. Nothing like a small panic attack to turn a mild hangover headache into a skull banger. "Should I even ask? I mean, is this what you've been preparing me for? How am I supposed to help anyone?"

"There's no need to look ahead. Just know that good things await you. Take it from moment to moment and have faith. You have more potential than you allow yourself to believe."

I laughed then, though it was bitter and tasteless. "I'm rocking a hell of a hangover. Again. And you just caught me with a guy in my bed. Are you sure you've got the right girl? I think you must be mistaken. I can't help anybody."

Cinder stroked a hand through my messy hair before leaning in to kiss my forehead. "You'll be surprised when you discover what you're capable of. Get some rest. We'll talk later."

He disappeared before I could give him shit for leaving me with such heavy thoughts. I'd been told my whole life that there was something different about me, but different didn't always mean good. In fact, it rarely did. Cinder's use of the term special wasn't fooling me.

I rolled over into the center of the bed. Immediately Rowen's scent rose up around me. I grabbed the pillow he'd used and dragged it close. The feel-good chemicals in my brain went off like an explosion. With a goofy smile on my face, I closed my eyes and breathed deeply. I didn't know what was yet to come, but I knew already that I would do anything to help Rowen. As for Arrow, well, he seemed to be beyond help to me, but it wasn't up to me to make that call.

I didn't really doubt Cinder's claims about me. Yet I still had a hard time believing that someone as deeply flawed as I was could be of any use. I did understand that the dark wanted me to think I could never belong to the light.

Wrestling with doubts and insecurities had never served me well in the past. So I snuggled in amid the mess of blankets, thinking only of good things.

I had a few decent design jobs to work on in the coming week, including a movie poster for an indie film. Crimson Sin was well on its way to a successful battle of the bands win. And I was going to see Rowen again. My mother had taught me young to count my blessings rather than my problems, something I'd fallen asleep doing since childhood.

Now I lay awake doing that very thing until all of Cinder's words flooded back to me with all of my questions. What about these two brothers was so damn important? And why me? What could I really do? Eventually the thoughts jumbled together, and I sank into sleep. The confusion followed me there, and my dreams were plagued with questions that left me restless and tired when I woke several hours later.

I needed a few moments to realize that my phone had woken me. I fumbled to answer it when I saw Jett's number.

"Tell me everything," she gushed into my ear. "Did you fuck him? I want details."

I rolled over with a groan. "No, Jett. I did not fuck him. He did spend the night though. We cuddled. It was nice."

Jett made a gagging sound. "Oh, barf. I was hoping for some orgasmic tales. So nothing exciting to share?"

"Well, there was something." I told her about Koda and the conversation it led to when Rowen and I returned to my apartment. I ended with Cinder finding us in bed together and the talk he and I had after Rowen left.

"Damn. No more playing human for you, girl. Time to shine."

"Ugh. Don't say that. I am so not ready for any of this."

Jett was quiet for a moment. "If we only did things when we were ready, we'd never do a damn thing, Spike. Remember our first serious show? How fucking scared we were? We almost backed out. But we didn't. And you can't now. Not if it's as big a deal as Cinder says it is."

"Yeah, I suppose. So what happened with you last night? You said the pack needed you." Changing the subject was the best way for me to get out of bed. If I didn't stop thinking about it all, I might never leave the comfort of my blankets again.

She turned away from the phone to shout at her cat to stop destroying the couch before answering. "We had to vote on a new pack member. Nothing too detrimental. Routine stuff. So are we jamming tonight? We need to be ready for Saturday."

With a longing glance back at the bed, I left the bedroom. "I have to tail Arrow tonight. Cinder wants me to keep an eye on him."

"Geez, that's shitty. What a crappy way to spend a night." Jett paused to puff on a cigarette. "Want me to come with?" It was tempting. Having a werewolf with me would lend some confidence, which I was seriously lacking. However, Jett was a wild card, an unpredictable loose cannon that could go off at any time.

"Thanks, but I've got this. I'll attract less attention alone. Your purple hair is too eye catching."

She seemed to accept this though she probably knew I was blowing her off. "That's true. It is pretty amazing. Give me a call if you need any backup. I'll be there. Otherwise, I'll talk to you later."

As I got ready to go out, I couldn't help but be skeptical. Arrow could be anywhere. What if he wasn't home? The fact that Rowen lived there too made me uncomfortable. If he saw me lurking outside his house like a total creeper, he'd never trust me again.

I dressed all in charcoal gray. A hoodie and yoga pants would guarantee my comfort. I didn't bother with much makeup seeing as the point was to go unseen. Nervous tremors shook my hands as I ran a brush through my hair and put it in a high ponytail. I slid a small, silver-coated dagger into my boot, hoping like hell that I wouldn't have to use it. Ensuring that my phone was on silent, I prayed that Cinder knew what he was doing by sending me on this mission. I slipped out of the apartment building with as much stealth as I could muster.

After parking my loud, old car down the street from Arrow's house, I tugged my hood up and crept closer on foot. This was a horrible idea. I could feel it in my bones. It was just past sunset. Arrow's BMW sat in the driveway. What if he stayed in tonight and watched TV or something? Was I supposed to sit here all night?

My worries were unfounded. Twenty minutes later, the door opened. When Arrow appeared, my heart raced, and I held my breath. He glanced around before descending the front steps to the car. When he got in I made my way back to the Nova. Following him might prove difficult since my old beater would never keep up with that BMW if he drove like a maniac.

I ducked in the driver's seat as he passed. Then I eased onto the street behind him, careful to keep a safe distance. This was so dangerous. I kept waiting for him to notice me, but if he did, he gave no indication.

Arrow was a better driver than I'd expected. He followed all of the road rules and even paused at a railroad crossing. Weird. He seemed to be trying not to attract attention from other motorists or passing cops.

When he headed to The Spirit Room, I wasn't all that surprised. A lot of us hung out there frequently throughout the week. It would be hard to go unseen there, but if he did see me, it shouldn't be obvious that I was following him. After all, us girls hung out there too. He didn't own the place.

None of Arrow's close circle of friends were there. I was relieved that Rowen wasn't with him. It soon became apparent that he was there to meet someone.

I ordered a virgin daiquiri and lurked on the opposite side of the room, trying to go unnoticed. A few people stopped to say hello, acquaintances I knew through the rock scene. Even as I made light conversation with them, I kept Arrow within my sights.

He lingered near the stage, feigning interest in the band playing. A few minutes passed, and he began to look annoyed. Muttering to himself, he checked his phone.

A pale brunette emerged from the crowd to touch his shoulder. She was gaunt, and even from where I was I could see her tremors. Head bowed, she leaned in to whisper something in his ear.

He appeared thoughtful for a moment before nodding. Arrow smiled and held out a hand for her to lead the way.

She headed for the restrooms, taking his hand and pulling him into the ladies room with her. I had an ill feeling that I knew where this was going, but I followed anyway.

The bathroom was busy. A group of girls clustered around the counter, checking makeup and gossiping. The scent of marijuana hung on the air. Nobody paid Arrow any mind as he slipped into an end stall with the brown-haired girl.

Taking a deep breath to calm my nerves, I entered the stall next to them and listened. Their voices were lost in the loud chatter, but I was able to make out some of their exchange.

"You know, Rose, eventually I'll have to stop taking blowjobs as payment," Arrow said with a chuckle. "As good as you are, they just don't pay the bills."

"Just this last time, Arrow, please. I promise. I'll have cash next time. Really. I'm good for it. I'm just waiting on some money I'm owed." Her voice was high and tinny, as if she was used to going through this routine.

"Someone owes you? Do you need me to smash some knees? I'm always happy to help a lady out." Arrow's voice was oily and smooth, meant to charm. It made me shudder.

He was absolutely vile. When the sound of a zipper was followed by his soft moans, I had to put a hand over my mouth to stifle the urge to vomit. Arrow was a nasty thing, more demon than human in my opinion.

I didn't hang around to listen to his big finish. I'd heard enough. Squeezing in among the gossip queens, I washed my hands and exited the bathroom before he could get a glimpse of me.

Waiting for him to come out fed my growing dislike of the guy. It was hard not to spew any venom his way. It was natural that I had a dark side like we all do, but if I fed it, it would grow. And that was Arrow's game, not mine.

When he strode from the restroom with a self-satisfied grin, I swore beneath my breath. Was there any redeemable quality in him at all? He had just taken advantage of someone with a drug problem, having her get on her knees in a dirty washroom for him. For drugs. And he was cool with that. I loathed him.

He didn't leave right away. He paused to talk with a few guys gathered around a table near the bar. His gaze swept the room, and I turned away, hoping to blend in among the rest. *Please don't see me,* I thought.

When I felt brave enough to turn back, he was gone. Shit. I scanned the entire vicinity but didn't see him. I was going to lose him. I hurried outside in time to see him turn the corner into the parking lot. I'd parked along the street a block away so I rushed to my car in a full out run. Something told me that Arrow wasn't going home, and now I was curious. I wanted to know what else he was up to.

My nerves had faded back in the bathroom stall. I wasn't afraid of being seen now, though I was wary. Arrow peeled out of the parking lot with a squeal of tires, and I frowned as I eased down the street behind him. A red light ahead would slow him down. I didn't need to race after him.

The sudden change in his driving was interesting. He'd gone from being calm and subdued to being feisty and maybe a little reckless. I wondered if it had anything to do with what had just happened. Maybe he'd gotten a thrill out of it.

When he headed to one of the richest neighborhoods in the city, my curiosity grew. He pulled up to a house completely surrounded by a perimeter wall. I watched with a sinking sensation as he walked up to an intercom with a bag in hand. The gate swung open to allow him entry.

Shit. What was I going to do now? I had no idea who lived here. It might not be worth hanging around. Still, I had to know what Arrow was doing in a place like this. Maybe it was his supplier's house.

Getting caught up in drug deal drama was not my intent, but I had a feeling that this went beyond drugs to demons. I could almost smell the sulfur as I walked up to the house. Wary of cameras, I kept my hood pulled up to hide my face. Of course where demons are concerned, cameras were the least of my worries.

"Spike," came a voice from behind me, and I whirled to find Koda standing much too close. He seemed quite pleased with himself for having caught me by surprise. "Can I help you with something?"

"Yeah, you can go away and pretend you never saw me." Hey, it was worth a try.

As expected, Koda laughed at me. "I think you owe me an explanation. For starters, what the hell are you doing here?"

I never considered anything but the truth. No sense lying to a liar. Really. "I'm following Arrow. What are you doing?"

"Following you."

Well that was certainly awkward. The demon clearly had much greater stealth than I did. I'd had no idea I was being followed.

"Why?" I asked, wondering if I could get to the dagger in my boot fast enough if needed.

Koda smirked, but the darkness in his red eyes lacked amusement. His expression was pure evil. "The question should be, why not? By protecting the undecided nephilim, you made the wrong choice. You can't save him. We will have him. And at some point, we'll have you too, if you don't get yourself killed first."

"Don't get your hopes up, Koda. I'm not going to abandon Rowen." I dismissed his threat with a shrug, refusing to let him of all people get to me. "I don't suppose you'd like to tell me what Arrow is up to in there."

A glare that promised terrible things marred his face. He grabbed me roughly by the arm, holding tight when I tried to jerk away. "Even better," he said slyly. "I'll show you."

Chapter Twelve

My protests went unheard as Koda dragged me over to the gate. After punching a code into the security box next to the intercom, the gate swung open for him. I was unable to get a look at the code but found it interesting that Arrow had called for permission.

Perhaps I should have been scared. I mean, demons were friggin' scary, but Koda's presence kept me calm. There was no way I would let him have the satisfaction of being the one to frighten me. Those days were long over.

The house was big, small mansion big. Large white pillars bordered the front door. I debated whether I should let Koda take me inside or go for my dagger. Arrow sure wasn't worth dying for.

I was about to reach for the dagger when Koda said, "Relax, Spike. Nobody will hurt you. Not as long as you're with me."

I really didn't like what he was implying. With the nastiest glower I could pull together, I spoke through clenched teeth. "I don't belong to you. I never will. Get that through your head."

"Well if you want to leave here alive, then you'd better just shut up. If you say something like that in here, there will be a battle for you. And no matter who wins, you'll lose."

No way in hell was I making the mistake of trusting Koda. So much for being stealthy. Now Arrow would know I had been following him. I sucked at this.

Koda pushed through the door, dragging me along beside him. The smell of sulfur was so thick I coughed. He rolled his red eyes at me and continued on through the large foyer, behind the spiral staircase, and down a hallway to a set of elaborate double doors.

When the doors opened they revealed what appeared to be a throne room of sorts, and fear slipped in to claim me. Koda shoved me along in front of him, and I struggled to keep my footing.

Crimson Sin

The room was vast with high windows and smooth, hardwood floors. A row of throne-like chairs stood at the far end, the center one seeming to command the entire room. Koda pushed me on through the room, into the middle where a group of demons stood gathered around a pentagram sunk into a circle in the middle of the room. The place virtually hummed with demon magic. I swallowed hard, knowing there was something bad going on here.

Koda dragged me forward, loudly announcing, "Look what I found lurking around outside."

I froze as the gaze of half a dozen demons landed on me. They all stood around the large pentagram etched into the sunken pit. Arrow stood among them, his expression unreadable though there was surprise in his eyes. What struck fear into the depths of my heart though was what was happening in the center of the demon circle.

A demon with dark hair and black eyes held a rooster by the legs. The head was missing. Blood dripped from the neck. The dark-red drops landed in the center of the circle where a hazy smoke slowly began to rise. The demon ran a finger through the blood before turning to a woman beside him and tracing a symbol on her forehead with it. She was the only human present, a black magic witch most likely.

Without looking at Koda the demon said, "Why did you bring that nephilim in here? She's a white lighter."

"Barely," Arrow muttered with a smirk, drawing everyone's attention to him. He shrugged and eyed me maliciously.

"No, I'm not. I'm undecided." My desperate claim went ignored. They didn't care. All that mattered to them was that I wasn't dark.

"She wanted to know what was going on in here," Koda said as if that were reason enough. "So I decided to show her."

The demon holding the rooster frowned. He did look at Koda this time, but it was with a subdued expression that told me he was inferior to the red-eyed Koda. "And what were you hoping to prove by doing that?"

Only one other red-eyed demon stood around the circle. I'd noticed that eye color was an indicator of their place in the hierarchy. Black-eyed demons were level three, while red-eyed demons were level two. It was near unheard of for level one angels to become demons so they were few and far between. I'd never seen one.

Koda stood tall, his chest puffed out as if offended that anyone dared to question him. "I wanted her to see what happens if she chooses the wrong side."

"Good luck with that." Again Arrow shot me a snide look to go along with his smartass remark. He was enjoying this, and my loathing for him grew.

"Well," said the red-eyed demon standing next to Arrow. "Now that you've interrupted the ritual for your own personal amusement, finish it off and kill her."

Wait, what? "Excuse me?" I spoke up, ignoring Koda when he shook me. "Kill me? I don't even know what's going on here."

"And you never will." The red-eyed demon studied me, an eyebrow raised as he assessed me and seemed to find me lacking. He wore the form of a thirty-something man with smooth, tanned skin. Spanish, if I had to guess.

I yelled, "Koda!" Despite the tight hold he had on me, I fought to break free of him. "You are fucking scum, you know that? I can't believe your ego is so fucking fragile that you have to threaten my life to prove yourself."

A titter of laughter rippled through the demons. The human woman was not amused in the slightest. She glared at me as if she'd happily kill me herself. Whatever we'd interrupted, it had been important to her.

"Dash, it's fine, really," Koda said, addressing the one with the scarlet gaze. "Spike is here as my guest. I want her to see why she should never underestimate us."

Dash didn't look convinced. He glared first at me, then Koda. Tension thrummed between the two of them that made the rest of the group stiffen. Perhaps they would fight. It might be my only hope for escape unless Cinder decided to drop in on me.

"We don't have white lighters dropping in for visits, Koda." Dash spoke between clenched teeth. "She may be undecided, but she's been working for the light. White lighters are not welcome here. Not even a half-breed like her."

Arrow frowned and pressed his lips together into a thin line. He stood stiffly, his shoulders squared. I found satisfaction in the half-breed remark because it got under his skin. I could see it picking at him.

"Can we please get back to my wedding?" The raven-tressed woman suddenly shouted, her voice high and shrill.

Wedding? Taking a closer look at her, I saw that she was indeed wearing a gown. It was black with a cinched waist and long, flowing skirt. The black-eyed demon who had smeared blood on her face held tight to her hand, making it evident that they were the happy couple. So to speak.

This was the worst wedding I'd ever been to. And I'd attended a few doozies. I couldn't imagine why a woman would want to wed herself to a demon, but she was a witch, thus not someone I could relate to.

"Hush a moment, Skylar," Dash admonished with a scowl. Then he glided over to me, his feet barely touching the floor. He got unbearably close, openly sniffing me like I was under inspection. "Who is your father, girl?"

I recoiled, leaning as far away from him as I could get. With Koda at my back, it didn't give me much room, but something told me that Dash was the greater evil of the two of them. It may have been the slither in his step or the oily tone of his voice. But more than likely it was the deep abyss of black that seemed to surround him like a second skin. I could feel it all over him, reaching for me.

"I don't know," I lied. There was no way in hell I was giving my father's name to a room full of demons. Not even Koda knew for sure who my father was. They already knew who Rowen's father was, and look how well that was working out for him and Arrow.

"Don't lie to me." His face frightfully blank, Dash reached out to touch me, and I jerked back. A small smile creased his sharp, angular face. "He was a fool to let you live. One so rare as you would have been better off never having been born."

A warm but clammy hand touched my face, and I muffled a shriek. My fingers tingled, and a bolt of fire leaped between us. It didn't last long, just seconds, but when it burnt out, Dash was furious.

"You dare to offend me in my own house?" He shouted, grabbing hold of me and snarling into my face.

Koda shoved him off me, getting between us. With both hands on Dash's collar, Koda growled, "This isn't your house, Dash. And Spike isn't anything to you. Back the fuck off."

"It's the house of my queen who I will serve until the end of time. In her absence, it is mine. Unless you'd like to contest that."

"Maybe I would. She's my queen too."

The two demons engaged in a silent war, each trying to intimidate the other into submission. We all watched them, everyone but Skylar, who glared at me. I hadn't ruined her wedding day—that had been Koda—but she didn't seem to see it that way.

"Be careful, Dash," Koda said, low and menacing. "If you keep on like this you're going to end up like Shya. A washed up has-been consumed by obsession."

This earned a snicker from a few of those present though I had no idea what they were talking about. I didn't need to know. I'd heard and seen enough.

"Never again speak to me of Shya. I'm not fool enough to think I can rule in Lilah's stead. I mean only to honor her empire in her absence, not to claim it." Dash vibrated with rage. His voice was calm and controlled, which made him that much more terrifying.

An angry scream rang out, ear shattering in its intensity. I covered my ears and winced. Only Arrow did the same. The demons stared at Skylar, who had clearly had enough. She stood there with palms up and eyes rolled back in her head so only the whites showed. A jumble of Latin rolled off her tongue, and a spell immediately began to take shape.

Her demon fiancé clapped a hand over her mouth to silence her, but it was too late. The spell hit me right in the chest, choking off my breath as it sought to get inside me. The crazy witch had thrown a curse at me.

As a witch, she was only a conduit of the power she had called. It didn't come from within her but from elsewhere. My power, meager next to these demons, was greater than what a human could handle. I gasped in relief when her curse fell away, unable to overcome the angelic essence inside me.

Retaliating wasn't an option. She was a human, caught up by the dark, a puppet of sorts. She didn't know any better. It was incredibly sad really.

Skylar's fiancé pulled her tight to him, pinning her arms down at her sides. He whispered something in her ear, but she only struggled harder.

"This is my goddamn wedding day," she hissed in his face. "I said I'd give up everything for you, but you can't even give me a decent wedding?"

The woman had a point. This was shittier than a cheap Vegas wedding performed by Elvis.

"I want her to be the sacrifice." Skylar pointed at me, nostrils flared. "Fuck the rooster."

Dash looked at me like I was a fish on a hook. Eyes glittering with evil glee, he nodded. "As you wish, Skylar. It is your special day, after all. Now calm down. It's not good to get so worked up. Your magic is erratic enough."

"That's not going to happen." Koda flared his wings in an unspoken threat. "Do you have any idea how valuable Spike is?"

I frowned, not liking the way this was going. Feeling eyes upon me, I looked over to find Arrow staring thoughtfully at me. Just looking at his smug face made me seethe. If I got out of this alive, I was going to rip him a new one.

"Valuable to you maybe," Dash sneered. "She means nothing to me. I have no use for more nephilim, regardless of gender. Her rarity might make her a worthy sacrifice." He seemed to ponder this, coming to an even worse conclusion. "Actually, maybe I'll use her as my own sacrifice."

My palms were slick with sweat. For the most part, demons didn't show a lot of interest in me. Every now and then I'd run into one like Koda who wanted to see what I was made of, but usually they treated me like they would any undecided nephilim, like a pain in their ass.

Arrow cleared his throat and raised a hand for attention. "I'm afraid that's not possible. You see Spike here, she and I are sleeping together. I wasn't going to say anything because it wasn't relevant. But it does mean that no harm can come to her by this coven."

Dash looked back and forth between Arrow and me. Lips pursed, he regarded us with heavy scrutiny. If anyone was going to blow the lie, it was me. The thought of touching Arrow made me ill, but for some reason he was trying to help me. I decided against making it hard for him.

"You expect me to believe that a white lighter lets you touch her?" Dash gave a bark of laughter, ignoring me when I again insisted

I wasn't light. He tried to push by Koda to approach me again, but Koda held him back.

With a shake of his head, Dash fixed his gaze on Arrow. "I don't know why you'd want to help her, but I know you're lying."

"I'm not though," Arrow said quickly, sticking a hand into his pocket. "Look, I have proof."

I cringed, knowing he was going to show them that damn photo. Somehow I was still hopeful when he held his phone out so everyone could clearly see the picture of me in my underwear.

"This is Spike in my bed after a show we both played. Why else would she be there if we weren't screwing?" Arrow was so calm and convincing that I almost believed it myself. "She followed me here tonight. It's my fault. Not hers. I should've known better."

Dash stared at the photo. He didn't look entirely convinced, but he couldn't argue against the sight of me in my undies passed out in Arrow's bed. "Yes, you should have. Get her out of here. I'll deal with you later." Turning on Koda with a black orb spinning in his palm, he said, "We are going to finish this wedding, and then you and I are going to talk about our priorities."

Koda's face darkened with unspoken promises of violence. "Count on it."

Neither of them looked at me again as Arrow grabbed my arm and pulled me from the room. Skylar burst into angry tears, and voices rose in argument as we fled. We paused only long enough to hit the gate button on the intercom system inside the door.

Arrow didn't say a word until we had exited the house. Once we were outside the gate, he pulled me around to face him.

"Why were you following me?" He hissed, anger causing his aura to buzz like he was consumed by bees. "You could've been killed in there, Spike. All because you were sent to tail me. What kind of guardian sends his charge on a suicide mission?"

"Ow," I muttered through clenched teeth. I glared at him. He held tight to my upper arm, refusing to let go. "Cinder isn't my guardian. He's a friend."

"Why did he tell you to follow me?" Arrow shook me until I yelped. "What the fuck are you doing here?"

His hand was like a vice around my arm, squeezing until my fingers began to tingle from numbness. Fury surrounded him like a storm cloud, raining all over both of us. I was angry too.

"I was following you so I could find out why you're trying so hard to keep me away from Rowen. He doesn't deserve to turn out like you." Honesty usually was the best policy. In this case I wasn't so sure, but I was above lying to Arrow. "Now will you please let go of me? I can't feel my fingers."

Arrow released me suddenly, as if he hadn't realized he'd been hurting me. His pupils dilated dangerously as negative emotions ruled him. I wasn't sure what he was capable of, and I wasn't too keen on finding out just yet.

"You just risked your life because of Rowen?" He asked in disbelief. "That is fucking stupid."

"And you just risked something too by helping me out, didn't you? What was that all about?"

With a snort of derision, Arrow spun on a booted heel and stalked off down the street toward my car. He pulled a pack of cigarettes from a pocket and stuck one between his lips. I followed along, surprised when he stopped at my car and leaned against the side.

A plume of smoke rose up as he eyed me, uncertainty heavy in his hazel gaze. "I do have some empathy you know, Spike. I may be dark, but I'm still half human."

"Could've fooled me," I muttered. When he glowered I held up a hand in surrender. "Thank you for getting me out of there. But you can't blame me for thinking the worst of you. You used your blackmail material to convince a bunch of demons we're fucking. I can't help but think that was a bad idea."

"Yeah, well you're out here now instead of in there, so you're welcome. Don't ever say I can't be a nice guy."

I choked on a laugh. "Good one. I saw you accept a blowjob as payment for someone's drug habit an hour ago. Whatever you are, you are not a nice guy. Why were you in there anyway?"

I plucked the cigarette from between his fingers and took a long drag. Son of a bitch, why did bad things feel so damn good?

"I don't force anyone to do anything. Free will, baby." He produced a joint and sparked it up, offering it to me after taking a drag. "I brought the rooster."

"No thanks. I don't smoke when I'm driving." It wasn't lost on me that he had just done the same thing to me as he'd done back at The Spirit Room, only on a much smaller scale. "I'm also not going to suck you off as a thank you either."

A scowl marred his face. Dark smudges beneath his eyes gave him a ghost-like appearance. His shoulder-length, black hair peeked out from beneath the knit cap he often wore. To look at either of us, you'd never guess we were anything but a couple of dirty rockers. Looks were so deceiving.

"You know, Spike, I actually kind of like you. You're a ballsy chick, and you play guitar like a fucking madwoman. It's beautiful really. But being pals with the light makes you the enemy, and I can't forget that. I don't want to see bad shit happen to you, but you have to stay away from Rowen."

I bristled at the hard edge to his tone. 'Enemy' was right. Arrow was so caught up in the dark that he didn't even know it was his own brother he sought to help them claim.

"I don't believe you have the authority to tell me who I can spend time with. Free will, baby." I repeated his words back to him, and he snatched his cigarette back with a snarl.

"Look, I know Rowen is a nice guy, and he's dreamy and whatever, but you'd be doing yourself a favor by forgetting about him."

"So would you," I countered, starting to get riled up.

"What's that supposed to mean?" Arrow blew a puff of smoke in my face and studied me. "Do you know something that I don't know?"

I was treading on dangerous territory. Telling Arrow what I knew might be a mistake, but if he knew, maybe he would be human enough to spare his brother the same hell he had to be living in.

Pulling my keys out with a loud jingle, I stormed around the car to the driver's side, needing to get away from Arrow before I did something to really fuck things up.

"Oh no, you don't." Hot on my heels, Arrow grabbed ahold of my arm again, gentler this time. "Tell me what you know."

It was my turn to study him. I searched Arrow's eyes for anything remotely human. Despite his actions a few minutes ago, there was little compassion or caring in him. If it was there, it was buried deep.

"You really don't know, do you?" I breathed, unable to hold the words back. It broke my heart to think that Rowen's brother would knowingly drag him into something he would never escape from.

"Know what? Spit it out dammit." Arrow tossed the remains of the cigarette and the joint, having attention only for what I might tell him.

He was unbearably close. My back was pressed against the Nova's door with Arrow hovering too close for escape. My heart raced as I fought with the decision to tell him or to keep it to myself. If he didn't know, he wouldn't have a chance to do the right thing. What choice did I have?

"Arrow," I said, tentative, knowing I couldn't take it back once I said it. "Rowen is your brother."

The moment that followed was heavy and long. He stared at me, unblinking. Then he started to laugh, a low ripple of noise that grew until his shoulders shook.

"You're fucking with me," he accused, his eyes lit up with a maniacal light as he chuckled. "Did your guardian tell you that?"

I was mildly surprised at his reaction. Also, somewhat concerned. "What could I possibly have to gain by lying to you?"

"How can that even be possible?" He leaned against the car, holding the door shut with a hand. "If you're lying to me, Spike—"

"Your father was the only fallen to ever father more than one child. With two different women. And I don't know why, but the dark is hell bent on having the both of you. Pun intended." Annoyed at his intimidating proximity, I gave him a shove out of my personal space and turned to stick the key into the door lock.

Arrow lunged forward to grab the door as I opened it. "Wait," he almost shouted. "Please. Just wait a minute. I'm trying to wrap my head around this."

I turned to him with scrutiny. "You really didn't know?"

With a slow shake of his head, he cast a glance back toward the gated house we'd just left. "No. I didn't know. They told me to befriend him. To watch him until the time was right to bring him into the fold. They never told me anything else."

Disgust filled me, and I let him see it in my eyes. "They dropped you into his life, and you just pretended to be his friend so you could bring him over to the dark side? Who needs enemies with friends like you?"

Arrow's gaze darted about. He seemed confused and maybe even kind of scared. "You don't understand. It started that way, but he really is my friend. I care about him. He's like a…brother to me."

Dropping the F-bomb like it was going out of style, Arrow turned away, pacing along the street beside my car. He pulled the cap off his head and ran a hand through his long hair. For just a moment, I felt sorry for him. Then I reminded myself of what a supreme prick he was, and the feeling faded.

I held the car door open, glancing uncertainly between the interior of the car and the dark nephilim cursing up a storm beside me. Part of me found some satisfaction in his torment. He deserved it.

As soon as I had that thought, I felt shitty about it. It wasn't my place to judge Arrow or enjoy his pain. Yet I did, a little. Hey, I don't claim to be perfect.

Feeling the need to offer some kind of advice, I said, "Arrow, you have an opportunity here. If you care about Rowen, don't let the dark have him."

"Oh right. Because it's just that fucking simple." Whirling to face me, Arrow's eyes flashed a deep, drowning black. Then it was gone, and they were hazel again. "Do you have any idea what would happen to me if I got caught encouraging an undecided to join the light?"

I nodded, understanding where his torment came from. "I see. This is all about you and not at all about Rowen. That is exactly why he needs protection. I won't be staying away from him. I don't care what you threaten me with."

Arrow stuck another cigarette between his lips and angrily puffed away. "Just leave, Spike."

I didn't wait for another chance to take off. Sliding into the driver's seat, I stuck the key in the ignition and hesitated. "Hey, Arrow. Not everyone knows who Rowen is. You should try to keep it that way."

He didn't speak again, just watched me with the vicious stare of a predatory animal as I pulled a U-turn and vacated the rich neighborhood. I couldn't do anything but leave Arrow to his thoughts. I hoped he made the right decision, but I wasn't going to hold my breath.

Chapter Thirteen

Nerves racked me over more than just the next round of the battle. This was the first time all week that Rowen, Arrow, and I would be under the same roof. Keeping secrets from Rowen was brutal. I kept wondering if I should come clean about Arrow being his brother, but I knew that was Arrow's secret to share. This was his choice, not mine.

Throughout the week Rowen and I had spent a substantial amount of time together. Though we weren't an official item, we definitely had a thing, as Jett liked to call it. Every moment I spent with him drew me deeper down the rabbit hole. Against my will I was falling hard for the boy.

From what I could tell, Arrow had said nothing to Rowen about their shared parentage. It was discouraging. I didn't think I could count on the dark nephilim to do the right thing. It wasn't who he had chosen to be.

"We play first tonight," Jett announced as she sidled up to me with a drink in each hand. "That sucks. I prefer to play last. Really bring things to a crashing halt."

"So we set the bar high instead and make sure nobody even comes close to comparing with us." It was too bad that beating Arrow meant beating Rowen. I was determined to have some victory to throw in Arrow's face, even if it was only this one.

My nervous gaze kept going to the door as I anticipated the arrival of Molly's Chamber. To Arrow's credit he hadn't yet shown the photo of me to Rowen. Perhaps he was saving it for something special.

"Would you chill out, Spike? Here, have a drink. You look like you could use one." She shoved one of the two drinks into my hand. Her tone was gentle. She knew about the dilemma I faced. She was the only one who did other than Cinder.

Arrow walked into The Spirit Room then. My heart skipped a beat when I spotted Dash at his side. Demons rarely take on a corporeal appearance and walk openly. They usually moved unseen among humankind.

"What the hell is going on?" I muttered as my nerves skyrocketed.

Jett followed my gaze, her glossy, pink lips pursed in curiosity. "What's up? Who's that guy? He's kind of hot."

"No, he isn't. He's a demon. The one from the wedding Koda dragged me into. If he's here, it has to mean trouble." My palms grew sweaty, and I shoved the drink back to Jett. My stomach was far too fluttery for alcohol. Something told me it would be a very bad idea to consume intoxicants with Dash around.

"You look fucking amazing tonight." Startling me, Rowen appeared from behind me, slipping an arm around my waist. He kissed me, a lingering press of lips that made Jett snicker. That swooning moment didn't last long enough, and unfortunately it didn't help me shake the increasing sense of dread.

I cast a glance down at my attire and smiled. "Thanks, babe." Jean shorts over fishnets with black stilettos and a Rocket Raccoon tank top completed my look. A cross pendant hung from my neck, and my wrists were adorned in spiked bracelets.

Rowen was casual in jeans and a Misfits t-shirt. Chains hung from his pants, and his blue 'hawk was spiked up with that adorable long piece falling into his eyes. I wanted so badly to sweep it aside, but knowing Dash was there made me hesitant to touch him. His arm was still around me, and I cringed, awaiting the moment Dash would see and know Arrow had lied.

I pulled away, hoping it wasn't obvious to Rowen that I was trying to escape him. It was for his own good though. Really.

"I hate to cut this short, but we play first, and I need to primp a little before sound check. Catch you later?" I grinned, doing my best to act normal.

"Yes," Jett cut in, grabbing hold of my arm. "We need to have a little girl time before we rock your faces off. You'll have to wait your turn, lover boy. Spike's all mine right now."

I let her drag me off, blowing him a kiss when I was sure Dash and Arrow weren't nearby. In fact, where were they? A quick scan of the room didn't reveal them. I had a terrible feeling about this.

"Jett, I don't feel good about this. Dash is going to find out Arrow lied."

"He doesn't have to," she said close to my ear to be heard. "Just play along. Do what you have to do."

"In front of Rowen? I can't climb all over his best friend in front of him because there's a demon sniffing about. He'll never understand." My pulse raced, and I felt ill. Should I have told Rowen about the incident at the demon wedding?

As we passed the washrooms on our way backstage, I was grabbed roughly by the arm and yanked away from Jett. Inside the men's washroom, Arrow pulled me into the corner behind the door and held up a finger for silence when I opened my mouth to ream him out.

"I couldn't shake Dash when he insisted on coming here with me tonight," he said in a rush. "I'm not sure what he's up to, but if he sees you all over Rowen then he's going to know we lied. Keep your distance until I can get rid of him."

"That sounds more like it's your problem than mine," I hissed, feeling defensive and cornered.

"You think so? Pretty strong words for an undecided. If they don't think I'm working on bringing you over to our side, then I'd say you're in the same position Rowen's in."

"What do you care?" Being undecided was dangerous. I knew that already. Koda was a prime example of that danger. However, Arrow was right that I didn't need another demon fixated on me.

Arrow's face contorted into an ugly sneer. "I'm trying to save my own ass here. You might want to do the same."

"And what about Rowen?" I demanded, hating Arrow for being so cold and selfish.

"Dash isn't here for him. He's here for us. In fact, as I was told earlier, we are under investigation for conspiracy." Arrow was surrounded by a cloud of negativity. It seemed to feed off him or vice versa. I couldn't tell.

His words chilled me. Conspiracy? The dark thought Arrow and I were plotting something?

"But why?" I murmured, more to myself than to him.

"Because we're shitty fucking liars compared to demons who have existed since the beginning of time."

No sooner had Arrow uttered those words than Dash appeared right behind him looking both angry and suspicious. Reacting quickly, Arrow kissed me, laying it on thick by slipping me some tongue. He tasted like cigarettes and beer. It was all I could do not to dry heave in his mouth. Faking my way through that kiss without punching him was one of the hardest things I'd ever had to do.

"Now get out of here before someone sees you in the men's room, you naughty vixen." Arrow followed up with a slap on my ass as he shoved me out the door.

Fuming but frightened, I met Jett's quizzical expression with one of my own. With wide eyes I merely shook my head, afraid to say anything in case Dash heard. This was bad.

I rubbed a hand over my left butt cheek where Arrow had slapped it, wishing I could rub away the echo of his touch. I couldn't shake the awful feeling that something terrible was going to occur.

Jett steered me toward the stage where we went through the motions of setting up our gear. Tash and Rubi hadn't arrived yet, but I expected them at any moment. Once I saw Dash and Arrow take a seat with Rowen and the other Molly's Chamber guys, I did breathe a little easier.

Jett said, "Maybe you should just tell Rowen everything, Spike. And maybe you should just make your choice already. Wouldn't that solve some of this problem?" She stepped up to speak into the mike, stopping when the guy in the sound booth gave her a thumbs up.

"It might." I shrugged and picked up my guitar, slipping the strap over my head. "I'm just afraid, you know. Once I choose and make that commitment, then everything changes. And I'm not sure I'm ready for that."

Jett glanced across the room to where Arrow sat between Rowen and Dash. The table of guys drank and laughed. Feeling my stare, Dash met my eyes across the distance. His expression was blank, but I knew without a doubt that he knew Arrow had lied, that he was here to catch us. I just couldn't figure out why it meant so much to him. The dark clearly had trust issues.

"Being ready might not have anything to do with it," Jett mused, spinning a large chunky bracelet on her wrist. "You've gotta do what you gotta do." Jett jumped as her phone buzzed. After a glance at it she said, "Tash wants us to come out and help her unload the amps from the van."

It was a welcome escape from the stifling confines of the rock club I'd once felt so comfortable in. I followed Jett out the side stage door, happy to escape Dash's watchful gaze.

Having Dash in the audience sucked some of the joy out of playing. When the stage lights flashed on in time with the first note out of my guitar, I was painfully aware of the demon's presence. Of course he wasn't the only demon in attendance. Others, those that clung to people, whispering temptation in their ear and silently stripping them of hope for tomorrow, were hard at work, existing only for their task. They weren't here for me. But Dash was.

I fumbled my way through the first song, unfocused and nervous. Jett shot me more than a few "what the fuck" looks. When Tash edged over with her bass and asked me if I was ok, I knew I had to get it together. Letting the band down was not an option. Dash was nobody. He could only steal my thunder if I let him.

That's what I told myself as I prepared for the upcoming solo in the next song. It was a difficult piece that I had written during an especially emotional time. After a particularly bad night where I'd witnessed the repercussions of free will, I had gone home and let out the anguish through my guitar. Getting this piece right meant a lot to me.

Taking on odd jobs for Cinder had been my way of fitting into a world that I wasn't sure I belonged to. It also meant seeing things that I could never unsee. One of those things was the body of a man who had hung himself after returning home from a tour of duty in the Middle East. He had been offered a choice. Death over life. Despair over hope.

There had been nothing I could do. Nothing even Cinder could do. I thought of that lost soul now, and I poured the echo of that memory into the guitar. I too had a choice. I could break under the pressure of Dash and the devouring darkness he represented, or I could bend and prove myself strong enough to stand up against the enemy.

The enemy? Had I already subconsciously made my choice? I knew I would never join the dark. Joining the light intimidated me though. It would mean putting myself out there, risking pain and suffering to fulfill a greater purpose. What if I couldn't hack it?

The spotlight followed Jett as she sang her heart out. Her tone was smooth, then gritty, growling out the anger of the lyrics. The crowd who had gathered around the stage jumped up and down, shouting and crashing into each other.

Feeling the weight of several gazes upon me, I took a deep breath, soaking in the power of the instrument in my hands. Never did I feel as alive as I did on stage with the magic of music flowing through me.

Right as I launched into the solo, Jett threw herself into the crowd, surfing atop the many hands that reached to hold her up. Closing my eyes, I gave myself over to the force inside me and let the solo explode out through my fingers.

It came out flawless, every note perfect, and it felt like my soul soared on wings I did not yet possess. I was breathless and sweaty when I reached the end of the intricate piece. And I was also renewed. The source of my strength was in the gift I'd been given. I met Dash's watchful stare across the distance, and I smiled.

He would not reduce me to a quaking mess. With my head held high, I held his gaze long enough for him to see my intent. Perhaps I was unaligned, but I was not going to be easily coerced.

Emotion filled me: anger at the dark, disgust at Arrow, something like love for Rowen, and fear of all of that. Determination kept my head up and my gaze set on what was right. I'd made it through so much. I would make it through what lay ahead.

Our set ended with an explosive finish. A drum solo from Rubi rocked the house. As the stage lights went dark, Jett collapsed dramatically on the stage.

The sound of the crowd filled my ears and brought a happy grin to my face. *Let's see you top that, Arrow.*

The emcee stepped up to the mike to encourage further applause as we exited the stage. Jett grabbed me in a crushing hug before doing the same to Tash and Rubi who both squealed at her superior wolf strength.

"We are not going home this round, ladies. I can feel it in my bones." Jett's exuberance was infectious. "Let's see Molly's Chamber compete with that."

Crimson Sin

Even though there was one other band left in the running, most of us felt this had become a Molly's Chamber versus Crimson Sin event. Even the radio station hosting the contest had played up the rivalry.

To Jett's bitter dismay, Molly's Chamber had been selected to play last, giving them the chance to end the night on a high note. That's when my nerves began to creep back in. Rowen would be in the crowd while the next band played. How the hell would I avoid him in front of Dash?

I tried to avoid going out into the club by fleeing upstairs to the backstage rooms under the guise of fixing my disheveled hair and smudged makeup. Jett followed along, griping at me while the other girls went to find us a table. They were getting used to the secretive nature Jett and I shared, though I was pretty sure they were ok with being left out of potentially life threatening issues.

"Spike, your hair looks fine, and you know it. Stop trying to avoid this. I've got your back. That demon can't do shit to you in here with so many witnesses."

"He knows, Jett." I whirled to face her, halfway up the stairs. "He knows that Arrow lied, and he's going to expose us. If the dark believes that Arrow and I are plotting something, there's no telling what lengths they will go to. I have to keep Rowen safe."

Jett bit her pink bottom lip, appearing thoughtful but uncertain. She shoved a sweaty lock of purple hair out of her eyes and sighed. "Yes, but you have to stay safe in order to do that. And that might mean doing something you really don't want to do."

"I'm not sleeping with Arrow to make our lie the truth. Please don't tell me that's what you're suggesting."

We reached the top of the stairs to find the backstage area empty. "No way," Jett spat, disgusted. "He is not worthy of the fabulous that is you. You might have to fake it though. Play a little more kissy face with him or something. And tell Rowen so it doesn't give him a heart attack when it happens."

"Gross," I muttered at the memory of Arrow's kiss. Standing in front of the mirror, I ran my fingers through my hair and fixed a small eyeliner smudge. "I really don't want to go back down there. How much of a wimp am I?"

"You're a warrior, Spike. A fighter. So... fight." Jett shrugged, as if it was that simple. It kind of was. Fight or don't. My options were limited.

"The warrior's greatest strength is knowing when not to fight." Arrow announced his presence by slinking in silently. "Trust me. You don't want to take on Dash."

"What are you doing up here?" I snapped. "Did you leave him alone with Rowen?"

Arrow stepped up beside me to peer into the mirror. He studied his reflection before turning to me with a frown. "They're not alone. Sam and Greyson are down there."

"Yeah and we know how skilled they are with demons. Are you out of your mind?" Hands on my hips, I stared at him aghast.

"I sure hope so. Otherwise this shit isn't doing its job." He tugged a small bag of white powder from his back pocket, offering it to each of us in turn.

Jett sat heavily on the couch in the middle of the room, glaring at him with that predatory gaze of hers. I waved a hand dismissively when he shoved the bag at me.

"You're useless, you know that? He's your brother, Arrow. And you're sniffing shit up your nose while a demon who wants him is alone with him." When he avoided meeting my eyes, I realized, "Oh, fuck. You were supposed to give Dash a chance to be alone with him, weren't you?"

I didn't wait for his reply. I turned to rush back downstairs, but Arrow grabbed me roughly by the arm and jerked me off balance. Jett leaped up with a growl to come to my aid, and he flung his free hand up at her, momentarily freezing her in her tracks.

"Settle down, ladies. Rowen isn't in any danger." His grip tightened when I fought to pull away. There was a glimmer of envy in Arrow's hazel gaze. "I almost wish I'd had someone willing to fight so hard for me."

"You should be fighting for him," I hissed. "He's your brother. Your blood. And you're just going to let them have him."

My palms tingled seconds before Arrow's hand burst into flames. He released me with a shout, and the flame went out.

"Bitch," he swore, shaking his hand though no mark remained. "The only proof I have that Rowen is my brother is your word. That's just not enough for me."

"So it doesn't even matter that he's your friend?" Jett kept her distance, wary of the angelic gifts we both possessed. "You're a horrible person."

Ignoring us both, Arrow shook some of the powder from his little bag onto the counter in front of the mirror. Then he took a twenty-dollar bill from his wallet and rolled it up.

"Do you really think you need more of that shit?" Judgment was heavy in my tone. I didn't care that it wasn't my place to judge. Arrow was a despicable creature.

"Hey, you're not really my fuck buddy, so mind your own damn business." With a wink, he bent to snort the small pile of coke up his nose.

I wasn't a violent person. Not really. Violence made me uncomfortable. But when Arrow straightened up and cast a wry glance my way, the punch just kind of happened.

My fist connected with his face. The pain was sudden and severe, and I could only hope that it had hurt him just as much. My entire hand throbbed, and I was glad I'd already played. I shook it and swore while Jett whooped her encouragement.

Arrow's hand went to his face and came away wet with the blood that dripped from his nose. "You know, Spike, I'm starting to really lose my patience with you. Give me a fucking tissue."

With his head tilted back, he held a hand out in expectation. I fetched one from the box on the counter and flung it at him, smirking as he groped blindly to catch it before it fluttered to the floor.

"You are a piece of shit," I said, my voice low and angry. "I don't care what Dash thinks. It's your lie. In fact, I'm going to go and talk to him myself right now."

"Like hell you are." Arrow grabbed for me again, but I used a self-defense move that Cinder had taught me to side step him, grab his arm, and twist it behind his back. He grunted and then laughed. "Go for it. And I show your photo to Rowen."

"What photo?"

All three of us froze before we slowly turned to find Rowen standing in the doorway. Confusion marred his brow. Dash was with him, hovering much too close. I released Arrow and stepped back, my face hot.

"This one," Arrow said without missing a beat. He pulled his phone out and began to search through the photos. "The photo that proves Spike and I have been sleeping together."

"It doesn't prove any such thing," I protested as fear crawled up the back of my throat. "It's a lie!"

Because Rowen was in the dark on so much going on around him, he would believe what he saw. Arrow was his best friend. How could I compete with that?

I pleaded with Arrow silently, begging him to have some humanity. He'd shown some the night he lied to Dash to help me. But it had come at a price, and this was it.

"Arrow isn't who you think he is." Jett spoke up, coming to my defense as Arrow crossed the room to Rowen. "He's like Spike, a nephilim. He's been lying to you."

Dash narrowed his gaze at Jett, unimpressed with the outspoken werewolf. Arrow shoved the phone at Rowen who briefly glanced at the photo before looking hard at Arrow and then at me.

"What the hell is going on here, Arrow?" he demanded, his amber eyes conveying his confusion.

"Boys, don't you have a show to play soon?" Dash cut in with a charming manner meant to put Rowen at ease. "This discussion may be best left for later." His gaze slid over Arrow and lingered, promising awful things.

"Don't think that I don't know what you are." Rowen turned on Dash with a cool stare. "If you're here because of me, you're wasting your time."

Dash smiled, revealing perfect white teeth. He swept a hand toward me and then Arrow. "Actually I'm here to investigate these two for conspiracy. I do believe I have caught them in a lie."

"The only one lying is Arrow." I was more than ready to throw the dark nephilim under the bus. He may have done me a small favor, but it paled in comparison to all of the shitty stuff he'd pulled. I didn't care what happened to him.

With a sly look, Dash glided over to study me. Our eyes locked, and I trembled beneath the weight of the darkness that poured over me.

"I don't recall you arguing his claim the last time we met. If you're changing your story now, that makes you a liar."

"I lied to get out of that house. There is no conspiracy here, and if I were to plot against the dark, it wouldn't be with Arrow." Turning to Rowen with growing desperation, I said, "The photo was taken the night of the house party. After I passed out. Arrow manipulated the entire thing. We didn't sleep together. I swear."

"Oh but we did. There's no sense denying it now. Let's just get it all out in the open." Arrow's insistence rang with such genuineness. No wonder the dark were so good at fabricating the truth. As long as they believed it, the lie was easier to sell.

Arrow dabbed the last of the blood from his nose and tossed the tissue in the garbage can near the door. He had thrown down, and now he waited for me to retaliate.

"You want to get it all out in the open? Then why don't we start with you and the secrets you've been keeping?" I tried to turn it back on him, hoping that Rowen would see through the lies.

Tension thrummed heavy in the room. Jett shifted uneasily from foot to foot. Rowen stared hard at Arrow, and the two of them shared something unspoken and unknown to the rest of us.

"We have a show to play," Rowen said before turning on a heel and storming from the room and down the stairs.

I watched him go, feeling a weight sink like a stone in my gut. Arrow turned to me with a scowl and snarled, "I hope you're happy, Spike. You just fucked everything up."

Chapter Fourteen

"**M**e?" Appalled, I wrestled the urge to throw another punch at him. My hand still throbbed. "You're the one who's been lying to him all along. This is all on you, Arrow."

I didn't realize how close my anger had brought me until Dash pushed his way in between us. His hand on my shoulder brought the sinking sensation of being pulled under water, unable to resurface. My instinctive reaction was to fight against the awful feeling. The force burst from me, needing no guidance. A bright white flame surrounded me in a protective glow. Dash recoiled, hissing like a pissed off cat.

"I'll be watching you, Ember." He emphasized my real name, ensuring I knew that he'd been gathering info on me. "An undecided can't help another undecided. You're just as fucked as he is."

I didn't give him a chance to continue his threat. Grabbing ahold of Jett's arm, I dragged her along beside me as I rushed after Rowen. He wasn't safe. Arrow had led Dash right to him, and though nothing had happened, yet, I knew that it would. It always did where demons were concerned.

The second band was starting their set when we got downstairs. The vibrant blue of Rowen's hair caught my eye, and I waded through the crowd headed for the stage.

"You go ahead," Jett said, pulling away. "I'll keep an eye out for Arrow."

The bass thundered in my ears as Sacred Stone gave it their all. It drove me on as I dodged bodies. I caught up to Rowen before he reached the table where Sam and Greyson sat chatting and laughing with a few groupies.

I grabbed his arm, demanding his attention. "Rowen, please. Hear me out."

His fiery eyes blazed. Shoulders rigid and jaw tense, he looked fierce and tormented. "I don't think this is really the right place for this, Spike. Can we talk about this later?"

"No, I need to say this now. I didn't tell you about the picture because I didn't want to start shit between you and Arrow. And I didn't tell you so many other things because it's not my place, it's his. Please believe that I would never do anything to screw you over." I had to shout to be heard over the music, but right then I barely noticed the band. All I could see was that skeptical look on Rowen's face, and it was more than I could stand.

His expression softened. "I believe that, but I don't know who I can trust right now. It's starting to feel like my entire life has been a lie."

I wanted to tell him that I understood, but I didn't understand. My mother had never hidden the truth from me. Maybe Rowen's mother wouldn't have let him be raised in ignorance if she'd known it would lead to this, but it was too late for maybe.

"I'm sorry. It shouldn't have been like this. You deserve to know the truth about everything. But only Arrow can give that to you." I would be crushed if he believed Arrow's lie, but Rowen's safety meant more than my personal comfort.

Rowen pulled me in for a hug, and a deep sigh escaped me. "I know you didn't sleep with him. I just wish I knew why he'd want me to think so. I need to talk with him after the show."

Cinder had told me once that everyone has an angel. Unseen and unacknowledged, they work hard behind the scenes to protect and guide their charges. So where was Rowen's angel now?

"You might not be able to trust him to tell the truth. But I hope for your sake that he chooses to do the right thing."

A melancholy wistfulness crossed his face, creating a yearning in me that was so new and raw. Falling in love came at a price for our kind. Cinder's warnings echoed in my memory. It made so much more sense now.

"That's the problem with Arrow," he said. "He rarely does the right thing."

"I noticed." I held tight to Rowen, not wanting the hug to end. My cheek was squished against his shoulder, and I paid little attention when a giggling gaggle of girls jostled us on their way to the front of the stage.

Eventually we retreated to the table where Sam and Greyson sat, doing their best to impress their lady friends. Rowen made a solid attempt to act as if nothing had occurred upstairs, and his buddies seemed to be none the wiser.

I couldn't stop myself from looking for Arrow and Dash. But neither one of them made an appearance. Arrow was probably primping for his show, trying to hide any telltale signs of the punch that his pretty face had taken. Or maybe he was in deep thought somewhere, working up the courage to face his brother. One could hope.

"And that's when Arrow took a piss off the side of the stage." Sam cackled, telling yet another ridiculous Molly's Chamber story that had the ladies wrinkling their noses and laughing. "So we have a lifetime ban at that joint."

"Yeah, but that was nothing compared to that time Slick here took a dive off the stage." Greyson joined in with a deep laugh, pointing to Rowen. "Landed right on his face. Blood everywhere."

"That's why drugs are bad," Sam said, nodding in mock seriousness before dissolving into a throaty chuckle.

Rowen shook his head and mustered a snicker. "You guys are blowing my good guy image. Spike's going to think I'm a fucking maniac."

Listening to the boys tell stories brought to mind the many memories I'd made with the girls, many of which were a blur now. The rock scene had a way of doing that to you. It got inside you and forced out the inner parts that you would rather keep hidden. And the only way to deal with the exposure of your artistic side was to drink or drug yourself stupid. Eventually, that all has to end, preferably by choice rather than by death.

Sam's dark eyes glittered, and his lips pulled back in a wide grin. "I bet Spike has some stories that would make ours sound PG. Don't ya? You girls have gotta be wild."

With a coy smile, I said, "You have no idea. But you'll have to wait for the book. I'm sure there will be one some day. Knowing Jett, she'll be able to write her own in no time."

Scanning the busy nightclub for Jett, I spotted her purple hair in the crowd where she was dancing up a storm. Normally I'd be right by her side, drinking and partying. I didn't feel normal anymore. Things were changing fast.

Sacred Stone finished their set, ending on cheers and screams that made me worry a little. Tonight the final two bands would be announced. They would face off next weekend. If we didn't make it, Jett would totally unravel. I could see it already.

"I guess this is where I leave you. For now." Rowen kissed me and stood. "Wish us luck."

"Are you kidding?" I laughed. "I hope Arrow forgets every lyric and bombs the entire performance. But good luck."

"Crimson Sin and Molly's Chamber," Sam proclaimed as he shoved his chair back. "You just wait and see. We're going head to head next week. Mark my words."

The guys left to go prepare to be the final act of the night. I sat alone at the table with a knot in my stomach. It should have been a fun night. It was a great opportunity for every band competing. Yet all I could think about was Dash and his unhealthy interest in Rowen. Arrow had led the demon right to his brother. Someone would pay the price.

"Can I buy you a drink?" Koda slid into the seat Rowen had just vacated. Without waiting for a reply, he held up a hand and immediately a waitress appeared.

"Raspberry vodka and sprite," I said grudgingly. Koda was not someone I especially wanted to see just then, but perhaps he could be helpful. "What are you doing here, Koda?"

He somehow managed to look both amused and offended. "Is it wrong to want to support you on such a big night? I saw you play earlier. You were fascinating."

Fascinating? I wasn't sure I liked that word choice. For demons fascination often meant obsession. Knowing Koda had watched unseen bothered me more than it usually would. Dash had stolen my focus. I'd been so aware of his attention that I'd been unaware of Koda lurking among the crowd. Damn demons. So easily illusive and deceptive. Even though I could see them when others could not, I was still human enough to be fooled.

"Thanks. I'm glad you find my God given talents so enjoyable." It took great effort not to smile when he frowned. "You shouldn't be here though."

"Why? Am I making you uncomfortable?"

"Pretty much always."

We sat there in silence until the waitress dropped off our drinks before disappearing into the demanding throng of rock n' rollers. The awkwardness grew by the second, but Koda sat there completely unfazed, watching everything from the guys doing sound check to the girl in a short skirt bending over to pick up a dropped cell phone. But mostly, he was watching me.

Koda sipped from the import beer he'd ordered and regarded me with a softness that meant he was going to get sappy on me, or as sappy as a demon can get. "I came because I knew Dash would be here. He has an unhealthy interest in you. I don't like it."

Dissension among demonkind was not uncommon. As well organized as they were, the conflict was constant among those power hungry liars. It really came as no surprise that they were so often at odds with each other.

I took a deep breath, trying not to lose my temper. Arrow had already worked my last nerve. "Koda, *you* have an unhealthy interest in me. Both you and Dash need to give up on me and Rowen. We don't belong to the dark."

"You belong with us. The nephilim are abominations, making you ours by nature. Accept it."

"Except there's this little thing called free will that states it is my choice. Not yours. There is nothing written in stone. I am my own person. You need to back the fuck off and respect that." My cheeks burned with the heat of my rising anger. "And if you can't respect that, then just back the fuck off."

Koda stared without emotion. It was as if my thoughts and feelings toward him bore no weight. It meant nothing to him that I despised him. In his mind he had a job to do, or whatever he used to justify being a constant thorn in my side. My absolute loathing for him slid off him like water off a duck's back. It was downright infuriating.

"I'm not going anywhere, Spike. Not until you've made your choice." Tipping his bottle to me, he drank back the contents, ignoring my hate-filled glower.

The level he was willing to sink to disgusted me. I leaned closer so as not to have to shout. With clenched teeth, I said, "If I were to choose the dark, Koda, it wouldn't be you. I will never choose to be with you. I'd rather be dead."

His lack of reaction was a front. The only visible change in him was the swelling of his pupils as they grew with sudden rage. Black, drowning pits outlined with brilliant scarlet, those eyes promised horrid things so depraved and cruel that my imagination refused to entertain the idea of what Koda was capable of.

He leaned in, swift and aggressive, pasting me against the back of my chair. Getting right in my face he sneered, "I'll keep that in mind."

Without wasting a breath on threats or filthy promises, Koda vanished, gone so fast it was like he'd never been there. His reaction had been expected, though the venom in his departing words sent a chill down my spine.

I shuddered and ran both hands through my hair. Exasperated and fed up, I pondered the idea of making my choice and proclaiming my allegiance. Putting it off was only causing Koda to linger in my life. However, making a choice would make me a sworn enemy of the side I turned my back on. Having Koda stalk and harass me would pale in comparison to what would come next.

A hand on my shoulder had me whirling around defensively. My palms burned, and I had to restrain myself when I saw that it was Jett and the girls.

"Sweet, you got us a table," she said, plopping down into the chair Koda had just abandoned. "What's wrong? You look pissed. Still mad about Arrow?"

I cast a quick smile at Tash and Rubi, glad to have my girls rallied around me while we awaited our fate in this band battle. Speaking low so only Jett's keen ears would hear, I said, "Koda was just here."

She nodded in understanding and patted my hand. Her skin was very warm. A werewolf's blood runs hot, or so I've been told. "Forget him. Your boy is about to play, and then we find out if we're playing them in the finals."

"Careful, Jett," Tash warned, chewing on the straw from her drink. "Don't get cocky, or your bad karma will ruin this for us all."

"Karma," Jett huffed, blowing a purple lock out of her eyes. "Such bullshit."

Tash shook her head and pointed the straw at Jett in a scolding gesture. "You won't be saying that when karma does get you. Just don't drag us into it."

Jett rolled her eyes and snorted. "You sound like a fucking hippie."

I barely paid attention to their banter. My gaze was on the stage where Rowen was doing sound check. His hands moved over his bass, sliding down the neck as he plucked through the strings. Feeling my eyes on him, he glanced up with a goofy, little half smile. Why did he have to be so damn irresistible?

The rest of the band joined him, even Arrow, who held himself with more attitude than usual. He'd cleaned up his nose pretty well, but some light bruising spread out beneath his eyes. Too bad that the bruise only served to add to his bad boy look. My hand still ached from the punch, but it was worth it.

Even from where I sat, I could see the tension between Rowen and Arrow. It must have been pretty palpable because Jett leaned over to me with a snicker and said, "Trouble in paradise. I hope they blow it."

Again I was torn, only partially sharing her sentiment. I drank the rest of my vodka and ordered another. I was going to need it to get through the rest of the night.

Dash was nowhere to be seen. The DJ cut the music when the band was ready to begin. The emcee announced them, and the drunken rockers gathered once again in front of the stage hooting and hollering, hands raised in the devil sign.

Arrow and Rowen stood close together, exchanging words nobody could hear but the two of them. When Rowen backed away to his side of the stage, he looked pissed. His arms shook as he held the bass tight, as if he might swing it at Arrow. But then Greyson pounded out a steady drumbeat, and everyone began to play his part.

I sat stiffly, unable to relax as I watched Molly's Chamber do what they did best. My gaze traveled over each of them in turn: Greyson, his face set into a focused grimace as he maintained the beat. Sam, head banging in time to that beat as his fingers produced an intricate riff. Rowen, his hands going through the motions of the notes buried in his memory while his gaze strayed to Arrow, who playing the part of the rock star, pretending to be unaware of his brother's dark stare.

It quickly became apparent that Arrow was very far from sober. A combination of coke, booze, and God knows what else made him careless and clumsy. The audience either didn't notice or didn't care. I cringed as I watched, wondering if perhaps karma was a thing and Arrow was about to get his.

They made it into their third song before Arrow lost his balance and fell into Rowen, almost taking him down. Anger creased Rowen's brow, and he used his bass to fling Arrow away.

It shouldn't have been a big deal. They should have kept going as if nothing had happened. Instead, they exchanged words, ugly words, judging from the look on Arrow's face as he spat something at Rowen.

I held my breath, sensing that this was going to get worse before it got better. Rowen said something back, something only Arrow could make out. Drugs, or maybe just his personality, had Arrow puffed up with sudden aggression.

Rowen held up both hands in a 'bring it on' motion. Greyson and Sam exchanged a look but kept playing. Arrow didn't hesitate. He dropped the mike and lunged at Rowen.

"Oh my God," I gasped.

Jett said, "Fuck yeah."

The crowd fell into silence as they took in the scene. Then they erupted in a cry of encouragement.

Rowen let his bass hit the stage. The brawl happened so fast, it was hard to keep up with each fist. I couldn't look away though I flinched with each landed punch. Security guys swarmed the stage, dragging the two of them apart before any serious damage could be done.

To their credit, Sam and Greyson didn't stop playing. They both looked as horrified as I felt. Arrow held up both hands in a show of surrender. He appeared to be pleading for a chance to finish the show. The crowd was going nuts.

A security guy looked to Rowen with a brow raised. Rowen, banged up but fine, nodded that he wanted to keep playing. Fetching his bass, he slung it over his shoulder and jumped back in as if nothing had happened.

Arrow ate up the fan reaction. He grabbed the mike and hurled himself into the audience, crowd surfing with a maniacal grin lighting up his face.

Eventually his high would wear off. Would he regret anything though? I couldn't imagine he had it in him.

"That was fucking spectacular," Jett gushed. "Kind of hot really." She nudged me with an elbow, but I couldn't share her amusement.

"They're definitely going to win now," Rubi mused, playing with her phone, unimpressed. "Nothing like throwing down on stage to win over the crowd."

I scanned the building, trying to use my sixth sense as well as my eyes. Where was Dash? It felt like something he'd have influenced. He might have been lurking, incorporeal, but there was no way of knowing for sure. I couldn't always tell.

Waiting for the rest of their set to end was tough. I couldn't sit still. The second that the lights went dark after their final song, I shoved through the crowd to get to the stage.

Arrow vacated the stage first. He pushed by me with a sneer, knocking me aside as he went. "Happy now, Spike?"

"Yeah, I'm really fucking thrilled." My sarcastic retort was spoken to his retreating form. *Asshole.*

Rowen exited the stage, sweaty and angry. He clutched his bass in a white-knuckle grip. "Let's get the fuck out of here."

"You don't want to wait for the results?" I reached to touch his face but stopped, uncertain. "Are you ok?"

"Someone will text us. I need to get the hell out of here right now." He stared off toward the backstage stairs, in the direction Arrow had gone. "Is it cool if I crash at your place tonight?"

Chapter Fifteen

Leaving before we heard the final results was not easy. Not because I wanted so badly to hang around but because Jett was furious.

"Are you kidding me?" She pulled me aside to ream me out in privacy, though the glare she shot Rowen didn't keep it all that private. "You're going to bail out and leave us because of a guy? That's not how this works, Spike."

"I know." And I did. We had formed a pact. The band came first. Men, we could take 'em or leave 'em. At least it had been that way until Tash got so heavily involved with Mr. Country. "But this isn't just some guy, Jett. This is a guy who is like me. Who needs me. I don't ride your ass every time you run off because of pack business. Well, this is nephilim business, and I need to leave."

Her dark eyes flashed dangerously. Winning this competition meant a lot to her, possibly more than it meant to anyone else. Still, life was more than climbing the ladder to the next rung. I wanted a music career as badly as she did, but I wasn't willing to sacrifice who I was for it. And right then Rowen needed me.

"Whatever," she muttered, shutting down like she often did when she was ticked off and trying to keep a lid on her temper. "Go then. I'll call you later."

Pretending not to notice her pout, I gave her a quick hug and stopped by the table to say goodbye to Tash and Rubi. They seemed confused but bid me farewell with much less drama than Jett.

"Sorry about that," Rowen said when we were outside, away from the loud noise. "I didn't mean to piss off your friend."

Both of us walked with a guitar case on our back. The vodka had left me a little tipsy, so I had to focus extra hard on walking with the guitar on my back and five-inch heels on my feet.

"Don't worry about her. She's high strung. It's kind of a werewolf thing. Or maybe it's just a Jett thing."

"Werewolf," he repeated, nodding to himself as if that made perfect sense. He was quiet for a moment, head down, watching his feet as he took each step. "This isn't the first fight Arrow and I have had. It may be the worst though, because of the audience."

"That was shitty of him." I readjusted the guitar on my back, unsure of what else to say. I could offer very little to make Rowen feel any better about the brother he still didn't know he had.

"You know what he said to me on stage, right before we started to play?" He didn't wait for a response, rushing on as if he had to get the words out. "He said he was supposed to protect me from you and that you seduced him the night of the house party to try to get some dirt on me. So he took the picture to use as blackmail, to keep you away from me. For my own safety."

"The fuck?" I stopped dead in my tracks, nearly losing my balance. It was the lamest attempt Arrow could have possibly made to redirect the blame, but it lit a fire of rage that licked a fiery path to the tips of my toes until I was engulfed in it. "That conniving piece of shit."

I spun on a heel, awkwardly, and headed back the way we'd came. Rowen caught my elbow, bringing me to a halt.

"Spike, don't. Please. It's not worth it." Rowen looked absolutely crestfallen, and I hated Arrow even more. "Let's just go."

As much as I wanted to slam my fist into Arrow's face again, I saw the pain in Rowen's amber-gold eyes, and my anger dissipated. I followed him for a block until we reached the side street where his Charger was parked. After laying down the back seat to create more room, we deposited our guitar cases in the trunk.

The tiny hairs on the back of my neck prickled as I felt someone watching us. Someone unseen. Dash, most likely. Or Koda. I wasn't sure which was the lesser evil. Neither probably. Evil was evil.

We got into the car and drove away, leaving our watcher behind. Rowen glanced back in the rear view mirror. "Who do you think that was?"

His gifts were becoming more pronounced. The veil between him and the rest of us was fading fast.

"Probably Dash," I said, staring out the window, seeking red eyes. "He's after you, Rowen. And only Arrow can tell you why."

"Why can't you tell me? You know something." When his question was met with my awkward silence, he added, "Spike?"

"It's because of who your father is," I said, propping an elbow against the cool glass of the window. "The dark wants all nephilim. They think we belong with them because we're the offspring of sin. But sometimes they want us for other reasons. Like a powerful father. Like yours."

Rowen pondered this in silence as we drove. I prayed silently that he wouldn't press me further. I could not be the one to tell him that Arrow was his brother. That was on Arrow. It had to be.

"And what about you?" he asked. "Why does Koda have such an obsession with you? Because of your father?"

I let out a breath in a rush of air and turned in my seat to look at him. "You noticed that, huh? I'm not sure what Koda's deal is. But I don't think it's about who my father is. I think it has more to do with the rarity of female nephilim."

"So we're both in danger," Rowen said, giving the car some gas, making it growl. "Once we choose a side, does that change?"

"Just the circumstances. The danger will never really go away."

Rowen fell into a thoughtful silence. The radio played the local station that put on the battle of the bands event. Broadcasting from The Spirit Room, the DJ broke in between songs to announce that the final two bands would be announced any minute. Rowen reached over and turned the radio off, plunging us into quiet. The only sound was that of the Charger as it prowled along the city streets.

"I think I want to choose. There's no point in waiting if it only encourages guys like Dash." He shook his head, knocking the hair out of his eyes. "Why haven't you chosen yet? What's stopping you?"

I was surprised to hear him say he wanted to choose a side. It made me feel insecure, ashamed really, that I'd known our situation for so much longer and was still undecided while he was ready to proclaim his choice.

"Fear." I wasn't big on lies, and Rowen felt like someone I could be honest with. "I'm afraid of being unable to live with the repercussions of my choice. Not to mention making the wrong choice.

That worry lingers in the back of my mind too. I don't handle commitment so well."

He nodded in understanding, glancing at me in the dark when we stopped at a red light. The glow of the dash lit up part of his face in an eerie light. "I think it's very clear what side we should choose. The more I discover about all this, the more I know that I don't want to end up like Arrow. I care about him, but…"

It was my turn to nod, knowing why he felt the way he did. If Rowen chose the light, it would be the absolute best thing for him, though it might never free him of Dash and others like him. If the demons realized he was close to making his decision, it would only encourage them to win him over.

"Choosing the light doesn't free us from the demons who seek us," I said. "But it does give us a strong foundation to base our resistance on."

"So why wait?" he asked.

I had no answer to that.

We arrived at my apartment to find it just how I'd left it. Cinder's ward was still in place. I led Rowen inside, flicking on the lights to kill the shadows, finding comfort in the illumination of the artificial bulbs.

Rowen propped his bass case against the side of the couch. "Thanks for letting me stay here tonight. I just know, if I go home, things will get out of hand."

"No problem. You're welcome here anytime."

We stood awkwardly in the middle of the living room. I was overcome with the urge to touch him but afraid to do so. Everything was so messed up, and I couldn't help but feel partially to blame. When Rowen pulled me into his arms and kissed me, a thousand voices rose up in protest, and I silenced them all.

His mouth was warm, inviting. A hand low on my back grasped a handful of my hair. The scent of his cologne reached inside me, becoming part of my memory forever. His tongue delved gently into my mouth, causing my blood to rush through my veins.

"Why do I get the feeling that this is somehow forbidden? Tell me I'm just being paranoid." Holding me close, Rowen pressed his face into my hair and sighed.

"You're just being paranoid," I said, hoping I sounded convincing. "There's no rule that we can't be together. Although it may tick off a few people."

"Like Koda." *And Arrow,* I added silently. There were others, like Cinder, who might not think it was a good idea, but this was our choice. "Fuck Koda." My temper flared as I recalled the demon's hissed threat. I wasn't an animal to be caged and owned.

Rowen tipped my chin up so he could gaze into my eyes. "You are the best thing to come into my life right now. I'm glad that I'm not going through this alone."

The glow coming from him could not be seen, but I felt it. It came from within, steady and pure. Rowen indeed belonged to the light. I hoped for his sake that the dark would not claim him as it had Arrow. They didn't deserve such a horrific victory.

I struggled to find the right words to say back, something as lovely and pure. When words failed me, I smiled, hoping he would see the things I couldn't say.

He kissed me again with a slow-burning passion that steadily grew in intensity. Throwing my arms around his neck, I held tight to him as the heat between us built into a blaze.

The caress of his fingers on my lower back was a warm, welcome touch as he slid a hand beneath my shirt. A small burst of adrenaline accompanied the sensation as his fingers found my spine. Rowen traced small circles on my bare skin. It tickled, and I shivered as nerve endings up and down my back ignited.

Our bodies communicated without the need of words. Pressing close against him, I felt his readiness and had to make the choice to pull away or to go on. I'd told myself I would wait, that jumping into bed with some random guy was not what I wanted. But Rowen was far from random, and every touch made me long for more.

His body was firm against me. The hard lines of him beneath my fingers gave me only a hint at what lay beneath his clothing. I wanted to see him, to feel him. All of him.

I steered him toward my bedroom, unwilling or unable to stop touching him. Our eyes met as we crossed the threshold. A dark brow lifted in a silent request. I answered with another kiss, one that surely conveyed my desire.

The bed was soft beneath me when we sank down upon it, but I doubted I would have noticed if it had been made of concrete. A shaft of light streamed in from the living room, allowing us to see one another without ruining the mood.

We spoke in low murmurs and gentle sighs. Rowen was a gentleman, taking his time, careful not to rush. His hand on my stomach released a flutter of butterflies. Excitement left me dizzy with want. The human side of us dominated with its lusty energy and drug-like desire. Yet the supernatural side of us was ever present too, guiding us through emotion and spirit, uniting body and soul in an act so often ruined by the worship of body alone.

Clothes came off, exposing tattooed skin. Protection was subtly slipped from the bedside table drawer. I traced a line along the bass cleft on his shoulder, down to the grinning skull on his forearm. He leaned down to kiss the feathers that curved onto my hip, and I felt myself cross over into total certainty. Rowen hadn't been in my life for long, but I knew that something deeper resided in him, something that spoke to me, and I wanted to explore all of it.

We moved slowly, ignoring the sound of our phones when they went off randomly. Every touch was a new sensation. Each taste of each other brought us to new levels of discovery. The saltiness of his skin and the musky scent of him would be locked away in my memory forever.

A strange kind of magic encompassed us. It was a spiritual movement that made us soar to heights I'd never imagined. When Rowen was naked between my legs, he paused to gaze into my eyes as if searching me to see if I felt it too. My soul seemed to swell with the overwhelming sensation. I felt like I might explode in a burst of power that came from a place more raw and real than I'd fully understood to this point.

A tingle in my hands was my only warning before the flames engulfed us. The fire consumed us, surrounding us in a protective glow. Rowen took me with a groan, filling my body with his. Untouched by the flames, he held me close, and we ceased to be two separate beings.

Every sensation was heightened. The part of us that had never been human took an experience that had once been pleasurable and made it otherworldly. It was like nothing I'd ever known with human lovers. Making love to Rowen was like connecting with the source of the universe itself. A word like pleasure couldn't possibly describe what I felt as we moved together, tapped into something bigger than the earth and its inhabitants.

Our bodies and souls fused together. As we reached for heights beyond our grasp, I could feel just how united we were. I became aware of my spirit and my body, aware of all they were and all they could be. In that dizzying moment, I realized that we were capable of so much more than we dared dream.

Slipping my fingers between Rowen's, I squeezed his hand and rolled us over so that I was looking down at him. He peered up at me with amber eyes that seemed to glow in the dim light. He was easily one of the most beautiful things I'd ever laid eyes on.

I dragged my free hand down his chest, memorizing every angle of him. The blue of his hair looked nearly black in the dark. The sounds he made as I moved atop him brought me to a state of bliss that I wished would never end.

It felt like hours had passed by the time we lay exhausted in each other's arms, though that was an illusion. For a long time we didn't speak. We didn't need to.

Finally Rowen said with a lazy lull, "Was it just me or was that fucking amazing? Like, out of this world amazing."

"That, so they say, is one of the perks of being with a nephilim. I guess what they say is true." I dragged a hand through his mohawk and smiled to myself. The fire had long gone out, leaving just the two of us in the darkened room.

"Think we should check our phones?" he asked, his breath warm against my shoulder. "I don't want to ruin this moment, but I'm a little curious about the results."

"You guys made it through," I said. "I'm sure of it. After that brawl on stage, you probably got one hundred percent of the votes."

Rowen laughed, a low, masculine sound that shook the bed slightly. "In that case, let's not look. I don't think I want to leave this bed or think about the shit with Arrow right now."

The arm he'd wrapped around my waist tightened, and he kissed my shoulder. I was perfectly ok with ignoring our friends. The results would be the same in the morning.

We spoke in hushed whispers, sharing what we'd seen and felt while enrapt in one another. I was fascinated that we'd both experienced something spiritual, completely beyond the physical. The lovers I'd had in the past had done little more than scratch a physical itch. With Rowen I'd been transported to a place where our souls dwelled or perhaps where they'd been born.

"I think I'm falling hard for you," he paused before adding, "Ember."

I closed my eyes, absorbing those lovely yet terrifying words. Of course it was what my heart wanted to hear, but my head was afraid. Life was much more complicated for our kind. Love meant danger. Always.

Afraid to say too much lest I tempt fate, I said "I didn't know what I'd been waiting for until I met you. It's not safe for our kind to love, Rowen. We must be careful."

I felt him nod. No further words passed between us. We lay there together as the night began to fade. Eventually his breathing changed, deep and even, indicating slumber.

Leaving him was the last thing I wanted to do, but my throat was dry. Wrapping myself in the fuzzy, black robe hanging in my closet, I padded out to the kitchen for a glass of water.

My gaze darted to my purse, which I'd left on the kitchen table. Ah, what the hell? I reached in to grab my phone when I spied the pack of cigarettes nestled beside it. Because quitting was fucking hard, I took my phone and a smoke and went out onto the balcony. I lit the cigarette and unlocked my phone, finding a text from Jett. It was short, to the point, indicative of her pending anger at being ditched: *You and lover boy face off next week.*

"Well, I'll be damned," I murmured to myself. So it was Molly's Chamber and Crimson Sin after all. I waited to feel something like excitement, and I did, sort of. But mostly I just felt ready to get this battle over with.

The awareness that someone was watching me settled in. Used to this kind of thing, I was careful not to move suddenly or indicate in any way that I'd felt the stare upon me. Only when I was sure that my watcher was not a demon did I look up.

I scanned the dark below. Sunrise was still a couple hours away. There on the sidewalk outside my building, staring up at me with a cigarette between his lips, long hair hiding most of his face, was Arrow.

Chapter Sixteen

"What the fuck are you doing here?" My fist was clenched tight, ready to connect with Arrow's smug face again.

I probably should've ignored him, let him stand on the street like the pathetic loser he was, but seeing him there made me so damn mad. In seconds, I left the balcony, zipped back through the apartment where I grabbed my keys, and trotted down the stairs.

Arrow held up both hands. A smirk pulled at his lips though he seemed to be fighting it. "Simmer down, angel girl. I just wanted to see Rowen."

"So you're creeping down here in the dark, watching my windows?" I cast a glance up at the second floor where my apartment was. The light in the kitchen gave a street gawker a good view. I'd have to make a point of closing my curtains more often.

"I saw movement in your bedroom window. Thought maybe I should wait until the lovefest was over." A plume of smoke passed through his lips as he spoke. He was unapologetic, as arrogant as ever. "So Rowen popped your nephilim cherry. How was it?"

He was trying to encourage my temper. I was sure of it. It appeared that Arrow had come here looking for a fight of some kind.

"It was better than anything you'll ever have. So I won't torture you with the details." Playing his game didn't make me proud of myself, but it did feel good to rub it in. "Jealous?"

Arrow took another deep drag off the cigarette, letting it out slowly as he regarded me in silence. Then he gave a clipped nod and let his gaze travel over my robe-clad body. "You know it."

"Dammit, Arrow! What the hell is wrong with you? Creeping around out here in the dark. Picking fights with Rowen. This is not ok. You owe him." I pointed a finger at him, and it burst into flames.

He sneered in the general direction of my finger, unimpressed. "I don't owe him jack shit. But I did come here to talk to him so cut me a fucking break, Spike."

"He trusted you, and you sold him out to Dash. Do you really think that's what your father would have wanted for you both?" Playing the father card was low. I knew it. Having it played against me always resulted in tumultuous and dangerous emotion.

Arrow's eyes flashed with fury, and immediately the darkness seemed to gather closer. "My father is locked up in a holding cell along with your father, waiting for judgment. I really doubt he gives a shit about any of this."

Despite his attempt to shrug it off with angry words, I knew my words had struck a chord.

The shadows moving around us crept closer, and the flame in my hand went out. I was discovering little by little what Arrow was made of. He was a manipulator of darkness and shadows.

I couldn't appeal to Arrow's compassion or humanity. He simply didn't seem to have any. I found this hard to accept. Sure he was dark, but he was human too. It had to be in there somewhere.

"Fine," I said between clenched teeth. "There's obviously nothing I can say to convince you to do the right thing. So stop wasting my time and get the hell out of my neighborhood."

I shivered in my robe though I wasn't sure of the cause: the chilly autumn night or the dark shadows that crept around us. He could stand out there all night being weird for all I cared. I was done. I turned to storm back inside.

Arrow's hand on my arm stopped me. I shook him off, rubbing the spot he'd touched as if that could wipe away the unwelcome sensation.

He frowned. "You're assuming that you know what the right thing to do is." He dropped his cigarette and ground it out under the heel of his combat boot. "But what really makes you so sure you're right about everything? Even if what you say is true, and Rowen and I are brothers, what good does telling him do?"

So Arrow was human after all. He'd been thinking about it, which was more than I'd expected from him. Maybe he even felt bad about leading Dash to Rowen, but it was too late for that. He still had responsibilities to the dark.

"You tell me," I said, making it a challenge. "If you love him, you should want to protect him."

"I do!" he shouted suddenly. The sky darkened overhead, and the streetlights flickered. "Trust me, I do. Do you think I really want him to end up like me? But my hands are tied. There is nothing I can do."

Arrow's desperation was palpable. I almost felt bad for him. No, I tried. I couldn't bring myself to feel bad for someone who'd exhibited such selfish behavior with total disregard for others.

"There might be. You can keep Dash away from Rowen until he can make his choice. He's eager to do it." Because I was too damn nice, I gave Arrow another chance to prove he wasn't a complete asshole.

"He is?" Arrow mulled this over. "You know which side he's going to choose."

It wasn't a question, so I didn't answer. I merely held his hazel gaze, letting him draw his own conclusions. We stared at one another until my teeth began to chatter. Then Arrow nodded and began to back away without a word. He knew. He'd seen the truth in my eyes.

I retreated back into the building, cursing as the warm air blanketed me. After ensuring the lobby door locked securely behind me, I darted up the stairs and slipped back into the safety of my apartment.

A glance out the window revealed Arrow's slowly retreating form as he crossed the street to his BMW. Feeling my stare, he looked up. Across the distance, I couldn't read his expression, but I didn't have to. I knew the Rowen situation was eating Arrow up because he hadn't said a word to me about the battle results. That just wasn't like the Arrow I knew. I still didn't trust him. Not for a moment.

I found it hard to settle down and think about sleep when I was such a mess of emotions, equal parts outrage and disappointment. The relationship between two brothers shouldn't have involved me, but it did. Cinder claimed there was a reason for that, and I trusted Cinder. I had to.

I slipped back into bed beside Rowen. Well into the wee hours of the morning, sleep began to pull me under, and I invited it. The motion of the bed roused him slightly, and he rolled over and reached out a hand for me.

I cuddled in close against him, enjoying the way it felt to have him in my bed. The dark could intimidate and taunt, threaten and stalk, but it couldn't force us to live like slaves. We were free to love, to live, and to choose. And we would.

* * * *

The alarm on Rowen's phone woke us several hours later. The vibrating buzz combined with a loud, annoying chime brought me out of sleep with a start.

"Oh, shit," Rowen muttered, groping about for his phone before realizing it was still in the kitchen. The bed shifted as he got up, and I groaned at his sudden absence. He came right back, phone in hand. Rubbing a hand through his hair, he blinked sleepily at me. "Sorry 'bout that. My damn alarm. I have to be at work in an hour. But hey, I got a text from Sam. We made it through. Crimson Sin and Molly's Chamber."

"I know," I said, smiling at the grin that lit up his face. "I was up earlier. Jett told me."

Rowen slid close, bringing back the warmth of his naked body. "Are you psyched? You should be. You guys will win."

"I am. Somewhat. It's a little nerve racking though, going up against you. You know, all things considered." I motioned to the bed. On one hand, it was just a contest, but on the other it was a serious opportunity. Bedding my opponent a week before the final showdown could make things a tad awkward come show time.

"It's just a radio station contest. It won't change anything between us. As much as I want to win, I don't think it would be good for Arrow. He's got enough groupies and drugs clouding his brain without the illusion of actual fame." Rowen hugged me close and made a pained sound. "I wish I didn't have to get to work. I doubt I'll even have time to stop at home to change first."

"Sorry?" I offered, unsure if I really was. I wasn't ready for him to leave yet.

"Never. I'm not. There's nowhere else I'd rather be." He kissed me with a tenderness I'd come to believe only existed in romance novels.

I sighed against his lips. "You have got to stop being so damn great. It's just setting me up for disappointment when you inevitably do something to remind me that you're still a guy."

His laughter set loose another batch of butterflies. He slid a hand into my hair and made me meet his gaze. "We're not all douchebags. Some of us want more than a quick lay. Some of us actually want to love and be loved."

Swoon. I'd given Rowen my body because I'd known deep down that he wasn't like the men of my past. But his words and the genuine way he spoke them made me give him my heart. I knew in that moment that I was already a little in love with him.

"You keep talking like that, and I'll never let you leave." I traced a finger over the single, black feather tattooed on his collarbone, curving up the side of his neck. It seemed strangely symbolic, that one lone feather.

"Promise?"

After much stalling and half a dozen lingering embraces, Rowen finally got dressed and left. I spent the afternoon watching Seth roam around the apartment while working on some website maintenance for a client.

A call to Jett went unanswered. She was still pissed at me for breaking our cardinal rule. I could have sent a text reminding her that she'd ditched me at the bar to go home with a guy last year, leaving me to cough up money for the cab ride we'd planned to split. Because I was a good friend who chose to forgive, I didn't. Once that feisty wolf temper finally simmered down, she would forget the whole thing.

I talked to Rubi and Tash who were bouncing with joy at having made it to the final round. Their enthusiasm was infectious. I couldn't help but get excited.

Part of me kept waiting for Cinder to pop by. His appearances could be quite erratic, though he tried to come by regularly. I was overdue for some training. It wasn't like him to go too long without scheduling a session, but in the past he had gone several weeks without coming by. "Angel stuff", he always said, but I knew he either didn't want to or couldn't tell me what he'd been doing.

As the afternoon faded into evening, I traded my computer for my guitar. I spent some time jotting lyrics into a notepad while strumming out a new song. It was nice to just chill. Alone time wasn't something I had a lot of these days.

I started yawning not long after I finished supper, which consisted of Chinese leftovers. I considered making coffee but decided an early night would be best. Catching up on sleep would be beneficial. Jett was likely going to insist on meeting for practice every night this week.

"What do you think, Seth? Should I just go to bed? It's not even nine o'clock yet. Would that be lame?" The little tortoise climbed over a throw pillow I'd tossed on the floor. He continued on his way, oblivious to the conversation I was trying to have with him. Seth was a surprisingly social creature really. I could always count on him to be a good listener.

My gaze strayed to the notepad. I studied the last line I wrote for a few minutes before picking up the pencil and erasing it. Something wasn't clicking.

I thought about Rowen and the song we'd played together the first night he'd spent at my place. Playing it warmed me, and I smiled a goofy smile all to myself. Inspiration filled me like a magic all its own. I kept playing and writing, pausing only to check up on Seth.

When I finally took a break to grab a snack, it was well after midnight. Amazing how creating makes time cease to exist. I was in my zone and loving it—

—until a bang on the window scared the shit out of me.

My heart pounded, and the roar of adrenaline was loud in my ears. I made my way to the window and peeked out the blinds.

"Is this a fucking joke?" I muttered upon spying Arrow down below. Alarm turned to anger, and I stormed out onto the balcony. "Dude, are you serious right now? What the fuck?"

His expression was pinched, shoulders held taut. Something was wrong. I felt it as soon as our eyes met.

"Rowen never came home," Arrow said. "I think he's in trouble."

CHAPTER SEVENTEEN

"It was Dash. I know it. Fuck. This is all my fault. I'm such a fuck up." Arrow scrubbed a hand over his face and streamed a few more obscenities all directed at himself.

He sat at the kitchen table. I stood nearby, leaning against the kitchen counter, facing him. Letting him into my apartment hadn't been much of a choice. Though I'd have preferred not to, the haunting fear in his eyes had convinced me. Of course, since demons were good liars and being dark made Arrow a natural liar too, I was worried but treading carefully.

"Wait, just calm down. Tell me everything. Slowly this time." I'd offered him something to drink, but he'd been too caught up in his panic to answer me. A close look at Arrow showed signs of drug use. He'd gotten high before coming here. That didn't earn him any points. I remained wary.

"I told you. He texted me and said he'd be home after work, that he wanted to sit down and have a talk, man to man. I was freaking out because I knew I had to tell him we're brothers. So I snorted a line, had a drink, and waited for him. But he never came home. He should've been there around eight or nine."

Arrow tugged the hat off his head and flung it on the table. His hair was a mess of long, raven black. He shoved a hand into it and regarded me with hollow eyes. Fuck, drugs were scary.

"And you tried calling him?" Even as I spoke I was selecting Rowen's number from my contact list. Putting my phone to my ear, I listened as it went straight to voice mail, an indication that his phone was off. Unreachable. My heart began to beat a little faster.

"Of course I tried calling him. Do you think I'm a fucking idiot? Ah forget it. Of course you do."

Of course I did, but I was nice enough not to say so. "What about his work? Did you try calling them? Maybe someone there will know something."

Arrow turned a sour gaze on me, and I had a hard time meeting it with his messed up pupils. It made him feel otherworldly, more so than usual, and I didn't like it. "They said he left at eight. Nobody there has heard from him."

Seeing Arrow looking so defeated should've brought some satisfaction. Instead, it scared me. I didn't know him well, but I knew it took a lot to rattle him. "So what do we do?" I asked, needing a goal, a plan of some kind.

Arrow's gaze dropped to the table, and he picked at a mark in the wood. "We don't do anything. I'll go to Dash. That house you tailed me to, I think that's where he might be."

"I'm coming with you. You can't come here and tell me Rowen's in some kind of trouble and then expect me to wait around to find out if he's dead or something." My temper was still cool but ready to ignite if Arrow fought me on this.

"He's not dead," Arrow said, his voice dull. "Dash doesn't want to kill him. He wants to recruit him. And if he's forcing Rowen's choice, there's no telling what he might do. It could get pretty nasty."

Sudden panic threatened to choke off my air supply. The thought of Rowen at the mercy of a demon made me break out in a cold sweat. "I wish they would just leave us alone." My voice cracked, and I had to pause, to focus on deep, even breaths.

Arrow was quiet for a moment before saying, "That's never going to happen. They need us to be their eyes and ears during the day."

Demons couldn't take corporeal form when the sun was out though that didn't make them any less dangerous. It just gave them limitations, proof they were not the gods they believed themselves to be. They too were subject to a higher power. Using the dark nephilim as their daytime bodies was clever and frightening.

"What do we do, Arrow? We can't just go to that house and expect everything to go fine." I needed Cinder's help. Surely he would have some kind of guidance.

"We go there during the day and look for him. We've got to start somewhere, and I can't think of a better plan. It could be dangerous for you, you know. Being undecided and all."

Not for a moment would I be fooled into thinking Arrow really gave a damn about my well being. Though it did appear that he felt guilty for leading Dash to Rowen, so perhaps there was hope for him after all.

"I'll take my chances." A glance at the clock revealed about five hours left until the sun rose. "So we meet at sunrise? On second thought, you shouldn't be driving like that. You're fucking wrecked, aren't you? I'm going to make you some coffee. You've got to try to sober up."

Busying myself in the kitchen gave me a task, which made me feel like I was doing something other than waiting in limbo for morning. Part of me couldn't believe that Rowen was really in danger though I felt the truth of it. I wanted it to be a bad dream. Cinder had warned me against getting involved with him. Could any of this be my fault? Or was it all on Arrow? Could any of us really point fingers?

"Or you could do a line with me. Just to take the edge off." The slyness of his tone was almost convincing in its smoothness. It was persuasive and dripping with darkness.

I stalked over to the table and held my hand out, shaking my head, unable to hide my judgment of his stupid decisions. "Hand it over. We can't help Rowen if you're high. Fuck your brain up on your own time."

The lights flickered as he stared at me, unmoving. Refusing to be intimidated, I thrust my hand closer. Finally he pulled a small bag of white powder from his wallet and flung it down on the table. I swiped it before he could rethink his decision and tucked it into my bra. With a brow raised, he smiled, so I moved it to my purse.

Making coffee helped me to hone my focus. The mundane task let me think things over. Was it possible that Arrow was purposely baiting me? No. I didn't believe that though I knew he was certainly capable of it. Something else was going on, and we couldn't sit back and do nothing while Dash tried to force Rowen's choice.

"Here." I shoved a cup of organic coffee at Arrow. He rolled bloodshot eyes at me but took it anyway. "I'll be right back. Don't leave and don't touch anything."

I retreated into my bedroom where I dug the dagger that Cinder had given me from my closet. It was designed to be easily concealed though the blade was still over a foot long. The sheath was designed to lie against my back where a hoodie and my hair would keep it hidden. I tossed it on the bed. My own gifts would give me a chance against any other nephilim though I hoped like hell it didn't come to that.

I sat on the end of the bed, gazing longingly at the place where Rowen and I had so recently made love. How could he just be missing? I spoke Cinder's name aloud, knowing that he'd hear but also knowing it didn't mean he would or could come. *Please.*

After waiting a few minutes, I returned to the kitchen, surprised to find Arrow standing over Seth's habitat. I froze, watching him gently stroke the back of the tortoise with a small smile on his face.

"You like animals?" I asked, announcing my presence.

He turned quickly and yanked his hand back. "Yeah, sure. Only a heartless dirtbag doesn't like animals."

"You know, some might say you're a heartless dirtbag, Arrow." It was a mean thing to say, but I didn't feel bad. That raised an alarm for me. Being shitty to him just because he was dark didn't make it ok. It only made me as bad as he was. I knew better.

"Yeah," he agreed. "I'm sure that's one of the nicest things people say about me."

"Sorry. I shouldn't have said that."

"Naw, it's cool."

Feeling awkward, I perched on the arm of the couch. It made me nervous to have Arrow in my apartment. I was even more nervous when he wasn't sitting down.

"Relax, Spike," he finally said, sitting on the opposite end of the couch. He'd abandoned his coffee. "I don't expect you to trust me, but I wouldn't let any harm come to my brother's girl. He means a lot to me."

"So you believe that he's your brother?" I was skeptical. He'd seemed so resistant.

Arrow shrugged and pulled a cigarette from the pack in his pocket. "I did a little digging. Found some signs that back up your claim. I should've believed you. You don't seem like the lying type." He studied me for a minute, the unlit smoke between his lips. "Why don't you choose the light already? I mean, you're going to eventually, right?"

"What makes you so sure?" Was I so transparent? True, I was close with the light. I was just afraid of making such a commitment to anyone or anything. Hell, even falling for Rowen scared the shit out of me. The fact that he knew already what side he wanted to choose made me feel even shittier about it. He'd had much less time to consider it.

"You're not cut out for the dark," Arrow mused. "You're too pure."

"Thank you." That was a compliment to me whether he'd meant it as such or not. "You know, you don't have to be one of them."

He regarded me with a strange expression, as if he wasn't sure if I was fucking with him or not. Then he gave a short, sharp laugh and twirled the cigarette between his fingers. "Trust me. I do."

"You can smoke that out on the balcony." I pointed to the glass door just off the living room. This conversation was odd, and I didn't really know how to wade through it.

With a head nod, Arrow let himself out, giving me a moment alone to figure out what the hell I was going to do with him until dawn. I didn't have much time to consider it. Cinder's voice in the kitchen had me almost collapsing in relief.

"Ember? What's wrong?" Tonight Cinder was channeling his inner geek with an X-Men tee. His shaggy, blond hair was disheveled. A smudge of something darkened his cheek. His expression was pinched and distracted, as if he'd just come from something chaotic.

"Rowen is missing. Arrow thinks that Dash has him. Can you help?" I went to him, casting a glance at the balcony, ensuring Arrow was unaware of the angel in the kitchen.

Cinder's face showed no surprise. He nodded as if he'd expected this news. "You're all right, though?"

"Yes."

Cinder's violet gaze went to the balcony where Arrow was leaning over the railing, staring down below. "You shouldn't have let him in here. He's dangerous. And now he can pass the wards. Because you allowed it."

Cinder's angelic wards would have worked on Arrow, if I hadn't given him an open invitation. That was all it took for a dark entity to get into your space, your life, your head. An invitation. The kind one usually doesn't realize one has issued.

"I know who he is, Cinder. But he's the one who told me about Rowen, and I really don't think he's lying."

"I'll be the judge of that."

Cinder strode over to the balcony door and flung it open. With one hand he grabbed hold of Arrow and dragged him back into the apartment. The lit smoke fell from Arrow's hand onto the carpet, and I rushed to grab it.

Arrow knew better than to fight an angel. Cinder slammed him down onto the couch and stood over him, preventing him from trying to rise. Arrow stared stonily up at the angel, unflinching. He had a certain readiness to him, as if he were accepting of potential death.

I properly disposed of the cigarette before standing awkwardly beside Cinder. I felt like I should interfere somehow but was afraid to do so.

"Tell me what you told Ember," Cinder demanded. "Look into my eyes and tell me."

Arrow clasped his hands and took an audible breath. Then he repeated what he'd told me, word for word. He barely blinked, and he certainly didn't move. Cinder studied him for a minute before nodding, satisfied.

"You're telling the truth. Impressive. Also suspicious. You could be speaking the truth because it serves a purpose. Are you trying to lure Ember into a trap?" Arms crossed, Cinder tapped a foot impatiently. I'd never seen him so harsh and aggressive.

"No." One word. Arrow's stare became more of a glower.

The angel and dark nephilim maintained their eye contact. A silent battle ensued as Cinder sought truth and Arrow awaited his verdict.

Turning his back on Arrow, Cinder fixed me with a fierce stare. I wondered what I'd done to get his temper turned on me. For an angel, he had a short fuse.

"I assume you mean to look for Rowen." It wasn't a question. When I nodded, he continued. "That is incredibly dangerous, and I would highly advise against it. However, should you choose to go after him, please know you're putting yourself in jeopardy."

"Does that mean you won't come with us?" I'd known it was a long shot. Angels couldn't simply be everywhere at once, and a Dominion like Cinder had many tasks, all of them of great importance.

He shook his head, his expression revealing nothing. "I can't. I'm sorry."

"Why the hell not?" Arrow spoke up with a sneer. "You're a guardian, aren't you?"

"You ignorant child," Cinder scolded. "You don't have any idea how this all works, do you? They've taught you nothing. All mortals have a guardian, even you. They protect, guide, encourage, and love. But they are not genies in a bottle ready to grant your every wish. They cannot protect you from all things. Some things are meant to happen, no matter how bad they seem at first. All things have meaning. Even death. And no, I am not merely a guardian. I'm a Dominion. So watch your tone and show some respect, demon."

Arrow's eyes flashed, and he came off the couch with anger spurring him on. "I'm not a fucking demon."

"Oh no? You chose the dark. They are your kin. With them you spread darkness and evil. What makes you any different than the rest of them?" There was such raw truth to Cinder's accusation that Arrow sat back down, averting his gaze by staring at the tortoise habitat.

I held my breath until I couldn't hold it another moment. The tension in the room had my palms tingling. Needing to break the tense silence, I said, "We have to do something, Cinder. We can't just leave Rowen. He told me that he wants to choose. If Dash knows that, there's no telling what he may do to force Rowen's choice."

Cinder nodded gravely. "That is true. The dark has already secured one of Rhine's children. There will be some urgency in ensuring they secure both."

"Rhine?" Arrow echoed. "Like the river? Is that my father's name?"

Without looking at him, Cinder nodded again. "It is." To me, he said, "I wish you would reconsider. But if you really must go, take this."

He produced a sword with beautiful wings on either side of the handle and a deep purple amethyst centered between them. The inscription engraved in the blade was in a language I couldn't read. I expected it to be heavy but found upon accepting it that it was surprisingly light and manageable.

"What is it?" I asked, ignoring Arrow's eye roll. Obviously I knew what it was, but coming from Cinder, there had to be more to it.

"It's a safety net," Cinder said. "Use it if you have to. But try not to have to."

Cinder pulled me in for a hug. He kissed my forehead before whispering something against my skin in a language that sounded very old. I felt a warmth there, beneath his lips, the sensation of something primordial taking hold. Something far older than me. Power.

I gazed up at him, an unspoken question in my eyes.

"Take care, Ember." It was all he said before he gave me a pointed look that could've meant anything. Then he was gone.

"Says he's not a guardian," Arrow muttered. "Then why put his seal on you? Seems like a guardian thing to do to me."

"Oh, shut up, Arrow. You don't know shit about the guardians." I hefted the sword, holding it up before me, letting my mind wrap around the way it felt in my hand. "Wait, what's a seal?"

The dark nephilim snickered. "Obviously there are things you don't know shit about either. A seal is the casting of your own energy over someone else's. So another angel or demon can see that you're under his protection. It's a warning. If they fuck with you, they fuck with him."

"Oh." I thought about that and couldn't help but feel warm and fuzzy. Cinder was special to me, a good friend. He cared so much, which meant a lot to me. "Good to know."

"So, what now?" Arrow's gaze held expectation. "Do we just sit here and find ways to insult one another until sunrise? I mean, I'm up for it if you are, but I'll need my stash back."

"Fuck your stash," I said, tempted to flush the bag. He had a point though. Sitting around waiting was going to get old fast. Though I wasn't hungry, I was interested in getting Arrow out of my apartment sooner rather than later. "Let's go for breakfast. I'll buy. Actually, I'll drive too."

We could get a cheap plate of bacon, eggs, and pancakes at any of a few decent twenty-four-hour diners. It would give us a purpose, something to do to pass the time so it didn't hold us prisoner inside my apartment.

Arrow eyed me uncertainly for a moment, then shrugged. "Fine with me. But we're not taking your car. It's a piece of shit."

"You don't get to talk about her that way. I love that car." Nothing annoyed me like people shitting on my ride. Only Jett got away with that. Still, I held my hand out for his keys.

As he dropped them into my palm, our hands touched briefly, and he pulled away, as if afraid I'd somehow sense his grief and guilt. That impulse revealed more about Arrow than he wanted me to know. For the first time since we'd met, I almost felt bad for him.

Chapter Eighteen

Sitting across from Arrow at the late-night diner, I watched as he noisily munched on a crunchy piece of bacon. I had picked at the things on my plate but left most of it untouched.

"Are you going to finish that?" he asked, pointing at my plate, his mouth full.

I shoved it across the table and sat back to watch him devour my food too. "I don't know how you can eat right now. Aren't you nervous?"

"Hell yeah. But you gotta eat, right? You can't survive on nasty coffee alone." He gestured to the mug in front of me. Stabbing a chunk of pancake with his fork, Arrow took a loud slurp of his own coffee.

My frown went unnoticed as he shoveled food into his mouth. Maybe this was how he dealt with tough situations. Who was I to judge? Still, did he have to be so noisy about it?

The diner was relatively empty, just a few other groups, most of whom seemed to be coming from the bar. This was a popular location for an early morning meal after a night of partying. Every time the door opened, I glanced up, worried someone from the rock scene would come in and see us together. Maybe that was mean, but I didn't want anyone thinking the wrong thing.

So of course the guys of Sacred Stone walked in. I sighed, and Arrow looked up, following my gaze. Then he glanced at me, understanding my reaction.

"I bet it's killing you to be seen here with me, huh? Don't worry. I never showed any of them your picture." He snickered between mouthfuls, pleased with himself. At least he seemed to be coming out of the strange, dopey haze he'd been in earlier.

"Fuck you, Arrow," I said with a smile, as if I'd thanked him instead. Because his mouth was full again, he shot me his middle finger as a response.

Paul Webber, the lead singer of Sacred Stone, led the pack through the diner. They strode toward us, every one of them with a forced swagger in their step. *Puhhlease!* In skinny jeans and a leather jacket, Paul looked like the punk he often acted like. I wasn't impressed. Ignoring him, I stirred another packet of sugar into my coffee.

"Well, well, well," he boomed, jerking to a stop beside our table. "Never thought I'd see the two of you out together. Alone."

Arrow fixed him with a withering stare. "Is there some kind of law against two people eating together?"

"There is when one of them is your best buddy's girl. But hey, that is clearly none of my business." Paul held his hands up in a "whatever" gesture. "I'm sure you'll all stop being so chummy after one of you kicks the other's ass next weekend anyway. Preferably Molly's Chamber. No offense, Spike. You girls are good and all, but let's be realistic. Music is a man's world for a reason."

A few of his friends snickered. My palms tingled. Oh, that wasn't good. Entitled male crap usually didn't set me off. I knew better than to let such narrow-minded idiots get to me. But I was already fired up because of Rowen. If he gave me much more crap, I'd be swinging at this asshole.

Arrow dropped his fork with a clatter that drew the attention of the other patrons. He too seemed to be feeling frisky because he stood up to face Paul, getting right in his face.

"Apologize to Spike. Right. Fucking. Now."

Paul laughed, but it was half-assed, like he wasn't so sure he liked where his insult had taken him. "You're kidding, right? Don't act as if you don't agree."

"Do I look like I'm kidding?" Arrow pressed closer, nearly chest to chest with Paul. His stance was so aggressive that I tensed. "Crimson Sin is still in the contest, and your band is not. There's a damn good reason for that. Now apologize."

The world stalled in intense silence as everyone who was gathered beside our table waited to see what would end this confrontation. I held my breath, knowing that Arrow was capable of things Paul couldn't even dream of.

Paul's condescending gaze dropped to me, then back to Arrow. "Fuck that."

The punch came fast. Fueled by cocaine and darkness, it was loud. Arrow's fist connected with Paul's jaw, dropping him like a sack of bricks where he stood. One of Paul's friends dropped down to help him up while the others blocked Arrow from throwing another punch. He made no move to do any such thing. He just stood there staring down at Paul with utter contempt.

A waiter rushed over with shouted commands for everyone to get out. None of us were welcome any longer. If we didn't leave, the waiter would call the cops.

"Fine with me," Arrow muttered, swiping his phone off the table. "Let's go."

Before I could reach for my wallet, he produced a handful of bills and tossed them on the table. I followed him out, glancing back to see Paul's friends helping him up. He was dazed, holding his face.

"What the hell did you hit him for?" I demanded when we were in the parking lot.

"You're welcome." Arrow didn't even look at me as he strode angrily to the black BMW.

I jerked to a halt. The keys were in my purse, so he was forced to wait. He stood beside the car with a hand on the door as if that would hurry me up.

"I'm welcome? Are you expecting gratitude? Do you think you just did something heroic in there by treating me like a weak female who can't defend herself?" I was furious that he was using me as a prop in his pissing contest.

Arrow gave a loud, exaggerated sigh and leaned against the passenger door. "Save the feminist bullshit, Spike. We both know you can defend yourself." He motioned to the bruises marking the side of his nose. "Paul is a fucking prick. And you don't deserve to be spoken to like that. I wanted to shut him up so I did. End of story. We don't have to pick it apart."

Because I wasn't the argumentative type and because I wanted to leave before Paul and his buddies came outside, I unlocked the car and got in.

"Did you really hit him because he insulted me?" I asked. "Or because you just wanted an excuse to do it?"

I started the car, and Arrow immediately jacked his phone into the speakers, fiddling with the volume. He didn't seem interested in answering. Just when I'd given up and put the car in gear, he said, "They don't get to talk to us like that. Any of us."

So it was a nephilim thing. Arrow wouldn't be the first to feel he was better than the average human. It was, in fact, something Cinder had warned me against. Having gifts that others didn't have and being linked to another world could give anyone a complex.

"Well... thank you for considering me to be worth defending. But please, try to lay off the violence. All you've done is convince him that we really are running around behind Rowen's back." With a glance at the skyline, I eased the BMW into traffic. It made me nervous to drive something so nice and new. I'd gotten used to driving a car always on the brink of breakdown.

"Who cares? Paul's a fucking tool anyway." Bitter and moody, Arrow stared out the window. Both of his fists were clenched in his lap.

"So where am I headed? South, I know. But then what? I don't remember exactly what neighborhood it was in." Focusing on the task at hand seemed best. I down shifted too soon, and the car jerked. I winced. "Sorry. I haven't driven a stick in a while."

Arrow raised a brow at that and opened his mouth to make a smart-ass remark.

"Shut up," I muttered.

"Shit, Spike, you have a filthy mind. I was just going to say that it's no big deal. I have an extended warranty, and I doubt you can really fuck it up. Anyway, head south. Cross the river. I'll direct you as we go." He lit a smoke and puffed away on it while drumming his fingers on the dash in time to the raucous music blasting out of the speakers.

Finally the night was coming to an end. The sky was beginning to lighten. My hands were tight on the wheel. I was scared. Arrow opened the window a few inches to let the smoke escape. He seemed calm, unfazed by what we were going to do. I was envious.

When he passed me the cigarette, I hesitated only a moment before taking it. Quitting would have to wait for another day, assuming I lived to see it. Right then I was anxious as all get out and needed a drag.

We didn't talk much as I drove. The loud music was helpful. It kept us from feeling forced to converse. The closer we got, the lighter the sky grew, and the shakier my nerves became. I had a bad feeling about this. By the time we pulled into the ritzy neighborhood, my hands were so tight on the wheel that I was sure they'd have to be pried off.

"Park a block away, down here." Arrow waved a hand toward a side street. "We'll leave the keys in the car and the doors unlocked. Nobody will touch it here. If we don't both make it out, then whoever does can get away. Hopefully with Rowen."

My breath caught, and my pulse pounded in my ears. We hadn't even left the car yet. I felt like a huge wimp. "There's a chance we won't both make it out? Exactly what are you expecting in there, Arrow?" I pulled over and killed the engine. Taking deep breaths was not helping.

"Well for one, Skylar," he said. "Let's just hope she's the only witch here. They have greater power in numbers, and they don't make it a habit to be alone."

"Skylar? Well that's fucking great." My hand went to the cross around my neck. The witch had been pissed that I'd interrupted her sordid wedding. I wasn't looking forward to seeing her again.

"I won't let her hurt you." With such sincerity in Arrow's declaration, I had to remind myself that he couldn't be trusted.

I watched with a lump in my throat as the sun crested the horizon. "Let's go before I chicken out and run screaming into traffic."

I grabbed the sword Cinder had given me from the backseat. It felt good in my hand, and I gave it an experimental swing. Could I use it on someone like Skylar if she threw another demon curse at me? I'd never killed anyone. I didn't want to start now, but in self-defense, I might have no choice.

"There will be hellhounds protecting the property during the day," Arrow said as we walked down the street. "I'll get rid of them. They know me."

"That has got to be one of the most fucked up things I've ever heard anyone say." We turned a corner, and I could see the house ahead, so normal from the outside, not unlike the houses next to it. "What's the deal with this house anyway? Dash and Koda said something about Lilah. Who's Lilah?"

Arrow slid a sideways glance at me as if wondering how much to tell an undecided. "Lilah is a demon queen, one of the most powerful in all the underworld. She's a prisoner now. Captured by the angels. I don't know the whole story there. What I do know is that the door to her kingdom is here, somewhere in the city. Some say that's why there's so much supernatural activity here."

"So why does she have a house in the rich part of town? Is that where the door to her kingdom is?" Every step that brought us closer to the house made my unease grow.

"She was cursed into the form of a vampire, forced to live as one of them. This is where she lived. Until she was killed, which sent her right back to the angels' prison. Or so they say. I don't know. I never met her myself." Arrow shrugged as if he couldn't care less. But Dash and Koda had cared.

"Dash seemed pretty worked up about her though," I said, hoping to coax something out of him that could help me with Dash in the future, provided I had one after today.

Arrow smoothed his hair down beneath the knit cap that hung off the back of his head. "Dash is always worked up about something. Far as I know, Lilah had a bunch of demons at her command. Now that she's gone, they're all fighting over who gets to take her place. So far, nobody's been able to access the kingdom she left behind and all the power that goes with it."

"That's a good thing, right?"

"Fuck yeah."

Perplexed, I snuck a studious peek at Arrow. His expression was neutral, revealing nothing. I thought it odd that a dark nephilim held such an opinion.

When we stood in front of the house, I felt overwhelmed by the evil presence inside. The iron gate was closed. I stared at the high, concrete walls surrounding the property and sighed.

"We have to go over, don't we?" With zero climbing experience, this was going to hurt.

"Sure do. Here, I'll boost you up. Then you help me."

"Oh, I really don't like that idea." I shrunk back when he came toward me.

Arrow huffed and rolled his eyes. He seemed to do that a lot. "Do you have a better plan?"

I swallowed hard and looked up at the top of the wall. It seemed so far away. "Not really."

"Alrighty, then let's do this." Arrow clasped his hands together, holding them like a small stool.

I rested the sword against the wall, tried to brace myself with my hands, and stepped onto his hands. He flung me up there fast, and I scrambled to grab hold of the top of the wall before I fell. I wasn't quite strong enough to haul my weight up. I almost fell backward, but his hand on my ass stopped my descent.

"That's great, Arrow, thanks," I muttered sarcastically. However, it was the encouragement I needed to drag myself up onto the top of the wall. The wall was about a foot thick, giving me enough room to balance but not much more.

"Hey, I didn't let you fall. Give me some credit." He passed the sword up and then backed away a few feet. Taking a running start, he leaped at the wall and managed to hook his fingers on the ledge.

I clung to the edge of the wall with one hand and used the other to grab hold of his wrist. He clambered up beside me, and we both sat there for a moment, gathering ourselves.

"The hounds should be coming," he said, peering down. "Wait here."

He jumped down into the yard. Right on cue a pack of dogs appeared as if out of nowhere though I was pretty sure they'd been in the backyard. With glowing red eyes, the horrifying black beasts were the stuff of nightmares. Even from here I could see that every tooth in their massive heads was razor sharp.

"No fucking way," I gasped.

The hounds raced up to Arrow, stopping short of an actual attack. He held a hand out to them, and their snarls ceased. Much to my surprise, they began wriggling and tail wagging, excited to see Arrow.

He whispered to them, trying to keep them from barking or howling or whatever hellhounds do. One of them sprawled on the ground at his feet, begging for a belly rub.

"It's ok, Spike. You can come down now."

"I really don't want to." Knowing I couldn't sit on top of the wall all day, I dropped the sword so it stuck point down in the grass. Then I slowly lowered myself down and let go. The drop wasn't as far as I'd expected.

Right away the hounds wanted to check out the newcomer. Cringing but trying not to stink like fear to them, I held out a timid hand. They sniffed me, shooting glances at Arrow. When they saw that he was cool with me, they backed off, losing interest in us completely.

"Those things are fucking scary." I picked the sword up and motioned for Arrow to lead the way.

"There will be wards on the doors," he said. "Nothing that will keep mortals out, lucky us, but they will alert everyone inside to an intruder. The windows too."

"So what now?"

He studied the house for a moment. Clearly flying by the seat of his pants, he didn't inspire a lot of confidence in me.

"You stay out of sight while I go to the door. Be ready for anything."

"I really don't like this."

Arrow eyed me as if he wasn't sure he could trust me not to fall apart. Well, he wasn't the only one. "I'm not real thrilled either, but we don't have a choice. I'm sure Rowen is in here."

I watched with bated breath as he strode up to the door. His fist fell heavy against the door, and I jumped, wary of who might answer. He rang the doorbell next, and right away we could hear the heavy fall of hurried footsteps.

The door jerked open with a whoosh followed immediately by a snide, "What are you doing here, Arrow? How did you get through the gate without using the intercom?"

Arrow's response was to throw both hands up, effectively freezing the owner of the female voice who'd answered. "Come on," he said, waving me over. We shoved past the woman, whom Arrow had temporarily frozen, and almost knocked her down in the process.

I cast a frantic glance back at her as he dragged me into the house. It wasn't Skylar.

The house was relatively quiet, which made it extra creepy. I followed Arrow from the large living room to the kitchen, the throne room, and then the library only to find them all empty. He stared at the spiral staircase, considering it before his gaze strayed to the closed basement door.

"Hate to say it, but I think we go down." Arrow started for the basement, and I hurried after him.

"How long will that hold her?" I asked, worried that we were going to be facing a coven of witches.

"A few minutes, but I'll hit her again if she comes after us. Be ready to use that fire of yours. We're going to need it."

The stairwell was dark. Arrow gripped the railing, taking each step with care so as not to alert anyone who might be down there to our descent. When we reached the bottom, the stairwell opened into a spacious entertainment room with a large screen TV and a bar off to one side. A desk laden with computers and various tech items lined the opposite wall. It was so dark that I was forced to create a small flame in my palm to light our way. The hallway stretched out straight ahead, and we continued on.

We passed a few closed doors that appeared to be bedrooms or storage rooms. A furnace hummed behind one of them. A set of heavy wooden double doors marked the end of the hallway.

Arrow said, "This is where the magic happens. Literally." Gingerly taking hold of one of the door handles, he inched it open.

At first glance the room appeared to be empty. A long, blocky table lined the wall to our left. It had a pentagram etched into the surface with a goat head inside. A gavel at one end indicated it was used for meetings of the evil kind. I shuddered at the black vibes coming off it. The walls were covered in tapestries and paintings depicting various scenarios of demons doing horrible things to humans of all genders and ages. My gaze passed over them, and my stomach turned. It was history, true stories on canvas. Sickening.

Arrow gasped, "Oh, my God."

His words were so surprising that I spun to see what had elicited such a statement from him. My lungs were crushed beneath the weight of the sudden shock. My brain needed several tries to accept what my eyes were seeing.

A large upside down pentagram had been painted on the tile floor. In the center of it stood a crucifix. Hanging from that crucifix was Rowen.

Chapter Nineteen

The shock was overwhelming. However, it wasn't merely that Rowen was on the cross that was so astonishing. The silver wings spread out behind him choked off my breath and momentarily stole my voice. Unconscious and half-naked, he slumped there with his head limp and his eyes closed. Blood and bruises marred his tattooed skin. Someone had carved an upside pentagram into the flesh over his ribs on the left side beneath his heart. Only the subtle movement of breathing told us he was still alive.

"Arrow, is he...? What do we do?" I whispered the words and still they sounded too loud.

"We get him down and get him the fuck out of here." My question seemed to snap Arrow into action, and he lunged forward toward Rowen.

Rowen's eyes snapped open, and his lips moved in a warning that came too late. Arrow's foot hit the side of the circle causing an explosion of light that threw him back. He narrowly missed me, instead landing flat on his back on the table.

"Are you ok?" I asked, voice low, watching as Arrow rolled off the table with a series of F-bombs.

"Those bitches have nothing on me," he said, stalking back over to the circle with extra venom in his step.

He bent down beside it with a hand out, drawing small circles in the air. His brow creased in concentration. At first nothing appeared to be happening, but then the shadows gathered close to Arrow. Something in the atmosphere shifted with an audible pop.

"Is that so?" came a female voice from behind us.

Skylar stood in the doorway. The light from my palm cast a fiery glow on her face, illuminating her black eyes. That was a bad sign; her demon husband was possessing her, using her body as his own during the daylight hours. We were so fucked.

"Fuck you, Ransom," Arrow said, addressing the demon by name. "Spike. Fire." Having disabled the curse on the circle, Arrow crossed it freely.

Staring into Skylar's demon eyes, I didn't need any further prodding. Palms tingling, I blasted her with the angelic flame. Flames licked up the doorway, climbing the frame until the entrance was encircled in fire.

Ransom jerked back out of the room, escaping the touch of flame. He looked out of Skylar's face with enough sinister intentions to shrivel my soul.

I held up the sword and said, "Back the fuck off, or your wife gets this in the guts."

"Do it, and I will make the rest of your short life a living hell." The voice that came out of Skylar was gravelly and terrifying. "Cinder's seal isn't going to protect you, undecided."

Despite Ransom's claim, he made no move to cross my fire or retaliate. I looked to where Arrow was untying the ropes that held Rowen in place, grateful that they hadn't used actual nails. I was torn between helping or manning the door. A clatter on the basement stairs announced the arrival of the woman who Arrow had frozen, so I stayed by the door, sword held ready.

She was a red-haired beauty with piercing, green eyes. On her heels, a frazzled-looking blonde wrung her hands and muttered to herself. They both jerked to a stop outside the door and looked to Skylar, who swayed slightly, blinking a few times. Her eyes went from black to blue in a blink. Ransom had left her.

Her focus turned to me, and she let out a shriek. "You! You ruined our wedding, and now you think you're going to steal our nephilim? Well your angel's seal doesn't mean shit to me."

The curse she threw was precise, her aim true. It hit me in the chest, choking off my air. The sword in my grip vibrated as it neutralized the effects, allowing me to draw a breath.

As she passed through the doorframe, the fire went out. The other two were quick to follow, and they surrounded me, chanting something I couldn't make sense of.

Arrow grumbled, "Oh, Skylar, really? Get bent, you bitch. This isn't your fight."

He paused his rescue of Rowen to come to my aid with a creeping shadow that slithered across the floor to wind itself around Skylar's ankles. Like a boa, it cinched her tightly before it wrenched her feet out from under her. It didn't stop there. With a screech, Skylar clawed at the tile as she was yanked out of the room and up the stairs. Her wail grew farther away, followed by the slamming of the basement door at the top of the stairs.

I would have gawked at Arrow in surprise if the other two witches weren't pressing in closer. So much about him remained a mystery to me. The extent of his abilities being one of them.

Lady Red uttered, "Away!" and waved a hand. It wasn't directed at me, however, but at Arrow. She succeeded in knocking him aside, which caused Rowen to collapse to the floor.

I dove toward him as he fell onto his hands and knees. A blanket of silver covered him as his wings spread wide. I needed to ask so many questions if, er, when we got out of here.

"You stupid witch!" Back on his feet, Arrow flung out both hands. Red was frozen in place, her mouth open to throw another curse. The shadows swirled around the blonde. Guided by Arrow, they flung her against the wall where she kicked and screamed as the shadow grew into a frightful, black mass.

I whispered to Rowen, "Come on. We have to get you out of here." I slung Rowen's arm around my neck and hauled him up. "Did Dash do this to you?"

A large silver wing brushed against my back. Sure, I'd seen Cinder's wings and even Koda's, but this was blowing my mind. So many questions.

"Dash did... a lot of... things to me." A cough racked Rowen, and he spat blood. "He thought... he could force... my choice. So I had to... prove him wrong. I had to... choose."

Arrow shouted, "Get your ass moving, Spike!" He grabbed hold of Rowen's other side. "And stop being so scared to fight these broads. They sure as hell aren't scared to hurt you. They'd sacrifice you to the fucking devil if they could."

We dragged Rowen from the room, careful with his wings as we passed through the doorway. The stairs seemed so far away. Knowing that Skylar was upstairs shook my confidence, but she was not yet our biggest concern.

A low, guttural voice behind us caused my quickly flagging courage to disappear completely. "I'm not done with him yet," the voice hissed in a low timbre that I recognized as Dash, albeit a much more sinister sounding Dash.

I turned to find Red standing there, her body held at an odd angle. Her eyes were redder than her hair. Dash commanded her form in an awkward and unfamiliar way that made the possession so much creepier.

"Keep going," Arrow instructed before turning to face the demon. "I'm not going to let you have my brother, Dash. You already have me."

"Brother," Rowen echoed, the word escaping on a rush of pained air exiting his lungs.

I urged Rowen on to the staircase though I didn't feel good about leaving Arrow to face the demon alone. But really, what could I do? The sword dragging along in my right hand began to grow warm.

"You were just a means to an end, Arrow. I used you to get to him. He's the one I really want. He's the child that should never have been born. The rarity. But you, there are so many more where you came from." Even though I couldn't see it, I knew the tone Dash used conveyed the condescending expression Red's face wore. What he said was despicable, and I didn't know which brother I felt worse for.

Hearing a grunt from Arrow, I risked a glance back to find him on his knees. Red stood over him while Dash's ugly power poured out of her. Arrow clutched his head and sunk down even closer to the floor.

"Your loyalty is sadly lacking, Arrow," Dash proclaimed. "You know what happens to those who betray the coven."

"Keep moving," I whispered to Rowen. "Get to the top of the stairs and wait for me. I have to help Arrow."

I didn't have a plan. Maybe this was a huge mistake. Arrow was a supreme asshole, a drug dealer who used blackmail to get what he wanted and took blowjobs for payment. Still I couldn't rush away and leave him to die. Was this what Cinder saw in me? The spark that made him believe I was capable of more than I'd dared believe.

Leaving Rowen clutching the handrail, I turned back toward the demon and said a prayer that this wasn't how I would die.

"Walk away, girl." Red eyes found me and glimmered with danger. "This doesn't concern you."

"Yes, it does." Slowly I inched closer. If Dash focused on Arrow and me, then maybe at least Rowen would get away.

Arrow rolled a pained gaze my way and shook his head, just once. "Spike, don't."

I stared at Dash, seeing him within the red-haired witch. The longer he possessed her the more she seemed to become him. Every second that passed caused my heart to pound a little harder.

"Had I known that you were one of Cinder's, I'd never have wasted a second look on you. However, if you interfere, I will do everything short of killing you. I promise, you don't want that." As he was speaking, Red's hand drifted to Arrow's shoulder. She barely touched him, and he was screaming. Blood welled up in Arrow's mouth and trickled down his chin. Dash had no intention of letting him leave here alive.

"No, I don't want that," I said, raising the sword. Could I really do this? Harm Red in order to drive Dash out? I didn't want it to come to that, but it already had.

"What is that you've got there?" Dash caught sight of the weapon I held, and he recoiled. "But you're an undecided. You're not worthy to wield that blade." He recognized it. I hadn't anticipated that.

"Well, you'll have to take that up with Cinder." I gripped the hilt tight with both hands.

"Do you even know what that is?" Dash's voice thundered out of Red. Distracted by the sword, he seemed to momentarily forget about Arrow. "That is the Midnight Star, a blade forged for the flame bearer. Every generation there is one who comes to liberate the nephilim from darkness. I suppose that's you then, honey. I never thought it would be a woman." Dash threw a lot at me with that declaration. No way, I can't be the flame bearer he spoke of. If anything, that was all a damn lie meant to distract me while he killed Arrow.

"Back off, Dash. We leave, and your witch lives. I don't want to hurt her, but I'll do what it takes to get out of here." The sword seemed to hum in my hands or perhaps that was the tingle of my palms, itching to throw a fireball at the witch. *The flame bearer.* Could that be me? I was only one of many who possessed power over the element of fire.

"There's always more where she came from. Not you though. You and that one," Dash nodded to Rowen who sat slumped on the stairs under his blanket of silver. "You're both mine."

Nothing got my hackles up like possessiveness. I wasn't an object. My mother had invested much time into ensuring that I believed that because she'd known eventually one of these assholes would tell me otherwise. *Thanks, Mom.* I growled, "Like hell we are."

Though my arms were trembling, I held the sword as if I would use it. And I hoped that I could follow through if it came to that. For a strained moment Dash and I stared at each other, waiting for someone to make a move.

Instead Arrow flung up a hand to freeze Red as the shadows swarmed her. Dash's greater power enabled him to fight back with much success, but Arrow's effort bought us a few precious seconds.

"Go!" Arrow demanded as he dragged himself to his feet.

I turned and ran for the stairs with Arrow right behind me. His movements were stiff and pained, but he didn't falter. Suddenly he was ripped away by an unseen hand and smashed into the floor so hard I thought for sure he was dead. But he was a fighter. He waved a hand at me to keep moving. I didn't want to, but I couldn't let Dash have all of us.

"Run," I urged Rowen, who blinked bleary eyes at me. His wings sagged heavily, and he struggled to get up.

The next thing I knew I was airborne, flung down beside Arrow like a sack of meat. My teeth smacked together before I managed to catch myself with a hand. With the other, I clung to the sword for dear life.

Red stood over us as Dash used her to pour his darkness into me. A million little knives buried inside me, sawing and slicing, cutting me down until I was too weak to fight back. A human could only conduct so much demonic power before burning out, but Dash never let up.

With great effort I tried to lift the sword, but it lay plastered to the floor. My strength was quickly sapped.

With a brilliant flash of light, Red tumbled back into the big screen TV. Both it and she toppled over, crashing down behind the television stand.

After a moment I realized that the blast of light had come from Rowen. He lay collapsed on the stairs, watching as Red began to rise.

Neither brother was in good enough shape to fend off a further demon attack. I had no other choice but to lay Red out.

With a grunt, I stood up. This time I didn't hesitate. I rushed her with my sword held ready. Dash saw it coming, and he smiled. Maybe he didn't believe I'd do it. Or maybe he enjoyed the fight. But when I plunged the blade into Red's middle, his smile crumbled.

He gripped the blade before I could shove it in deeper, but it was already deep enough. Blood began to drip from the slices on the witch's hands, but neither she nor Dash seemed to feel it.

"You're making a grave mistake, girl. You can't kill me." As Dash spoke, blood filled Red's mouth. He was fighting to hold on.

"I don't need to," I said. "I just need to stop you."

The blade gleamed as a brilliant silver light engulfed it. Dash roared, an anguished sound. Demons might not die, but they feel pain. Right then that pain was enough for me. I wanted the asshole to hurt.

Dash fought to remain in Red, but it was useless. She was seriously wounded, and he was weakened by the silver buried inside her. With an angry cry, he let go, forced back to the other side where he would regain his strength and, at sundown, his body.

The crimson color faded from Red's eyes, returning them to their natural green, but they were dull and unfocused. I jerked the sword free, and she hit the floor.

I stared at her, feeling a strange sense of surreal detachment. I hadn't wanted to hurt her, but my self-defense had been vital. We'd never have had a chance to escape if I didn't do it. Still, I felt horrible.

"Don't feel bad," Arrow said, holding his head. "She was a willing vessel. She knew the risk she was taking."

I held out a hand to him, ignoring the parts of me that hurt. He was in much worse shape. We still had Skylar to deal with once we emerged from the basement.

Arrow's bruised face had some new additions. He looked like shit. Wiping the blood from his face with the back of his arm, he headed for the stairs with an awkward limp.

"Come on, buddy," he said to Rowen. "Let's get you out of this shithole."

"Let me go first." I paused to wipe the blood from the blade on the arm of the couch. "If Skylar's waiting for us up there, I can distract her while you two get out."

Arrow didn't argue but said, "We're not going to leave you behind, Spike."

I squeezed by the two of them and hesitated with my hand on the door. When the two of them were as ready as they were going to be, I turned the knob and flung the door open.

Silence met us. The quiet was eerie despite the sunlight streaming through the main floor. I stepped out of the basement and turned in every direction. Nothing. Where was Skylar?

Slowly I inched forward, waiting for her to appear. Arrow and Rowen followed. I paused so they could head for the door first, watching their back as they went. This didn't feel right. It was too calm.

"Spike, get the gate, will you?" Arrow called, unfazed by the quiet. "There's a button for it there." He pointed to an intercom system on the wall near the spiral staircase that led to the upper floor.

I moved toward it, still turning slowly, unwilling to leave my back unguarded. Arrow opened the front door and dragged Rowen across the threshold. No sooner had I hit the button for the gate than Skylar appeared at the top of the stairs.

The first and only thing I noticed before she jumped on me was that her eyes were blue. Though no demon resided inside her, that didn't make her any less crazy. She leaped from the top step, clearing the rest as she crashed down atop me, sending us both sprawling across the entryway floor.

The sword slipped from my grasp and skittered away despite my attempt to hang onto it. Flat on my back, I rolled over to get up, but Skylar was on me before I could. With black hair hiding most of her face, all I could see was her crazed eyes as she sat on my chest and wrapped her hands around my throat.

She began to speak in Latin, a spell. Letting her finish was not an option. I threw a hand up, and a ball of fire exploded in her face. Her scream was sharp in my ears, but they'd taken much worse from amps and drums.

The stink of singed hair was satisfying. Her face turned red and mottled from the flame. My fire didn't stop her for long, but it did give me a chance to get up. Instead of going after her, I dove for the sword. Anticipating that move, Skylar shouted a command, and the sword slid further out of reach.

Arrow lingered on the front step looking uncertain. His shadows were useless in the sunlit room. Rowen slumped against him, sides heaving. He was too weak to help me. All they could do was watch.

Using my gifts required a lot of energy and focus. I couldn't do much before I burned myself out, both literally and figuratively. Being half-human, my power supply was limited and currently in need of replenishment. I had no way of knowing which one of us would last longer, Skylar or me. I knew of only one way to find out.

A flame burned in the center of my palm. With careful intent, I pushed it out around me until I was surrounded by fire. Then I lunged for the sword, unwilling to leave it in the demons' den.

Skylar threw a spell at me, then another, frowning when they did nothing. "This isn't over," she declared, hands on her hips like she was about to have a hissy fit.

"It is for now." Holding the sword once again, I couldn't help but notice how nicely the winged handle fit in my hand. "Unless you want to end up like your ginger friend downstairs, it's probably best that you fuck right off."

I was mad as hell and ready to show it. Sweat dotted my brow. My body ached, and I was tiring quickly.

Her fierce expression faltered, and she looked toward the basement. "What did you do to Michelle?" She didn't wait around for a response. Forgetting me entirely, Skylar rushed to the basement door.

I didn't waste the opportunity to get out without further incident. I let the fire cloaking me go out and joined the boys on the front step. The warmth of the sun cut through the slight chill in the fall air. Grateful that we were all alive, I sucked the fresh air deep into my lungs.

"You think you can do something about those?" Arrow nodded to Rowen's wings as we passed through the open gate. The hellhounds had gathered to watch us, but none of them moved beyond the perimeter.

Rowen shook his head. His voice was raspy, and his shoulders slumped with exhaustion. "I don't know how. I really don't feel so well."

We needed Cinder, but first we had to get Rowen out of sight, somewhere safe. "Let's just get him in the car," I said, urging them to move faster. "We'll be safe at my place."

I couldn't be sure if anyone had seen us. Only one car passed as we struggled to get Rowen down the street and into the car. Thankfully that driver was too busy on his cell phone to gawk at us. Typical.

Those silver wings took up the entire back seat and then some, but Rowen settled in against the leather seats with a sigh. I peeled away with a squeal of tires, no longer concerned with the newness of the BMW.

From the passenger seat, Arrow stuck out a hand. His head was bowed, his brow creased in unspoken pain. "Now," he said through clenched teeth. "Can I have my stash back?"

Chapter Twenty

"Rowen?" I glanced at him through the rear view mirror. "Are you ok? Do you need a hospital or something?"

He wasn't looking so good. His breathing was shallow, and his amber eyes were dull and listless, lacking their usual fire. The purple and red bruises adorning his body appeared much worse than they had indoors.

"Don't be stupid," Arrow said as he used a credit card to cut a line of coke on the dash. "He can't go to the hospital with giant fucking wings. Oh, and thanks for the concern. I only got my insides fried back there."

A hard frown furrowed my brow. I told myself Arrow wasn't worth getting frown lines at an early age, but it was impossible to relax.

"Pretty sure you're fine. Keep treating yourself with drugs and cigarettes. I'm sure that's the cure for someone like you." Somehow I managed to keep from screaming in his stupid face despite being tightly wound and ready to snap.

"It's cool." Rowen's voice was hoarse, as if he'd spent a lot of time screaming. "I'm ok."

He wasn't at all convincing, but I headed for home, silently repeating Cinder's name. I couldn't do this on my own, and I sure as shit couldn't help Rowen with the wings. They'd manifested shockingly soon after he'd made his choice. As far as I knew, it didn't generally work that way.

"Someone like me?" Arrow repeated, leaning over to snort the line through a fifty from his wallet. "That sounds awfully judgmental. Haven't I earned at least a little bit of respect from you yet?"

I sighed and blew a long piece of layered bangs out of my eyes. "Is that really so important to you?" After what we'd just gone through, I wasn't in the mood to have this conversation. My only concern right then was Rowen. Not for a moment did I wish anything bad on Arrow, but he seemed to be doing just fine.

Arrow ignored me, choosing to drag on a cigarette rather than answer my question. Fine by me. We drove the rest of the way to my apartment in silence.

He also seemed to be just as curious and surprised about the wings as I was. I caught him sneaking glances in the side mirror, peeking into the backseat to eye the silver feathers.

Only true angels had white wings. Demon wings were black as sin. Those in between, the fallen and the nephilim, their wings were silver although I'd seen them a drab grey as well. Cinder had said it had to do with the soul of the individual. Black soul, black wings. Made sense to me.

We arrived at my place in the late morning just after rush hour. Hopefully we wouldn't be running into anybody in the elevator or the hall. I went first, ensuring the lobby was empty before waving Arrow and Rowen over. I darted up the stairs to the second floor while they took the elevator. The hallway was empty, and not a sound penetrated the walls from nearby suites.

We'd made it halfway to my apartment door when a sound at the opposite end of the hall startled me. I held my breath, fearing the worst. The fire exit swung open and in staggered my neighbor, Jez. My breath whooshed out in relief. Jez was a shapeshifter. Judging by the number of times I'd seen her come in bloody and bruised, she'd already seen her share of weird shit.

Her bright green gaze swept over each of us in turn. Strands had escaped her golden-blonde ponytail, and the pungent scent of alcohol wafted around her.

"Hey, Spike," she said, casual and chill, like a man with wings was no big deal. "Arrow," she added, a hardness in her tone that hadn't been there before. I hadn't been aware that they knew each other.

"Hi." I squeezed out a small smile. Though we were only acquaintances, it was somehow reassuring to have someone else in the building who was more than human.

She paused at her apartment door, key poised in the lock. "Let me know if you need anything. I'm just a few feet away."

"Thank you," I said as I jammed my key into my own door. "Ditto."

Throwing the door open, I stepped back to allow the guys through. The scrumptious aroma of fresh bread greeted us. Cinder!

"Oh my," I heard from the kitchen as Cinder caught sight of Rowen. "Let's get you settled somewhere comfortable."

I locked the door as if the deadbolt was what made it safe rather than Cinder's wards. The deadbolt might have been useless on anyone other than humans, but it gave me a sense of security anyway.

A peek in the kitchen revealed a loaf of bread fresh out of the oven, a tray of fresh fruit, and a tub of organic vanilla yogurt. I couldn't find enough words for the gratitude I was feeling. Cinder was the best friend I'd ever had, though I wouldn't have said so to Jett. She's so touchy.

Arrow stepped back, seemingly happy to let Cinder take over. The compassion flowed from the angel as he got Rowen settled in the middle of the couch, wings splayed out on either side.

"Did anyone see you come in?" Cinder directed the question to me.

"Only Jez." I propped the sword against the wall, sat heavily on the armchair adjacent to the couch, and began pulling my boots off. The adrenaline was wearing off, leaving me nauseous.

Turning back to Rowen, Cinder placed a hand on each of his shoulders. He spoke in low, calming tones, assessing the extent of Rowen's injuries. With a gentleness that I'd never seen among humankind, Cinder guided Rowen in commanding his wings.

"It's no different than any other limb," he said softly. "They are yours to command. Will them to move, and they shall. Will them to be unseen, and they shall. Take a deep breath." Cinder turned. "Ember, fetch him some water, will you?"

"I'll do it." Arrow rocked forward, springing into motion.

I turned in my chair to watch him search through the cupboards until he found the glasses. His hands were shaky. He listed too far to the right, lost his balance, but caught himself on the counter. His head jerked up, and he caught me staring. Maybe he was in rougher shape than I'd thought.

I turned away quickly, just in time to see Rowen's wings vanish. He breathed a sigh of relief and grabbed Cinder's hand in a thankful squeeze. He held his other hand out to me, and I went to him.

Rowen looked better already. Cinder's encouragement and guidance had lit a light that burned inside Rowen. He had chosen the light, as he'd said he would. It suited him. I was happy even though I was also jealous of his ability to be so certain with his choice. I knew my procrastination was an obstacle that I had to get over. Why did I have to be so damn afraid to commit?

Curled up next to Rowen, I had to ask myself how deep my fear went. I couldn't mistake the way I felt about him. I was falling in love, which was scary, but it was also exciting. My fears had cost me good things in the past. In fact, they still did. At some point, I had to face that before it took everything from me.

Arrow returned with a glass of water, which he handed to Rowen before sitting down in the chair I'd just vacated. He rubbed his hands over his face and stared at the carpet.

The brothers needed to talk. Now was as good a time as any.

"Cinder, will you join me outside for a minute please?" I kissed Rowen's temple before getting up and heading for the balcony.

Cinder closed the door behind us and took a seat in one of the lounge chairs. I leaned against the railing and sparked up a smoke. His lips quirked like he wanted to lecture me, but somehow he refrained.

"You did good, Ember. I'm proud of you."

"Really? But I just lit a cigarette after dragging in two broken nephilim."

"I know." Cinder nodded and propped a foot on the opposing knee. "That's why I'm proud. Well, not the smoking part. That's a vile habit, and you should know better. But you did what you set out to do. You succeeded."

"Yeah, I guess." I sucked smoke into my lungs and gagged when it only increased my nausea. The concrete felt cold beneath my socked feet. Now that I was home, I was unbearably exhausted.

"Tell me what happened."

I recounted the events of the morning for him. He listened attentively, waiting until I'd finished before asking any questions. Then it was my turn.

"Cinder, what is the Midnight Star for? And why did Dash think it was meant for me?"

Cinder looked mildly surprised that I knew the sword's name. "Because it is. I wasn't supposed to give it to you until you'd committed yourself to the light. But I couldn't send you in there without it." Again that commitment thing. Why did choosing have to be such a big friggin' deal? I already knew the answer to that.

"Dash told me that it was to be wielded by the one meant to liberate the nephilim from darkness. Care to shed a little light on that?" The cigarette had burned down to the filter though I'd barely smoked it. I squished it out in the empty coffee can that served as an ashtray and sat down on the chair next to him.

"Dash spoke the truth. Unfortunately, now he knows who you really are. So I suppose you should as well." Cinder paused, gazing down at the quiet street below. "Every generation has a flame bearer, one born to bring the lost nephilim back to the light. The nephilim were once known as abominations, and all were condemned to darkness. But things changed. Humankind can be made right with God, and as mortals, so can the nephilim. The demons resent that though. They strive to claim as many of you as they can." He waited then, allowing me to mull this over.

And I did, expecting it to somehow shock or alarm me. It didn't. Somewhere deep inside, something clicked, like I'd known all along. "Is this common knowledge?" I finally asked. "Is this why Koda has been after me for so long?"

"No," Cinder said, his voice thick with disgust. "The identity of the chosen flame bearer isn't widely known. Koda's sick obsession is all his own. Though I imagine it may get worse if he learns of it."

My gaze strayed to the door. Rowen and Arrow were talking inside. Arrow had moved to sit beside Rowen, and the two of them seemed to be in deep discussion.

"What do I do now?" I asked. "And more importantly, how do I do it?"

Cinder's hand was warm on my shoulder, and I shivered as it made the chill in the air seem that much sharper. "You keep being you and doing what you know to be right."

I peered into his pretty, violet eyes and saw my own reflection within them. "The part you're not saying is that I have to hurry and choose, don't I?"

"It's not my place to pressure you, Ember. Your choice is your own, and you know in your heart what it must be."

"I do, I know. But I'm scared, Cinder. I don't do commitment so well. There are so many what-ifs running around in my head. What if I can't stay loyal to my commitment?" I nodded toward Rowen. "I'm actually jealous of him for being so sure."

Cinder made a sympathetic noise and patted my shoulder. "What-ifs belong to the devil. Any sentence or thought that begins with what if is a product of doubt and fear. You must banish it."

I nodded and bit my lip, unable to voice my frustration at being unable to quell my irrational inner fears. My silence didn't prevent Cinder from understanding though. He smoothed a hand over my hair, exuding a sense of calm that settled over me.

"Many share your struggle. It's not so different from those who don't believe marriage is more than a piece of paper. They fail to realize that the paper is solely for the human legal system. The vows, on the other hand, are for the soul. Making such a declaration before God and man adds vitality to our commitments. That's what makes it real, the oath to withstand all that life brings until the end. That's what makes it mean something. What's holding your soul back, Ember?"

Tears filled my eyes and ran down my face. Something he'd said had reached through the fog and chaos in my head, penetrating to the source of the problem, finding it and setting it free. Cinder didn't offer me the false words of comfort that humans were so quick to dole out, thinking them helpful. He let me cry, which was just what I needed. I seldom allowed myself such a luxury.

"I'm afraid that I won't be able to cut it, that I'll be a total failure. I'm not exactly living the sin-free life here, and I'll never be perfect." There. I said it. All my silly, irrational fears were on the table. I knew perfection was a myth, that it didn't exist. Still, the pressure to achieve it was there, a rotten seed buried in my soul.

Cinder pulled me in for an awkward half-hug across the span of our chairs. He chuckled, a gentle sound that soothed. "Do you think I'm perfect, Ember? I promise you that I am not. Nor is the preacher who leads his flock, the family who adopts an orphan, nor that sweet boy in there." He pointed to Rowen. "All you can do is your best. Perfection is not a requirement to serve the light. Only dedication. Ask yourself where you belong. You already know the answer. Just come to terms with accepting it, and you will become all you are meant to be."

I stared at Rowen, my mind racing. "How is it possible that he has wings?"

"His soul was ready to embrace all of who he is. I daresay it was a mistake for his talents to be hidden. Somehow they were never hidden from him. He will be a vital addition to the light." Cinder's smile was filled with joy.

I wanted that smile for me one day. Cinder was right. I knew where I belonged. Maybe I did have much work to do on myself, but I had to start somewhere. Another glance at Rowen confirmed that I wanted to be as secure in myself as he was. I wanted more than what my life was offering. So I would have to take the reins to control my fate.

"So what makes the Midnight Star so special?" I asked, curious but also ready to move past my little cryfest. "It has a pretty fancy name."

"You do," Cinder said as if that explained everything. "You and every other flame bearer who possesses it. It will take care of you, if you let it. It forces demons back to the other side."

The memory of plunging it into Michelle surfaced, and I tasted bile at the back of my throat. "I used it to hurt someone, a human. I didn't want to, but I didn't have much choice."

"That woman chose to serve Dash knowing that it put her life in jeopardy and, more importantly, her soul. We all have a role to play. She played hers, and you played yours." Cinder rose and pulled me up with him. "You're shivering. Get something to eat and get some rest."

Maybe some food would settle my stomach. "What about them?" I jerked a thumb toward the living room. "Dash did a real number on them both. They need healing, and I don't think they're safe at their house once the sun goes down."

Cinder considered the guys who appeared to be deep in conversation. Arrow had tossed his hat on the chair and his long hair fell to hide his face. His shoulders were squared and stiff. Rowen slumped against the back of the couch, his arms crossed and his brow pinched. I wondered what exactly they were talking about.

"I don't suppose you want to have them stay here," Cinder suggested, his head inclined in thought. "I can't put wards on Arrow's house since he's dark. Rowen won't be safe there any longer."

I studied the brothers through the glass. Arrow was clearly in more pain than he wanted to show. It was more than just the drugs that had him losing his balance in the kitchen. Dash had seriously hurt him. He could be bleeding internally for all I knew. Rowen too was in rough shape, but he didn't seem to be as obviously distressed. His agony appeared to be more of the mental kind.

"Will you heal him?" I asked. "Arrow. I mean."

Cinder regarded me with a studious look that dissected my words, seeking out the root of my intent. "You would ask me to bless him? After all that you know him to be."

I knew the angel wasn't trying to make me second-guess my request. He merely wished to verify it. Feeling my stare upon him, Arrow glanced up to meet my gaze.

"Yes," I said, hoping it wasn't a mistake. "He's as lost as anyone, Cinder. I think he even knows it. If I don't make a request on his behalf, who will?"

With a broad smile, Cinder turned to go inside. "You never stop amazing me, Ember. I hope you can see the depths of your genuine nature. You may be a sinner, but your heart dwells in a place of beauty." He stopped with a hand on the door and turned back to me. "You're no stranger to commitment, you know. That little tortoise in there will live many human years, yet you promised to care for him through them all."

I opened my mouth to protest then clamped it shut, finding that he was right. Adopting Seth hadn't felt like a commitment. Not for a moment had I paused to consider the length of years he would live. In fact, the idea of having decades with the little guy had appealed to me.

"I see what you did there." With a laugh, I gave him a playful shove. "Let's go inside. It's freezing out here."

The guys fell silent as we entered. They exchanged a look. Fatigue lined Rowen's eyes, giving them a hollow, sunken appearance. Arrow was wired on coke when he should have been tired as well. Exhaustion was quickly overtaking me.

Cinder extended a hand to Arrow. "May I?"

Arrow shot me a wary glance before putting his hand in Cinder's. Nothing obvious or visible happened. The room seemed to grow warmer, and Arrow let out a small gasp. Then it was over. Cinder did the same with Rowen who watched him in wide-eyed wonder.

"Stay safe," Cinder addressed us all. To me, he added, "We'll speak soon." Then he was gone.

"We all need to get some sleep," My gaze landed on the Midnight Star, surprised that Cinder had left it behind. "We're safe here behind Cinder's wards. You guys can crash here if you want. The couch pulls out into a bed."

Arrow got up too quickly and put a hand to his head. "You guys chill here. I'm heading home. Hiding from Dash is pointless. He'll catch up with me eventually."

"Arrow, don't. Just stay. At least until you've slept." The hard edge to Rowen's tone made me think they'd argued while I was outside.

"Naw, it's cool. I'll sleep in my own bed. And maybe die there too." Arrow shrugged like it was all part of life, no big deal. Then he headed for the door without a look back.

Rowen got up too, wearing a scowl. Instead of following Arrow, he went straight into my bedroom and closed the door. With raised brows I stared at the closed door. Did this mean we were an official item? He was sleeping in my bed as if we were.

The smothering sensation of commitment crawled over me, cutting off my breath. Were we supposed to have a talk about this or just let it be whatever it was? I was too confused and too tired to make sense of it all.

I caught up with Arrow when he was halfway down the hall. He kept going, ignoring me when I said his name. Breaking into a sprint, I caught up to him. I grabbed his arm tighter than necessary.

"Do you think going off alone is the best idea right now? I don't think you're in the right state of mind to be alone."

He shook me off with a force that bordered on violent. "I don't really give a shit what you think, Spike. Stop acting like we're the same. Rowen is light, and you are so sickeningly light that you may as well just choose them and get it over with. I'm dark. The enemy. So thanks for asking your angel pal to heal me, but I'll be on my way now."

He stormed away with such anger in his stride that I decided it was best to let him go. Who was I to try to stop him? Arrow was in charge of his own destiny. Still, I felt bad for him. Perhaps my pity drove him away in such fury.

After stabbing the button for the elevator half a dozen times, he cast a scathing glare my way. "See you in a few days. When we kick your ass on stage."

So he wanted to be like that, did he? Fine. I got it. Arrow didn't know how to react to the kindness of others because he wasn't used to receiving it. Lashing out was all he knew.

I watched him disappear into the elevator, feeling both sad for him and pissed at him. *I hope you live to see that night, Arrow,* I thought. *Really, I do.*

Chapter Twenty-One

Rowen stayed for a few days. It gave him a chance to rest, us a chance to recover, and Arrow some time alone. Rowen didn't say much about his talk with Arrow, only that the discovery that they were brothers had been shocking. He needed some time to adjust.

In between work, jamming with the girls, and training with Cinder, we didn't actually spend all that much time together. Still, at the end of the third day, when he announced that he was going home, I was both relieved and worried.

We hadn't had 'the talk,' the awkward breakdown of our relationship that analyzed the future we might or might not have together. Every moment I spent with Rowen brought me closer to a feeling of certainty that he was the one. Still, the voice of doubt lingered in my head.

"If this is moving too fast for you, let me know," he'd said to me one night after we'd made love. "I don't want to scare you away. But I don't think I could ever feel for someone else what I feel for you."

I'd held him close and kissed his words away, content to let my body say the words I couldn't give voice to. I did feel deeply for Rowen, but I didn't do love so well. I feared hurting him.

Once he'd decided to go back to Arrow's, I made him promise me he would be careful. That night, we'd sat outside Arrow's house in my car, holding hands and dragging the moment out as long as we reasonably could.

"If anything happens, Dash or anyone else, don't hesitate to call me. I'll come." I kissed him several times before letting him get out.

"I promise," he'd sworn with his hand on the door. "You know, Spike, you are the one who made me so sure of where I belong. I want you to be that sure too. It's ok to take a leap of faith. You might be surprised at how well it works out."

I watched him walk up the front steps and disappear inside. Arrow's car wasn't out front, but it could have been in the garage. I had to admit that I'd love to have been a fly on the wall when they spoke next.

When I pulled up at the jam space to meet the girls, it felt like it had been ages since we'd been together when it had only been a few days. Once Jett was brought up to speed on the latest goings on in the nephilim world, she forgot that she was mad at me for some silly-ass reason.

"Next time shit like that happens, Spike, you let me know. I'll have your back in a fucking heartbeat. I mean it." Jett had been adamant, insisting she wasn't afraid of Dash, adding, "Fear is for suckers."

She was currently singing her heart out as we put the finishing touches on a new song. Playing it for the final show meant a lot to Jett. I'd never seen her so intent on proving herself. I wondered if she would've been this hell bent on winning if we'd been up against a band other than Molly's Chamber.

Even though the final band battle meant a lot to me, it was difficult to stay focused. My mind kept straying. Rowen's text that Arrow was gone didn't help any. Arrow had left a message saying he'd try to make it to the show. No guarantees. What in the ever loving fuck?

We took a break after that song, and I told Jett about the text.

"Are you fucking kidding me?" Jett stared at me with growing ire. "Arrow's bailing on the show? We can't win by default. I want to kick his ass!"

"He didn't say he was bailing," I corrected, accepting the joint Tash passed my way. "He said he'd try to make it."

I mulled this over. Where the hell would Arrow go? And why? It definitely had something to do with Dash.

"Oh, he better fucking make it. I will gut that fucker if he ruins this final night for me. For us." Jett snatched the joint away and puffed angrily on it. I hid a smile. She was always so easily angered. The wolf made her impatient and bossy, or maybe that was just Jett. I hadn't known her before she was a wolf.

We played well into the wee morning hours. Finally Tash packed up her bass and announced that she was going home. I'd been yawning for some time already.

"Me too," I agreed. "Jett, I think we're more than ready for the show. Let's call it a night."

"Fine." Her eyes glittered wolf. She was still cranky though her mood had worn thin. "When we win, I'm taking us all out to celebrate. Somewhere swanky where they frown on people like us."

I wasn't sure if she meant us as in rock musicians or us as in beings other than mere humans. It didn't really matter.

We locked up the jam space and headed to our cars. I was in the middle of the parking lot when Koda appeared without warning. It was so sudden that I'd had no sense of him. He appeared right in front of me with black wings spread, his red eyes seeming to glow in the darkness. Jett waved for the other girls to take off quickly as she hurried to my side.

"What now, Koda?" I asked tiredly. "I'd appreciate it if you didn't show up like this in front of my friends."

His gaze swept over me before lingering on Jett who glared furiously at him. With wings flared, Koda maintained an intimidating stance.

"I came to warn you about Dash," he said. "He's going to be at your show this weekend."

"Am I supposed to be surprised? Or scared? Because all I am is sick of demon bullshit." My palms tingled as I instinctively grew defensive. Throwing a fireball in Koda's face might feel good, but the results would be short lived. Not worth it.

"You have been nothing but a bitch to me, and still I'm here with good intentions. Is it too much to ask that you speak to me with some respect?" Somehow Koda managed to look hurt.

I wasn't buying it, and I snickered, unable to resist. "But I don't respect you, Koda. And let's not forget what they say about good intentions. The road to hell is paved with them."

"Actually," he retorted with a sinister smile. "The road to hell is paved with the souls of snotty nephilim who spit in the face of those seeking to help them."

Jett scoffed. She wasn't the type to let a stupid comment like that pass without a remark. "Is that how you think you get into a lady's pants? No wonder you've never scored with Spike."

My elbow jerked of its own accord, finding its way into the soft tissue between Jett's ribs. She grunted, but it came out as more of a laugh.

Koda spared an evil smirk for Jett. "I bet that mouth of yours gets you into plenty of trouble."

"You have no idea," she quipped, thrusting her hip forward and crossing her arms. Jett wasn't one to be easily cowed.

"I haven't been looking for a new pet, but I would make an exception for you." Koda's cool tone had taken on a malicious note I'd heard before. Though he was seldom more than a royal pain in my ass, he was still dangerous. Taunting him was unwise.

I jumped in before Jett could reply and make things worse. "Tell me why I should care about Dash coming to the show. It's a public place. What can he really do?"

Koda stared hard at Jett for several more seconds before allowing me to redirect his gaze. "That's not the question you should be asking. You stabbed his witch and swiped his nephilim. You should be wondering what it is he won't do."

The intensity of his stare bore deeper into me than usual. I was uncomfortable beneath the weight of it. "Dash told you, didn't he?"

"That you're the keeper of the Midnight Star? Yes, he did. There have been many, though it's been ages since it's been a woman. But never an undecided." The sound of feathers rustling was loud in the stillness as Koda's wings settled against his back.

I couldn't tell if there was a veiled threat in Koda's words or not. The way he looked at me was as intrusive and vile as ever. I had a sinking feeling that this news had only fed his weird infatuation with me. "Ok," I said, drawing out the word, feeling uncomfortable and desperately wanting to be away from him. "So if we're done here, I'll just be leaving now."

"I came as your friend, Spike. I don't want you to be caught off guard by Dash. I can help, you know. If you'd consider striking a deal."

Jett scoffed but said nothing.

I looked at Koda like he was out of his mind, which he evidently was. What kind of a blasted fool did he take me for? My laugh was sharp and deadly. "Really? You're trying that? Come on now, Koda. Even you're smarter than that."

He bristled, drawing himself up to his full height and twitching his wings. "I can keep Dash away from you," he insisted defensively. "I can arrange it so he never dares to look your way again."

I didn't doubt that Koda could do as he claimed. No two demons were the same, each possessing their own powers and authority. However, Dash had proven himself as one who fights back, which made me think he wouldn't give up as easily as Koda seemed to think.

"I don't need your help," I said.

At the same time Jett asked, "What would you want in return?"

Now that was a question I didn't want the answer to. Too bad because I was going to get it.

"One night," Koda said, his expression deadly serious. "I just want one night with you." The fire that smoldered in his eyes conveyed his intent very well. I needed no further description. Talk about an indecent proposal.

"What the fuck, Koda?" I blurted. "Do you think I'm the kind of person who sells herself? You can take your deal and stick it. Get out of my face and leave me alone. Or you'll be the next one I gut with the Midnight Star."

It was a feisty threat, one I didn't think through before anger forced it out of my mouth. Koda was getting on my last nerve. Allowing him to anger me was weakness. It brought me to his level. A few deep breaths helped me to regain control of my temper, but it didn't stop a flame from sparking to life in my palm.

Koda's eyes narrowed, but he otherwise didn't react. The lack of reaction was worse than if he'd erupted in temper. I clamped my mouth shut and prayed he would leave.

"I see." His tone was ice-cold steel. "Your constant rejection of my affection is growing tiresome. You're terribly mistaken if you think you'll have a happily ever after with your white lighter. The dark will never allow that one to slip away."

The menacing glimmer in Koda's eyes was starting to scare me. I touched Jett's elbow lightly, hoping she would pick up on what I wasn't saying. She hesitated a moment, unsure. Then she turned around and walked to her car. Good. I wanted her to go before Koda could get it into his head to hurt someone close to me.

"Rowen can handle himself," I said, allowing the fire in my hand to grow. "So can I. Without your help." Taking a risk, I shoved past him and continued on for my car. The flames engulfed me, coating me in a protective sheen of fire as I went.

Koda turned to watch me retreat, but he didn't give pursuit. "I guess we'll see about that." His remark was simple enough, but it was loaded with threats and dark promises.

I kept an eye on Koda as I deposited my guitar into the backseat of the Nova. Jett's Mustang tore away down the street, giving me a small sense of relief. I didn't understand Koda's obsession with me. Cinder had surmised that it had something to do with the rarity of nephilim women. He also suggested that Koda was drawn to the fact that I was both angel and human. The way Cinder described it made me think Koda had some kind of twisted fetish or something.

Koda could never be trusted, no matter what kind of nasty deal he was willing to strike. He was evil. Evil could never be trusted. It could only be battled.

As shitty a guy as Koda was, he had given me a heads up. It was no surprise that Dash wasn't done with either Rowen or me. I'd expected him to come after us, but now I knew when that would be.

I wasn't ready. Not by a long shot. Between the performance, Arrow's disappearance, and the demons, the final battle showdown was shaping up to be a crazy good time or a total nightmare.

Chapter Twenty-Two

"Try not to look too hot tonight. It's going to be hard enough for me to focus. If you look even half as good as you usually do, I won't stand a chance." Rowen's playful, sexy tone emanated from my phone. On speaker, it sat on the bathroom counter beside me. We chatted while getting ready for the big night.

"Ok. I'll wear ratty pajamas and put my hair in a messy bun. No makeup." I smiled to myself in the mirror as I carefully applied my favorite velvet-red lipstick.

His chuckle was light and warm despite everything that had recently gone down. "You'd make even that look sexy. I can't wait to watch you play."

"Stop that. You'll make me nervous. Then I'll fuck up, and we'll lose. That's what you want, isn't it?" I teased him, knowing that neither of us cared who won tonight. All I cared about was seeing the night through to its end without incident.

I left my long, black hair down, teasing it up just a little to give it a wild, tousled look. My grey blue eyes were heavily outlined in black and silver shadow. Taking the phone with me into the bedroom, I tossed it on the bed and began to dig through the stuff in my closet for the right attire.

"So what are you going to do if Arrow doesn't show up?" I asked. "Have you guys planned for that?"

He sighed, a heavily dramatic whoosh of escaping air. "Sam will take over vocals if Arrow doesn't show. It won't be the same, but we aren't going to let him ruin tonight for us."

I nodded, even though he couldn't see it. "Good. I think he's done enough."

Nothing but silence came from Rowen for a moment. He sounded defeated when he finally said, "Agreed. Somehow I suspect it's far from over. But I'm not letting him ruin the great mood I've got going on, so let's not talk about him."

I nodded again, felt stupid, and said, "Ok. What about Dash?"

"What about him? I've been right here for days. If he wanted to kill either me or you, he's had ample opportunity. I don't think that's what he wants." The sound of a lighter's flint was followed by an inhalation of smoke. It reminded me that Rowen's good choice didn't mean he'd never make bad ones.

Why couldn't I stop feeling so pressured to be perfect? Where had that even come from? My mother had raised me to be content with who I was, but society had tried to crush that. The men I'd risked dating had never been content with me being myself. Koda and others like him had encouraged the belief that I wasn't good enough for the light.

Feeling a sudden surge of frustration, I reached into my closet and dragged out the first thing my hand touched, a Motley Crüe t-shirt. I paired it up with tight leather pants and my favorite knee high boots. I was ready, on the outside anyway.

"I wish I could bring the sword with me," I said, gazing longingly to where it sat propped in its sheath in the corner of my bedroom.

"I think you should. Can you fit it in your guitar case?" The loud clink of ice falling into a glass came through the phone.

I eyed the sword. "Actually, yeah, I think I can fit it in there. Are you drinking?"

"Just a little. I need to take the edge off. Don't worry. I'll catch a ride with Sam."

On the final night of the band battle, drinking was bound to happen. Still, I couldn't shake the concern rooted in the back of my mind. "Well, I guess I'll see you there then."

Rowen's laugh was low and throaty. I almost wished we could blow off the whole evening and just stay in together. "I can't wait to have my ass kicked by you."

After we hung up, I worked on squeezing the Midnight Star into my guitar case. It was tight, but I managed. That sword wasn't the kind of thing I could just pull out and start brandishing like a wannabe warrior woman, but having it with me gave me some comfort.

I checked on Seth before I left, ensuring he had fresh food and water. Then I gave his little head a kiss and locked up on my way out.

Guitar case and bat wing purse slung over my shoulder, I headed down the hall with a strange, growing excitement in my step. I was still wary about what the night might bring, but I was kind of looking forward to it.

The elevator door slid open. Cinder stood inside with arms crossed and a playfully scolding expression. He was channeling his inner '80s rocker with a Poison t-shirt and blue bandana tied around his shaggy blond hair.

"Taking the elevator, Ember?" He teased. "Really? You live on the second floor."

I stepped in and hit the button for the lobby. "Hey, this sucker gets heavy." I eyed his clothing with an inquisitive stare. "What's with the threads? Are you coming to the show?"

Cinder didn't often come to my shows, and I'd always accepted that it wasn't an ideal scene for angels. On second thought, maybe it was. Still, I hadn't expected to see him tonight.

"I am. For the most part I'll be unseen. I fully believe you and Rowen are more capable than Dash realizes. However, should it be required, I intend to be there to fight at your side." Cinder's readiness showed in the way he held himself, rigid though calm.

I threw an arm around him in a hug, finding it funny that he smelled of baby powder. "Thank you. For everything."

"No need to thank me. I wish I could do more, but I am confident in the woman you have grown into. You have all you need to succeed. And though I probably shouldn't be, I'm eager to see Dash again. It's been a while." Cinder's gaze slid over me. With lips pursed, he said, "Can you actually breathe in those pants?"

"Yes," I laughed, momentarily distracted by the revelation that Cinder wanted a piece of Dash. I suppose kicking some demon ass was pretty satisfying for the angels though Cinder would never say as much.

Cinder could have popped over to The Spirit Room in an instant, but he rode with me in the Nova instead. The engine sounded a little rougher than usual. Probably time for another oil change. As long as The Piece didn't leave me stranded and waiting for a tow truck, it was all good.

A line had already formed to get into The Spirit Room before we arrived. As I parked, my belly flipped a few times, but otherwise I was feeling good about the show.

Arrow would be sorry if he just handed us this win. Of course, the fact that he was willing to do that made me think something was very wrong. But what could I do? He'd left on his own. Hadn't he?

"I'll see you later," Cinder said when I began dragging my stuff out of the car. "Break a leg. That's what they say, right?"

I nodded and smiled, happy for his good wishes. "Yes, thank you."

He was gone before anyone could take notice of him. Jett was waiting at the side door where the bands enter. She thrust a vodka and sprite topped with a cherry into my hand.

"Here's to our big win." Her grin was huge. Her deep-burgundy painted lips made her teeth appear dazzlingly white. "Can you feel it, Spike? I can fucking feel it."

"I feel it, Jett. It's going to get interesting."

She did a little happy dance that I had to admit was infectious. Our chances were good but not guaranteed. Still, I wasn't going to ruin the positive vibe she had going. Positivity could breed very good things.

The DJ pumped classic rock into the building while Sacred Stone set up. Being the last band to be eliminated, they'd been brought back as the opening act tonight. Hopefully Paul would keep his chauvinistic trap shut if we ran into each other.

I scanned the growing crowd. It was too soon for Dash yet. He wouldn't appear this early in the evening.

"Tonight we win. Then we get signed. And then we tour and live it up." Jett's eyes sparkled with big dreams. "I can't fucking wait."

I'd grown up sharing that exact dream. I still did, but now I wondered if it was doable. Once I chose a side, I would have new obligations. No. I shoved those thoughts aside and focused on everything from Jett's lilac perfume to the notes being plucked on stage as Sacred Stone did their sound check. Live in the moment.

I drank back the vodka quicker than intended. I needed a little relaxation, something to take the edge off. The alcohol spread through my veins with more force than I'd anticipated.

"Is this a double?" I asked.

Jett tossed her purple bangs out of her eyes. "Damn right it is."

I followed her upstairs to the dressing room. It was empty other than Rubi and Tash who primped in the mirror amid giggles and girl talk.

"Dude, don't let him do shit like that to you," Rubi admonished as we entered. "It's unsanitary."

"Shut up." Tash slapped her with a hairbrush. "I like it."

"Do we want to know?" Jett asked, plopping down on the couch. She pulled a joint from her cleavage and sparked it up.

I propped my guitar case near the door. Instead of joining Jett on the couch, I paced around the room. My excited energy made it impossible to relax.

"Tash lets Mr. Country violate her no-no area," Rubi said, bracing for the next hairbrush smack.

Jett let out a puff of smoke. "No such thing as a no-no area, Rubi. Don't be so uptight."

"Told you," Tash joined in. "You need to get laid, Rubi. I think you've forgotten how much fun it is."

I laughed but said nothing. This wasn't a conversation I was going to weigh in on. Teasing Tash was kind of our thing, but I wasn't about to say anything to get this turned around on me.

Except Jett said, "Spike's finally getting her itch scratched," She passed the joint to Tash. "Let's hear about how good Rowen is in bed. I bet he's good."

My cheeks warmed. "Let's not discuss Rowen's sexual prowess. Some things need to stay on the down low."

Jett snorted. "Oh, please. Since when do you not fuck and tell? I bet he has a big—"

"Oh, I do," Rowen broke in, drawing every gaze to where he stood in the doorway. "At least, I like to think so."

My cheeks burned, but the girls laughed. Girl talk in public places was dangerous.

"I didn't hear you come up," I said.

"Yeah, well, I seem to be a lot more stealthy than usual." Rowen cast a glance toward the stairs. Sam and Greyson clambered up, making enough noise for a herd of elephants.

Rowen was ridiculously hot. His hair was perfectly spiked with that piece I loved falling into his eyes. In a black leather jacket with a

Crimson Sin t-shirt and black jeans, he gave me a rush that filled me to overflowing. So swoon worthy.

I gestured to his shirt. "Are you kidding me right now? You are going to get so lucky tonight."

"Hey ladies." Sam shoved by Rowen into the room. He had a beer in each hand, a guitar case strapped to his back, and a giant grin on his face. He shrugged off the guitar case and sat down beside Jett. "Damn, Jett, you're looking fine tonight. What are you doing after the show?"

Jett eyed him like the predator she was. Assessing the cute, fun-loving, but somewhat goofy Sam, she cocked her head to one side and smirked. "Not you, sweetheart. Nice try though."

"Come on, baby, let me rock your world." Dimples gave Sam a cherubic appearance. That grin probably worked on a lot of ladies.

"I don't think so." Jett's dark-red lips quirked as she enjoyed his attempt at flirting. "You couldn't handle me. Really. I'd eat you alive."

I suspected that statement had some truth to it. Jett wasn't a violent monster, but she was as spirited as they came. Being part of a pack kept her wolf under control and allowed her animal side to flourish. Still any guy that got involved with her had to be able to hold his own. I wasn't sure Sam was up to the challenge.

"I am totally ok with that," Sam said before pounding back one of the beers he held.

Rowen and I exchanged a look. He rolled his eyes at Sam and said, "Trust me, Sammy. There's more to these girls than it seems. You'd never stand a chance."

Voices and laughter quickly filled the room. Rowen leaned his bass case against the wall and steered me into a corner that barely gave us the illusion of privacy.

"I've been looking forward to this all day." His kiss started off tender and sweet, deepening with emotion and desire. Our friends whistled and shouted at us, but we ignored them all. I slid my arms around his neck and pressed closer. His hands were warm on my hips. Drums began to thunder beneath us, announcing the start of the show.

Jett and Sam said almost in unison, "Get a room."

"Who plays first?" I asked when we finally broke apart. "Do you know?"

"We do," he said, running a hand over his mohawk. "Still no word from Arrow. He's not replying to messages or answering his phone."

"Fuck him," Sam muttered while Greyson nodded his silent agreement.

"Are you worried?" I whispered, searching Rowen's amazing, fiery eyes. His reluctance to show any feeling regarding Arrow was worrisome. They were friends and brothers. It felt like he should be more concerned.

Rowen glanced toward the other guys. Anger lit up his face. "I care about Arrow. I hope he's ok, but he's fucked up too many times. The lies. That shit he pulled with you. I can't let that go. Not yet."

I nodded, totally understanding where he was coming from. With a hand on his face, I kissed him again before whispering against his lips, "For the record, he didn't know you're his brother until recently. From what I've observed, he's such a fucking asshole because nobody ever genuinely gave a shit about him. Just try to remember that. And don't forget that he went in after you."

He frowned and shook his head. The anger melted away, and he sighed. "See what I mean? That beautiful heart you have is what made me so sure of my choice. It's why I fell so hard for you."

Our friends were engrossed in conversation, but I could feel Jett's watchful gaze upon us. She knew me so well. I was sure she could see the doubt that flitted through me, which I tried desperately to hide behind a smile. Catching my eye, she gave me a pointed look, which I took to mean, 'Don't be a chicken shit.'

"You're sweet, Rowen." I ducked my head to hide the uncertainty that I was sure was painted all over my face. It wasn't that I didn't have feelings for him. It was that those feelings scared the shit out of me.

"Hey." He touched the side of my face. "Are we cool? I mean, are we on the same page here? I know we haven't really made it official, but it didn't feel like we had to. Are we… together?"

I hadn't expected this moment to happen in front of our friends. Thankfully only Jett appeared to be paying any attention. Her keen wolf ears could likely pick out every word too.

I had just seconds to form a response. To take any longer would reveal my inner doubts and fears, and Rowen would form his own assumptions from that. I knew that if I didn't take this chance, I never would. I could take a risk and possibly be disappointed, or I could shy away and never know what might have been. What I had to ask myself was if Rowen was worth the risk.

"Yes," I heard myself say as my pulse pounded in my ears. "We are on the same page. I'll be honest. This scares me. But I want to be with you. I want to discover what we could have."

Rowen pulled me into his arms and kissed me with a ravenous passion. Then he chuckled, a sensual sound that drove me a little crazy. "Will you still feel that way if we kick your ass tonight?"

I shoved him and laughed. "Not gonna happen."

"Care to wager on it?" With a raised brow, he shot me a naughty smile.

Before I could answer, the stage manager appeared with orders for Molly's Chamber to get downstairs. The DJ broadcasting live for the radio station hosting the event wanted to have a short interview with each band before they went on.

"Hold that thought," Rowen said, giving me one last lingering kiss before he and the guys disappeared downstairs.

"We should head down too," Jett said, waving a hand at Rubi who still stood in front of the mirror back-combing her hair. "If you bitches are finished here, I'm on the prowl for a boy toy tonight."

"Well, Sam was willing." I hid a smirk, expecting the withering look she shot me.

"Oh, please," she scoffed. "That boy would jizz his pants before I even got my clothes off."

The Spirit Room had filled up considerably in the short time we'd been upstairs. The air buzzed with anticipation as people drank, laughed, and waited to see if their preferred band would reign.

Right away people started coming up to us, wishing us luck and offering to buy us drinks. By the time we got seated as close to the stage as we could get, we had more than enough booze on the table to supply a dozen people.

"Thanks for coming out, sweetie." Jett accepted a silver Sharpie from a bearded rocker guy who'd asked us to sign a t-shirt he'd grabbed from our merch table. Tash's sister Tanya was manning it tonight. When he'd gone she gushed, "Now that is what I'm fucking talking about. People love us. Arrow can eat his fucking heart out."

"Don't be a cocky bitch, Jett," Rubi warned, ignoring the glare she received in return. "You're going to give us bad karma."

"Fuck your karma. You're starting to sound like Tash." Jett shoved a shot of tequila in front of each of us. "We will win this because we're good. Not because we kissed the universe's ass."

The tequila burned like a son of a bitch, but the effects were calming. I kind of needed that. I wasn't getting in the middle of this argument. Those girls could go back and forth for hours about that shit. Luckily they were both too excited to bother.

My gaze kept straying to the door. I wasn't sure what I expected. Part of me was sure Arrow or Dash was going to make an appearance soon.

Then I did see someone unexpected. Gabriel shot through the nightclub, heading for the back exit. His dark head was ducked as he avoided eye contact with everyone he passed.

Jett followed my gaze to the recently turned vampire. "Well, look who decided to show up."

"Looks like he's on his way out already. I'll be right back." I hurried after him, knowing that if he didn't want to be caught, I'd never reach him. Vampires were speedy things. Fucking scary things too.

To my surprise he was standing right outside the back exit, talking hurriedly on his cell. He hung up when I appeared and started to turn away, then stopped.

"Spike? Why are you still undecided?" It sure wasn't the greeting I'd expected.

"Is everything ok?" I asked. "You look like you're in a hurry. Not staying for the rest of the show?"

"Seriously? Why? Are you nuts?" Gabriel's eyes were wide, his nostrils flared. Standing beside him felt like standing next to a blanket full of static. "This is a bad time to not have a side."

"What's going on, Gabriel?" Careful not to get too close, I made my question more of a demand.

"What isn't?" he replied, shooting an anxious glance at the door we'd just exited. "This city is fucked. It's crawling with bad things, and you need to not be one of them. Ok?"

Because I didn't know what else to say, I said, "Ok. Noted. Are you in some kind of trouble?"

Gabriel inched away, as if being this close to me were painful. Maybe it was. I didn't know the first thing about being a vampire.

"You never saw me," he said. "Cool?" This conversation was going about as well as the last one we'd had at The Wicked Kiss. Gabriel never had been a big talker. He'd always been the strong, silent type. Still, this urgency and paranoia wasn't normal for him.

"Got it. I never saw you." I stood there puzzled, watching as he disappeared into the night too fast for my eyes to follow.

It wasn't news to me that the city was a mess. It was a place that drew and harbored many supernatural things. Rumor had it that the government had set up a supernatural task force here, though I had yet to see proof of that myself. It wouldn't have surprised me. In a city crawling with such darkness, there was great need for those that walked in the light. Like Cinder, and now Rowen.

And you, my conscience added. *You should be among them.*

I went back inside, both disappointed and disturbed by the brief encounter with Gabriel. He was in deep. The dark had gotten their hooks into him some time ago, yet somehow he retained enough of himself to know how far he'd fallen and to warn me not once, but twice.

Sacred Stone rocked the rest of their set without incident. I rejoined the girls at the table where we laughed, drank, and counted down until the big moment when we would take the stage for our final performance of this showdown.

Molly's Chamber was setting up their equipment when Rowen broke away to come by our table. He pulled me into his arms with a noise of aggravation. "If Arrow doesn't walk through that door right now, I'm going to knock him the fuck out when he does show up."

I gasped, not because of what he said but because of the eerie timing. As the words left Rowen's mouth, Arrow did indeed walk through the door, looking like something the cat dragged in. Arrow strode through the building with a cigarette in his mouth and a scowl on his face. He ignored the security guy who tried to stop him from smoking, shooting him down with a disdainful glare.

Dressed all in black, his disheveled hair exploded from beneath the hat he always wore. His black liner-smudged eyes were red rimmed. A purple bruise outlined one of them. It curved along his cheekbone, disappearing before it reached his chin. He cast a glance our way. His gaze was somehow haunted and vacant at the same time. Without a word to the people who tried to speak to him, he continued on to the stage where Sam and Greyson were.

"You better go talk to him." I gave Rowen a gentle shove, unable to tear my eyes away from Arrow's retreating form.

With a sour expression, Rowen said, "I have a really bad feeling about this."

Chapter Twenty-Three

Rowen wasn't the only one with a bad feeling. As I watched him go, I had the distinct sensation that something wasn't right. He approached Arrow who was speaking with the other guys. Nobody looked happy.

"I hope they throw down on stage again," Jett observed, watching the tense exchange. "That was hot."

I didn't quite share that sentiment. It had been alarming to see Arrow and Rowen throwing punches at each other. I didn't want to see it again, but the two of them glared at one another. Then Rowen held both hands up in some kind of appeal, and his expression softened. Arrow shrugged and turned away. Oh boy.

Jett stole my attention. "Excuse me a minute. I spy something I may want to sink my teeth into later." She slid from her seat, adjusted her cleavage, and strutted up to the bar where a guy with long dreads waited to order a drink.

Rubi disappeared into the ladies room, and Tash stared at her phone, most likely texting Mr. Country. I sipped another vodka and sprite, watching Molly's Chamber finish setting up their gear. Feeling a nerve-racking mix of stress and excitement, I headed outside for a cigarette.

I shoved through the crowd just making their way inside. Someone grabbed my arm, and I turned, expecting to see a fan or friend. It was neither. The man who held my elbow was tall with fair hair and silver eyes. He held my gaze for a moment before releasing my arm.

"You're angelkind." It wasn't a question. The brief moment of contact had given me a glimpse of him. He was angelkind as well.

"And you are?" I continued on outside to escape the mass of people lingering near the entry. He followed.

Once outside, I headed toward the parking lot, away from the door. Sparking a smoke, I leaned back against the building and waited for him to speak. Something about him insisted that he was neither angel nor demon. Since he wasn't a nephilim, I could only surmise that he was a fallen angel, no longer angel but not full demon either.

"Falon," he said with a cool, appraising stare. "And what might your name be?"

I studied him, trying to determine if he was a threat. He held himself with confidence, shoulders squared and posture stiff. Despite the arrogant set to his features and the cruel curve of his lips, I suspected that whatever had brought him here had nothing to do with me.

"Ember." I wasn't sure why I told him my real name. It came out before I could rethink it. "But my friends call me Spike."

"So what can I call you?"

"I guess we'll see." I drew the smoke into my lungs, feeling my body resist, promising myself I'd try to quit. Again. "Is there something I can do for you?"

Falon studied the people gathered around the door, waiting their turn to pay their cover charge and join the party. "I hope so. I'm looking for someone. A vampire, to be specific."

Damn. He was looking for Gabriel.

"Oh yeah? I think you might be in the wrong place for that. The vampire bar is downtown." Keeping a straight face, I puffed on my smoke, meeting his silver gaze. Nothing would make me admit that I'd seen Gabriel.

"Yeah, well, he's not known for spending a lot of time there. I've found him here before. It seemed like a good place to start." The curious expression Falon cast my way caused me to stiffen, but instead of pressing me about Gabriel, he asked, "Can I ask you something?"

"Shoot."

"Why are you undecided?"

This was starting to become a recurring theme this evening. What the hell? "Can I ask you why you're fallen?" I countered with a smirk.

"Seriously," Falon continued, ignoring my jibe. "Let me give you some advice. Being undecided is no different from being fallen. You belong to neither side. By not choosing, you still choose. And when it all goes down, you'll be claimed by the dark. You're a self-made casualty, kid. All because you didn't want to make a choice."

I considered this. It wasn't the first time I'd heard such a thing. I was puzzled and somewhat intrigued. It wasn't everyday a fallen angel tried to steer me in the right direction.

Even though it wasn't any of his business, I felt inclined to clarify my position. "It's not that I don't want to choose. I'm afraid of what comes next. Maybe I'm not good enough for the light and maybe I don't want to be dark. Also, I have commitment issues."

Falon laughed, a light, happy sound that surprised me. Now I was even more curious about him. "We all have commitment issues, kid. The difference between you and me is that you still have a chance to make things right. Second chances are a gift. Don't blow it." He shrugged as if it was no bother to him that he was beyond redemption.

Fallen angels were not given the same mercies as humankind simply because they had made their choice knowing full well what they were turning their back on. Humans lived in ignorance and deception that clouded their view. They rarely knew the depths of their decisions. The world cast a shadow over the truth. Humans were granted forgiveness for their lost and misguided ways.

I nodded and flicked the ash from my cigarette. "Well, thanks for the advice. It's hard though, you know. I have angels in one ear, demons in the other. Sometimes I just feel like I'm so over it. All of it."

"Running from who you are doesn't change anything. Trust me. I've tried." Falon offered me a hand. His handshake was firm but friendly. "Own it. And never apologize for who you are or what you have to do."

"I'll keep that in mind. Thanks." The brief exchange didn't give me much of an opportunity to analyze Falon or decide how I felt about him and his advice. The fallen weren't known for being trustworthy. Still, I sensed that his words came from a place of truth.

He turned to go but hesitated as if he had more to say. We stared at one another until it grew uncomfortable. Then he said, "There is only one keeper of the Midnight Star at a time. Right now, that's you. Don't fuck it up. Oh, and don't lie. You suck at it."

Without another word, Falon walked away. He rounded the corner into the parking lot and vanished with the sound of wings.

I stood there dumbfounded. He'd known I was lying about Gabriel, and he'd offered me guidance anyway. The signs were starting to stack up. I felt the significance of the fallen angel and the vampire he sought giving me pretty much the same advice.

"Yeah, I get it," I muttered to no one in particular.

A chill stole over me. I attributed it to the falling temperature even though I knew it was the icy hand of fate sliding over me. Standing there on the sidewalk alone gave me a few minutes to mull this over. I already feared failure with Rowen. My failure, not his. Now the pressure to choose was mounting. I was beginning to tire of my own issues.

By the time I went back inside, the emcee was announcing Molly's Chamber. He stirred the crowd up, telling them to scream if they wanted Molly's Chamber to win. The audience erupted in a deafening roar.

Lost in thought, I wandered closer to the stage to watch from the outskirts of the crowd gathered there. The rumble of the bass boomed through the building, so low and smooth I could feel it in my bones. Guys held drinks up in salute. Girls screamed and struggled to get as close to the stage as possible. A few flashed their breasts, earning a passing smirk from Arrow. I watched the ensuing chaos feeling both pride and trepidation.

Arrow's voice snarled, an accent to the menace in his mannerisms.

Master of shadows
Don't fear what you don't know
Keeper of secrets
The illusion is part of the show
Be careful if you touch me
I get inside your head with ease
I won't remember you in the morning
But you will never forget me.

He gripped the mike stand with both hands, and the passion poured out of him. As we all watched, he worked out his personal issues through singing, screaming, and making the crowd his. They wanted him or wanted to be him.

I watched him for any sign of what he'd been up to the past few days. He had more aggression to his actions than usual. He whipped off his hat and threw it into the crowd, swinging his black hair wildly.

Our eyes met, and he made a gun out of his thumb and forefinger, pointing it at me. Crossing my arms, I stared back until he broke contact to flirt with a girl in the front.

My gaze slid to Rowen who was playing his heart out. His fingers moved on the bass strings. So much more than an instrument, it was an extension of him. His very soul poured out through his fingertips. I knew that feeling.

Watching Molly's Chamber play, I was blown away by how good they were. All four of them brought something special to their sound. Even at odds, Rowen and Arrow were magic together. Light and dark. Empathetic and arrogant. They were so different but when the music flowed, they became something greater than they each were on their own. I didn't want to lose, but if we did, it would be to worthy musicians.

I still couldn't wrap my mind around what everyone was saying about me these days. Having the Midnight Star didn't make me anyone or anything different. Rowen attributed his choice to join the light to me, but that was misplaced credit. He'd done that all on his own. Arrow was so far gone. I didn't see how I, or anyone else for that matter, could do a damn thing about that.

Time moved swiftly. With each passing moment, my nerves grew until I was roiling with excitement. I was eager to get on stage.

Jett swaggered up to me, drink in hand, announcing that we needed to do a short interview on the radio. We answered questions about our songwriting, how the band met, and how the experience had been for us so far. We talked over one another, laughing a lot, and I knew that no matter what choices I made, leaving this band and these girls would not be one of them.

I didn't get a chance to speak with Rowen before we went on. As soon as Molly's Chamber left the stage, we were rushed on for sound check.

The emcee approached us with a huge grin. "Ladies! I've got some news for you. There's a rep from Dark Mountain Records here tonight. He seems interested in you. He saw the video of your last show." The bearded, long-haired, hippie-like emcee waited expectantly for a joyful reaction.

My stomach flopped, but Tash and Rubi gushed jubilant exclamations. Jett's gaze narrowed in suspicion, but the smile she tried to hide broke through. Of course we were excited by that. We were also a little intimidated and a lot wary. These things always seemed great at first, but they often didn't pan out.

"I'm sure he said the same damn thing to Molly's Chamber," Jett said when he'd left us. "I'm not letting that shit get inside my head. Right now all I care about is wiping the floor with Arrow."

"You and me both." I strummed my guitar, picking through the strings and tuning the pegs until the notes were just right.

"Glad to see that love hasn't made you weak." Her tone was joking, but she meant it.

We shared a look and, with it, the rush of those precious moments before we stepped on stage with hundreds of eyes upon us. I replied, "Me too."

I was head over heels for Rowen, but I was not going down without a fight. The guys deserved to win as much as we did, but that didn't mean we had to hand it to them. They'd given it their all, and I knew Rowen would expect me to do the same.

"I am so fucking stoked." Jett threw a few air punches and hopped up and down, unable to contain her enthusiasm.

I felt a definite buzz to the atmosphere. We were dreamers. Artists. We might have been playing a small stage in a city bar, but the place was packed. The raucous audience was more than we could ask for. Gratitude filled me. I was happy just to be able to play. Having people like it was just a really amazing bonus that I would never take for granted.

At last we were ready. The stage lights went dark, and the DJ's booming music died. A cheer went up. Several drunken shouts, whistles, and cries filled the silence.

The emcee stepped up to the mike at center stage. The rest of us hung back in the shadows. I was shaking with adrenaline. The need to pour out this pent up energy into my guitar was dire.

"Our final band of the night, these ladies have rocked your faces off for weeks now. Tonight they could win it all. Give it up for Crimson Sin!"

Crimson Sin

The emcee jumped off the stage, and as one, we launched into our first song of the night. The second that first note left my fingers and exploded out of the amps, I sighed. It was the elated release of a held breath that could be held no more.

We brought it loud, and we brought it hard. People rushed toward the stage, abandoning the bar and coming in off the street where they'd been smoking. As one giant wave, they joined those already packed in as close to the stage as they could get. With a giddy thrill, I caught sight of several Crimson Sin t-shirts among them.

I watched with a huge grin as people crowd surfed. Guys, girls, it didn't matter. Everyone was rocking out and partying their asses off to our music. We even got a couple of boob flashes, which had Jett and me exchanging a wry smile.

Sweat trickled down the side of my face. Each breath came fast and hard. My hands moved with the memory of songs I'd played so many times before. My soul was on fire with life.

People crowded into the building. I glanced around for Rowen but didn't see him though I knew he was out there. Despite how deeply entrenched I was in the music, I couldn't help but be aware of certain eyes upon me.

I ran across the stage, dodging Jett's mass of purple hair as I went. I jerked to a halt beside Tash and together we ripped through the bridge of the song. On my way back to my side of the stage, I happened to look out at the crowd, and my gaze landed on Koda.

Surprise almost caused me to stumble. Somehow I recovered before falling on my face. The demon stood off to the side of the stage, arms crossed and gaze narrowed. He bore the hard expression of one who'd been shot down too many times.

His presence wasn't a total shock, but it wasn't a good sign. He wasn't the highest demon on my radar, but demons often traveled in groups like insects or rats. Where there's one, there's gonna be more.

Once my demon radar went off, I became more aware of the dark beings that lurked among the rest of us. I sensed a lot of clingers, the hangers-on that latched onto people, encouraging bad thoughts and even worse behavior. They gained a lot of their power simply by being so often overlooked.

I spotted Arrow at the back of the crowd. He watched us with blatant contempt. He was alone. His gaze swept over the stage, landing on me. I was tempted to give him the same finger gun he'd given me, but I didn't dare risk a fumble by taking my hand off the guitar. For just a moment his eyes changed. They'd flashed red so fast I almost second-guessed whether I'd really seen it or not. Red.

So Dash was here. He was just conveniently hiding out inside of Arrow.

With a big solo coming up, I couldn't let my gaze linger. Distractions would pull me out of the moment and steal this win from us. I refocused my attention on the crowd gathered closest to the stage, and I let the solo rip from me with a staggering force.

This was my moment. It was my brief time to shine, to share this magical moment with my closest friends. Dash was not going to take it from me.

The power of the solo drove me to my knees. My long, black hair fell into my face, but I didn't need to see. My fingers flew over the frets of their own accord. I was vaguely aware of Jett leaping into the crowd, surfing on raised hands. Tash was standing in front of the drums, whipping her hair in time to Rubi's beat. *Fuck, yeah.*

Our set came to an end much too quickly. I wasn't ready for that last note. We ended on screams and applause that bordered on deafening. I knew no feeling in the world could compare to what I felt right then. Amazing.

"We got this." Jett dropped her mike and threw her arms around me. We shared a sweaty hug that got a few whoops and catcalls from the crowd.

The emcee returned to tell the crowd that the bar would be serving two-dollar shots for the next half hour. Then the winner would be announced.

"Dash is inside Arrow," I said as we retreated from the stage. "At least, I'm pretty sure he is."

Jett's brow creased in thought. "Why? What's he trying to achieve by doing that?"

"I don't know. I think I'm going to find out. Help me keep the girls away from him, ok?"

"Of course."

I searched the crowd for Koda and found him backed into a corner near the restrooms by Cinder. The fact that they were both in

Crimson Sin

corporeal form indicated to me that Cinder was trying to deal with Koda as peacefully as possible.

The girls and I swept through the room, receiving high-fives, handshakes, and hugs. Jett, Tash, and Rubi dispersed to join the party. Rowen stepped out of the crowd and caught me in his arms, lifting me off my feet. The kiss he planted on me was dizzying.

"Dash is possessing Arrow." I pressed my lips against his ear, ensuring he heard me.

Rowen took it in stride, completely unfazed. He was already more at home in his skin as nephilim than I was. "That explains a lot actually. So what do we do?"

"We drive him out. If we can."

Rowen slipped an arm around my waist and guided me toward the bar. "Let me buy you a drink. Play it cool, or he'll know we're onto him."

I let Rowen steer me along until Arrow appeared in front of us with a wicked smile and eyes that flashed red. I sputtered, "I think he already does."

"This doesn't have to get violent," Arrow said in Dash's voice. "In fact, I prefer that it didn't. You've already seriously harmed one of my people." Harmed. Not killed. So Michelle had lived. My heart soared. I hadn't killed anyone.

My gaze traced the bruises marring Arrow's face. "Looks like you've already gotten violent. What the hell have you been doing to him?"

"I'm not here to talk about him," Dash snapped. "I've waited patiently until now. I'm here to speak with the two of you. Is there somewhere we can go? It's rather loud in here."

Yeah, that didn't sound like a trap or anything. I thought about the Midnight Star upstairs where I'd left it, safe in my guitar case. I couldn't very well use it when he was possessing Arrow. Still, if we could drive him out of Arrow, I might get the chance.

"Outside?" Rowen asked, likely thinking it would be safer there.

"No." I shook my head, knowing this was a risk. "Upstairs."

Arrow's eyes flickered again, becoming hazel. He shook his head and uttered, "Rowen, don't."

He was fighting it, which meant that unlike Michelle, Arrow was not a willing participant in this possession. His fight was as terrifying

211

as it was reassuring. Dash wrestled for control, and Arrow's eyes turned red once again.

Though I couldn't rely on him to always come to my aid, Cinder's presence gave me courage. He was right where I'd last seen him. If Rowen and I didn't deal with Dash now, he would keep coming back. That's how demons worked.

"Let's go." Rowen took my hand, and we went upstairs with a demon wearing our friend's skin. This could end terribly in so many different ways.

The dressing area was empty. Everyone was downstairs partying. I wished I was among them.

"Let's not play games or waste time," Dash began as soon as it was clear we were alone. His red stare fixed on Rowen. "It's you I wanted all along. I still do. Arrow was a means to an end. Since he failed, now he's useless. I'm willing to offer you a deal. A good deal."

Rowen made a sound of disgust. He backed us away from Dash, putting the length of the room between us and him. "Go to hell. I'll never make a deal with you."

Dash looked out through Arrow's eyes. Something about it made my skin crawl. He looked at me and very calmly said, "What about you? You're not my first choice, but you've got a few things going for you. You're female. Rare. And the keeper of the Midnight Star. Actually, the more I think about it, the more useful you could be."

"Forget it," I spat the words at him. "I'm not negotiating with you. You don't even have the balls to face us yourself. Let Arrow go."

Dash nodded and slowly advanced on us, stopping in the center of the room. "I intend to. Since he betrayed me, I also plan to kill him. But because I can be a nice guy I came to offer his brother the chance to save him."

Rowen and I exchanged a look. A demon was always up to no good. Dash had likely spent the week cooking up this scheme, knowing how to get the response he wanted.

"Ok, I'll bite," Rowen said. "What do you want?"

Those red eyes were so wrong on Arrow. The cackle that followed was equally foreign. "I want you, Rowen. The son Rhine was never supposed to have. Join my coven in Arrow's place, and I will let him live. You too, sweetheart," he said to me. "Feel free to get in on this."

"Never." The word came as a ragged breath, but Dash heard me. Rowen stood silently at my side.

"Well, you have the right to exercise your free fucking will. As do I." Suddenly Dash materialized beside Arrow who wobbled unsteadily as he regained control of himself. Venom seeped from the demon. "Arrow dies."

Chapter Twenty-Four

Rowen didn't wait to see what would happen. He flung himself in front of Arrow. Dash circled the two of them with the slow stride of a predator sneaking up on prey.

I eyed the guitar case in the corner. I had to just go for it. As soon as Dash turned his back to me, I dove for the case and flung it open. Nothing.

"Oh, is this what you're looking for?" Holding out a hand, Dash produced the sword. He never touched it though. Instead it hovered above his open palm. I suspected that he couldn't touch it, that whatever law that made it mine somehow prevented him from using it.

Rather than waste words on the demon, I projected a stream of fire that thrust him against the mirrored counter, causing my sword to clatter to the floor. Rowen quickly joined me. He cast a circle of light that surrounded Dash, but it didn't hold the demon long. I'd just wrapped my hand around the hilt when he broke free.

Wearing a grim smile, Dash attacked all three of us at once. He barely moved, barely so much as twitched a hand, but we all fell to the floor, writhing in pain. Heat swept through my limbs, threatening to scorch me from the inside out. Hellfire burned inside me as I screamed.

"I'm sure this is the part where you think Cinder will rush to your aid." Dash stood over me, watching me try desperately to hold tight to the sword. "Koda makes a very good distraction, what with his obsession with you and all."

"Koda?" I gasped. "Fuck Koda." I was in too much pain to get anything else out.

Dash leaned down closer. "You've spurned his advances too many times. His soft spot for you has hardened."

Of course Koda was going to take any shot at revenge that came his way. I wouldn't have expected otherwise from a demon.

Crimson Sin

Summoning as much strength as I could muster under Dash's assault, I wildly swung the sword. I missed, but he did step back, out of my face.

Too busy sneering at me, Dash failed to notice the shadow that coiled itself around his ankle. It jerked him off his feet and flung him into the ceiling half a dozen times before slamming him on the floor. A demon could withstand loads of physical damage, though eventually they would weaken to the point of having to return to the other side to regain their full strength.

Arrow rose, dragging Rowen up with him. Though he had a head start on Rowen and I in developing his gifts, his quick recovery definitely made a good argument as to why one should not delay making a choice.

"Well, look at you, biting the hand that feeds. It's too late to pretend you're better than you are, Arrow. You'll always be a piece of shit." Dash chuckled as he pushed to his feet. A gash on his forehead healed up as we looked on. We would tire long before he did.

"Rowen is light. You couldn't torture him into choosing dark, and you won't coerce him into it now. Kill me if you want. I don't even care." Arrow held his arms open wide, inviting further attack.

I regained my footing, thanks to Arrow, but I felt faint and mildly confused. Being undecided made me the weakest one here. I was very much aware of what my hesitation could cost me.

Dash and Arrow glared daggers into one another. I didn't want to watch Arrow die, and from the distress on Rowen's face, neither did he. The only way to drive Dash to the other side was to impale him with the Midnight Star. If we simply tried to out power him, it would never happen. He could run circles around us in a power match. Even at three on one, we were outnumbered.

"As you wish." Dash's smile faded. With eyes vacant of emotion, he merely stared at the dark nephilim.

For a moment nothing appeared to happen. Then Arrow coughed, and blood ran from his mouth. Then from his nose. As I looked on, his eyes turned scarlet, and blood seeped from them too.

Rowen hurled himself at Dash. He crashed into the demon with a body check so hard I cringed. The two of them went down. Rowen's body lit up with a brilliant light, as if the sun itself burst from inside him. He held tight to Dash and fed him punch after punch. I quickly realized that Rowen would tire before he could cause any serious damage.

I hurried to Arrow, who had dropped to his knees. I'd seen him come back from this before. He could do it again, couldn't he? A closer look showed me that he was much worse off than he'd been last time. Dash had truly intended to kill him.

"Arrow? Stay with me, ok? We're going to take care of you."

He shook his head. He tried more than once to speak until he croaked out, "No. Take care of Rowen."

Because I didn't know what to say or do, I grabbed him by the shoulders and shook him until his eyes focused on me. "In twenty minutes, one of us is going to win the opportunity of a lifetime. Don't you dare die and let me win by default."

The corner of his mouth curved up like he was trying to smile but failing. "You deserve it more anyway."

"Shut up."

He was giving up, and I couldn't just step back and watch it happen. Blood dripped from his face. It splattered my hand before trickling between my fingers to slide down the blade of the sword. The silver-coated blade seemed to glow in response to the dark blood. Its energy field grew substantially, until I could feel it demanding more. The Midnight Star was hungry for demon blood.

Dash and Rowen grappled on the floor. Tired of tolerating Rowen's repeated blows to his face, Dash had taken the upper hand. He pinned Rowen to the floor, one hand tight on his throat. In the other he dangled a live snake over Rowen's head. The snake bared vicious fangs that dripped venom. It wriggled inches above Rowen's face.

Without thinking twice, I merely reacted. With the sword firm in my grip, I lunged forward and swung.

Thanks to hours of training with Cinder, my aim was dead on. The blade sliced the snake's head off, sending it flying. It landed on the carpet with a wet plop.

Immediately, I swung again, this time at Dash. The blade caught his hand, slicing off his fingers. Not good enough. I swung a third time, but he sent me flying. I crashed into the mirror and hit the floor. Miraculously, the mirror only cracked rather than raining shards down around me.

I knew what I had to do. I had been told repeatedly all night. There was no more time. To hold off any longer would mean death for all of us.

"I choose the light," I said, the words were barely audible as I spoke through clenched teeth. Louder, I repeated, "I choose the light."

Dash forgot Rowen then. He came at me with his bloody hand outstretched as if he could grab me without fingers. I wasn't sure if he planned to kill me or merely to silence me. He never got the chance to do either.

A bright white light struck me and surrounded me in a comforting warmth, like a fireplace on a cold winter night or a hot shower after a cold rain. The light offered such assurance that I felt safe. My entire body began to tingle. The warmth spread through me, filling my extremities. My hand clenched on the Midnight Star as the light shot down the blade, making it gleam as if lit with an inner fire. Though no audible words filled my ears, I heard a whisper telling me that I'd done right by embracing my destiny. *Destiny.* Such a strange word, filled with so much promise and so much left unknown.

A sense of expansion filled me. My lungs swelled, and my heart raced. Deep within my psyche, a sudden and new awareness jolted through me as my talents increased in potential and skill. For just a moment I knew who I was supposed to be with perfect certainty, something I'd known all along despite my confusion and fear.

The light slowly faded, and I turned on Dash with a fierce cry. Fire exploded from my hands to crawl along the Midnight Star engulfing it in flames. When I swung the mighty sword, the flame lashed out to strike Dash, knocking him further from Rowen.

Rowen stood unsure, wondering if he should come to my aid or his brother's. Being the empathetic person he was, he knelt down beside Arrow and helped him stay upright.

The demon had blazing red eyes only for me. "You just made a huge mistake," Dash hissed. He advanced on me, each step calculated.

"Oh, I don't think so." I held the sword out in front of me, daring him to take a run at me. I stood ready to lop his head off.

Dash was enraged. He flung a psi ball at me, an orb of energy meant to maim. I deflected it with the sword, sending it right back to him. Unfortunately, he simply reabsorbed it.

His next attack tried to wrench the sword from my grasp. He used his demonic power and why not? If I had the kind of power that Dash had, I'd never use my hands either.

When I refused to let go of the hilt, the force dragged me off my feet. It slammed me into the couch before tossing me onto the coffee table. Dash grabbed me by the back of the head, tightly clutching a handful of my hair.

Jerking my head back so he could glower into my face, he snarled, "I have way too much at stake to put up with more nephilim bullshit. I'd rather not kill you. Having Cinder up my ass for the next decade doesn't really appeal to me. But I have no problem killing these two. Choose your next move very carefully."

He held my head at a precarious angle. I was sure he could break my neck with just a twist of his wrist. I couldn't see Rowen from where I sat, but I could feel his worried gaze.

Instinctively, I reached back with one hand to grasp Dash's wrist. My breath caught as a force flowed between us. I didn't understand what was happening, but Dash did.

He jerked free of me, releasing my hair in the process. "You've got to be fucking kidding me. You're a replicant? A thief? I know who your father is."

A thief? I felt the slither of a demon inside me in answer to my silent question. Thrusting my hand toward him, Dash was thrown off his feet and dragged around the room, exactly what he'd just done to me. I'd stolen his power.

I had no time to marvel at this new talent. I knew about a plethora of powers and talents, but I wasn't familiar with this, whatever it was. Yet. I'd have to figure out my moves from moment to moment.

"Good for you," I said. "At least somebody does. Can't really say Daddy and I were close over the years."

Dash landed flat against the wall. His big, black wings unfurled, spreading wide behind him. He regarded me with curiosity that became disdain.

"Spike." My name was a ragged sound on Arrow's bloody lips. Pale and weak, he extended a shaky hand to me. "Take it. Rowen's too."

Thief. My mind raced to put it together. I'd stolen Dash's power, but what I'd taken I'd already used. This wasn't a gift with much longevity, but it could come in handy if I could learn how best to use it effectively.

I dropped down beside the guys. They grabbed my offered hand, first Arrow, then Rowen. After a brief wave of dizziness that passed as fast as it had come, shadows crawled through my mind while light lit up my focus. Awesome.

Rowen and I stood up together. His silver wings flared as a shelter over Arrow. I stepped forward to meet Dash as he came toward me. But his eyes weren't on me. He was looking at Rowen.

"I don't want to kill you," Dash said, hands up in feigned surrender. "Your father is my brother. Rhine and I fought side by side many times. It would be a great honor to have you among us. Please, consider it."

Confusion filled Rowen's face. He blinked a few times and shook his head. "My father... Then that means he wasn't an angel when I was conceived. He was a demon." Shock took the place of confusion, followed quickly by anger.

The nephilim could be born of either angels or demons, though lore often left the demons out of it, spinning the stories into tales of angels in love and lust with human women. That lust came from a dark place, so in my mind, they were all the same, all sinners who had allowed their offspring to bear the burden of their debauchery.

Dash nodded. "That he was. Rhine was a demon long before either of you were born."

Arrow gave no indication that he was hearing this for the first time, but he didn't look so good.

"Don't let it get you down, kid," Dash said with a sympathetic expression that looked so real I almost bought it. "Eventually, you all end up dark or dead."

The torment in Rowen's eyes was almost more than I could stand. I wanted to kiss it away, to hold him, to promise him that demons were liars and that everything would be ok. But the sad truth was that demons were just as good at speaking the truth as they were at twisting it.

Rowen's face hardened into a mask of loathing. "Either way, death will catch me one day. The dark never will."

Dash shrugged. "It's too bad that you feel that way. I have goals. Plans. If you're not with me, then you're against me. I'm sure Rhine will understand. You leave me no choic—"

I didn't let him get the last word out before I flung up my free hand and released the mix of nephilim talents I held inside me. A bright light struck the demon in the chest, paralyzing him in place. A shadow coiled itself around his body, squeezing tight so he couldn't abandon his corporeal form. Flames started at his feet, licking their way up until he was ablaze.

I stumbled back a few steps, and Rowen reached out to steady me. As wondrous as my new talent was, I was still very much a mortal and starting to feel my limitations. My strength was quickly being sapped.

"Go," I said to Rowen. "Get Arrow out of here. Find Cinder."

He grabbed Arrow but seemed conflicted. "I can't just leave you here with him."

"He won't kill me. Go. Now. You don't have much time."

Rowen and Arrow made it into the other room. They were almost to the stairs when Dash broke free. With the light out and the fire extinguished, he shook off the shadow, but sweat lined his brow. The effort left him temporarily flustered, meaning that the three of us together in one shot had managed to weaken him. Still I didn't think it was enough.

Dash shoved me aside and went after the guys. Arrow used his waning strength to throw a hand up, freezing the demon in place. It would hold him for seconds at best, but he bought us enough time for Jett to appear at the top of the stairs, assess the situation, and jump into the fray.

With fangs bared she lunged at the demon. A deadly claw found his eye and dug deep. Those vicious wolf teeth ripped into the skin of his throat, not once but several times in succession. She tore his throat out, leaving a gaping hole, but it began to heal even as blood spilled over both of them.

Dash broke free of Arrow's freeze and swung a fist at Jett who jumped out of reach. I didn't waste a moment. Swinging the Midnight Star with all I had, I brought the blade down against the gaping wound Jett had made.

The blade buried itself in his neck, sticking so that I had to wrench it free to swing again. Even as I severed his head from his body Dash lashed out with a blow that threw me. I landed hard on my back, slamming the breath from my lungs. While I struggled to breathe, I watched Dash's body fall to the floor and disappear on impact.

"Jett, what the fuck?" The first words out of my mouth were strangled and forced but accompanied by a grateful smile. "Nice timing."

She helped me up before casting a scowl at her blood-soaked shirt. "I'm your best friend, Spike. Did you think I was going to leave these two to have your back?" She gestured to Rowen and Arrow who clung to each other in the next room.

I was exhausted and bruised but, for the most part, unscathed. I hugged Jett and said, "Thank you. But don't ever do that again. I don't want anything to happen to you."

"Hey, I don't get a lot of chances to rip someone's throat out. That was fucking great." Jett peeled off her bloody shirt and wiped her face with it. She stood there in her black bra and eyed the guys. "Would one of you care to give me your shirt? I could go downstairs like this, but I don't want to blow the crowd's mind anymore than I already have tonight."

Rowen stripped off the Crimson Sin shirt he wore and tossed it to Jett who slipped it on. "Thanks, dude. Damn, your cologne smells good. What's with him? Did he get his ass kicked?" She pointed to Arrow who'd collapsed at Rowen's feet.

"Yeah," I said, dropping the sword. "Did you see Cinder downstairs? We need him."

No sooner had I said his name than Cinder appeared. His violet gaze fixed on me first. Before I could brace for it, he pulled me into a crushing hug.

"You chose," he whispered against my hair. "Oh, dear, precious child. You have no idea how relieved I am. Welcome to the light, Ember. You will be a valuable asset to our cause."

I clung to him, enjoying his baby-powder scent. So much warmth and love emanated from him. Closing my eyes, I soaked it all in. Finally I pulled back and met his joyful gaze with my worried one.

"Cinder, you've got to help Arrow. Please. Dash tried to kill him. I don't think he's going to make it without help."

Cinder gave me the wide-eyed look he often got right before telling me no. He gave a slight shake of his head, opened his mouth to speak, but merely sighed. Instead of denying my request, he went to Arrow. He had a hard time getting Arrow to make eye contact. The dark nephilim was fading in and out of consciousness.

"Arrow," Cinder snapped in a voice that could reach through the foggiest brain haze. "Look at me. Now. I've been asked to help you. Ember has made this request on your behalf. But you must allow it. I need your consent. Do you understand?"

Arrow's eyes rolled back in his head, and he mumbled something nonsensical. Rowen spoke softly in his ear. I watched with growing unease. My heart would break for Rowen if he had to watch his brother die.

"Don't you dare die, you mother fucker," Jett muttered. "Not before you hear them announce Crimson Sin as the winner."

Cinder frowned at her vile remark, but it seemed to bring Arrow back to himself. He rolled his hazel eyes toward her and scoffed. Blood trickled from the corner of his mouth, and he coughed.

"Arrow," Cinder repeated. "Answer me if you consent to healing."

"Fuck yeah," Arrow said, his gaze sliding to me. "I didn't come this far to let these bitches win so easy."

Cinder frowned again at the foul banter we all seemed to share, but he didn't hesitate. He took Arrow's hand and pulled him to his feet. By the time Arrow stood, his bleeding had stopped, and his breathing had evened. Cinder stopped short of healing the bruises on his face. That would be too suspicious among humankind.

Arrow clapped a hand on Cinder's shoulder, saying, "Thank you. Again. I know you're not really supposed to help shitheads like me."

Cinder smiled, genuine and warm. "That's where you're wrong. People like you are exactly who I'm supposed to help. You can thank Ember. She's the one who keeps speaking on your behalf."

"Where's Koda?" I asked. I didn't have the spunk to deal with another demon tonight.

"Koda won't be bothering you tonight." Cinder scrubbed a hand through his shaggy, blond hair. "He got the jump on me. I wish I'd realized he was sent to distract me while Dash cornered you. But it looks like you handled it on your own."

He glanced around at the mess. Blood stained the floor, and the mirror was broken. The Spirit Room's owner was going to be ticked. Oops.

"We couldn't have done it without each other," I replied. "All of us. Jett too."

"Three nephilim and a werewolf," Cinder mused, appraising us each in turn. "Interesting. You guys may really have something there." He was thinking something—I could see it—but whatever it was, he kept it to himself.

"Ok, boys," Jett clapped her hands together. Other than a blood smear on her chin, she looked like her human self again. "Put those wings away, Rowen. We have to get downstairs before they announce a winner and we're all missing." She was so peppy and unfazed by what she'd just done. I'd be having nightmares about this for weeks.

I stuck the sword back into the guitar case and gave Cinder another hug before following the others downstairs.

Chapter Twenty-Five

"You feel different," Jett remarked when we were standing with the other girls to the left of the stage. "Like less human than usual."

"I feel different to me too. Still feel pretty human though. Fuck, I'm tired." I stifled a yawn and glanced over to where Rowen stood with Molly's Chamber on the other side of the stage. "I'm a little bummed that I didn't get wings like Rowen did."

Jett nodded and slammed back a drink. "Yeah, those wings are pretty badass. Your turn will come."

I clutched a beer bottle, preferring to take it slow. I felt like I needed to sleep for a few days. The emcee gave the five minute warning, and people crowded the bar, trying to get another drink before the big announcement. Despite the tiredness, I had enough energy to be nervous. We'd been working up to this moment for weeks now.

People kept coming up to us with wishes of good luck. This wasn't about luck though; it was about talent and hard work. I smiled and said thank you so many times I thought my face would break. The good wishes were genuinely appreciated. I'd take all of the positive energy I could get. But if we lost, I'd still have to face everyone, have them gauge my reaction. I would still have to hold my head up.

Of course, winning a radio show contest wasn't the defining moment of my life, not by a long shot. In fact, I thought I might have just had that moment upstairs despite feeling a lot less fanfare than I'd anticipated. But this contest meant the chance to see a part of my dream come true, so it meant a lot. We would always find other opportunities, but we'd fought hard for this one.

Tash grabbed us all in a giant group hug. Someone splashed beer on my boots, but it didn't matter. "I love you ladies," she said. "No matter what happens, it doesn't end here."

Feeling the weight of a watchful stare, I glanced up to meet Arrow's eyes. He didn't say anything. He just gave me the rock n' roll devil horns and turned away.

I caught Rowen's eye and gave him a nervous smile. He pointed a finger at me and mouthed the word, "You." He seemed so certain we'd win and didn't appear to be the least bit threatened or disappointed. With a saucy wink, I blew him a kiss, feeling incredibly satisfied when his smile grew.

The emcee returned to the stage. A cheer went up from the gathered crowd. My stomach tightened, and I felt a little nauseous. "Are you guys ready?" The emcee held up a white envelope, and the volume in the building shot up. "Someone is about to win a chance to record their debut album with Dark Mountain Records and open a show for an upcoming headlining act. Are you guys friggin' excited?"

"Just get to it already," Jett muttered, but I could tell by the way she was shifting from foot to foot that she was anxious too. This meant more to her than it did to anyone else here.

Rubi grabbed my hand, and I grabbed Jett's. Resisting, she tried to tug away at first but then reached out to grab Tash. We stood there with heads bowed, holding tight to one another, as sisters united through the magic of sound.

"Both bands did fabulous tonight, didn't they?" The emcee's voice thundered in my ears. "But there can only be one winner." He slid a card out of the envelope, as if this were some kind of awards show. "And the winner is…

"Crimson Sin!"

It didn't sink in at first. The words echoed in my ears, but I couldn't make sense of it until Jett grabbed me and shrieked. We won? We won!

My feet refused to move. Frozen, Rubi pushed me along from behind. Together the four of us climbed the stairs to the stage. The room seemed to spin, and I blinked a few times, trying to center myself. We fucking won!

Jett acted as our spokeswoman. She grabbed the mike and told the crowd how fucking awesome they were for being so supportive. After answering a few questions from the emcee about how psyched we were, we left the stage in a blur of camera flashes and encouraging shouts. It all happened so fast. My head spun.

We were shuffled around. First we were posed for the photographer from the radio station who would be taking our photo for their website. Next we were introduced to the well-dressed rep from Dark Mountain Records who seemed genuinely pleased to meet us. He congratulated us on our win and promised to have us into his office within the week to discuss the album we would record.

Lost in the whirlwind of excitement, I was almost able to forget about what had just happened upstairs.

Well after midnight, I was able to break away and go to Rowen. He sat at a table with the rest of his band. He looked up with a grin at my approach. "Congratulations. I knew you would win. You guys deserve it."

I planted an eager kiss on him, squealing when he pulled me onto his lap.

Sam and Greyson mumbled their congratulations, which they really didn't mean. I couldn't blame them though.

Arrow placed an unlit cigarette between his lips and glowered. "Congrats." The word was forced. The glower never changed. Arrow was as happy for me as he could possibly be.

"You guys know this is just one competition, right?" I tried to coax a smile from them. "It doesn't mean shit. Besides, it's usually the runners up on reality TV competitions who go on to have the most fascinating careers."

Arrow's glower became a scowl. Greyson chose to drink rather than respond. Sam shrugged and muttered, "Yeah, that's kind of true."

"I'm sorry." I got up despite Rowen's attempts to keep me planted on his lap. "I'm probably the last person you guys want to talk to right now. I'll catch up with you later."

"Actually," Arrow spoke up. "Jett is the last person we want to talk to right now. So keep her busy, will ya?"

With a salute, I turned to go. "Will do. Have a good night, guys."

Rowen caught my hand and pulled me back for a kiss. "I want to see you later. Can I come by your place?"

Those fiery, amber eyes weakened me in all the right places. I caressed the back of his neck, trailing fingers through his 'hawk. I marveled at how I could touch him and feel the talents he possessed, knowing I could swipe a sample if I chose to. "I'll meet you there."

"Hey, Spike," Arrow called as I started to walk away. "You're really not so bad, you know."

"I know. You could use a little work though." He met my teasing grin with an eye roll. Arrow and I had reached some kind of understanding. Maybe one day we'd even be friends. Well, that was a long shot, but stranger things had happened.

My ears rang, my head spun, and I clung to Jett as we giggled about stupid shit we wouldn't remember in the morning. The night had been a gong show, a shitstorm of rivalry, demons, and celebratory booze, but Crimson Sin had survived. I partied with my girls until almost three in the morning.

When the house lights came on to signify that it was closing time, management started ushering people out. Rowen had left already, but I hadn't seen him go. Rubi, the sober one, rallied us girls together and led our way to the door. The van full of our gear was ready and waiting to chauffeur us home.

Then Cinder stepped in. He had my guitar case slung over his shoulder. "Car keys," he said, hand extended. "Come on. I'll drive you home. We need to talk."

I hugged the girls and shared one last excited squeal. Then I let Cinder lead me to the Nova.

"I didn't know you could drive." I tripped on a concrete divider in the parking lot. When had I gotten so drunk?

"I can do many things if required of me, Ember." He gripped my elbow until we reached the car. "I understand that you had something to celebrate tonight. However, you seem to have imbibed a little too much. It's not my place to lecture or to judge, but I must remind you that being intoxicated compromises your ability to defend yourself."

I fumbled with the seatbelt. A yawn escaped me, and I slumped back against the seat and closed my eyes. "I know, Cinder. You're right. You're always right." I reached out blindly feeling around for his arm, then patted it with drunken affection. "You're so good."

Cinder laughed in spite of himself. "You gained a new talent tonight. I can feel it. We'll have to work on that. The skills of a replicant can run away with you."

"More training. Why doesn't that surprise me?"

"It's better to be prepared for things you may never face than to be caught off guard. What happened tonight with Dash is just the beginning I'm afraid."

I frowned. The movement of the car turned my stomach. The drinks Jett had plied me with threatened to make a reappearance. Somehow I made it home without getting sick. The elevator didn't make that challenge any easier. I staggered down the hall with Cinder at my side.

Rowen sat on the floor, leaning against my apartment door, playing on his phone. He looked about half as drunk as I felt.

"I sure hope you didn't drive." Cinder's greeting was typical. He never stopped being the concerned guardian.

"Nope. Took a cab." Rowen pushed to his feet and stood back to allow Cinder to unlock the door.

Once we were safely inside, Cinder studied Rowen and me in turn. "Should I bother trying to speak with you both? Or would it be wiser to wait until you've slept off your poison swill?"

Rowen produced a crumpled joint from a pocket. "I'm sorry, but I really want to blaze this thing."

"I suppose I have my answer." Arms crossed and violet eyes narrowed, Cinder followed us to the balcony. "You two are going to make my job a real challenge, though I guess I should be grateful. Your choice of recreational activity could be far more dangerous. Still, try to keep the narcotics and alcohol to a minimum. Ok? It may seem like harmless fun, but anything that clouds your thoughts or judgment can be dangerous."

"How do you do that, man?" Rowen sparked up the joint and took a long pull. "Come across so genuine. No judgmental crap. It feels like you really care."

Cinder leaned against the doorframe wearing a wry smile. "I do care. I understand that such things are often part of the human experience and especially part of the rock music experience. But it doesn't have to be. Besides, only God can judge and contrary to popular belief, He's much more interested in positive reinforcement."

Rowen offered the joint to me, but I held up a hand to decline. If I indulged any further, I'd probably fall off the balcony. He studied Cinder for a moment before saying, "What about Arrow? Is it too late for him?"

"No. It's not. His humanity means that as long as he's alive there's a chance for him to find his way out of the dark." Cinder held Rowen's gaze. "Don't give up on him."

"Arrow's a good guy somewhere in there," I said. "I've seen it."

"I believe that's true," Cinder agreed. "But I'm afraid I can't come to his aid every time he gets in over his head. I was stretching the rules tonight."

"But why? Why does saving someone's life have to be against the rules?" I leaned on the railing, looking down below. The ground below began to spin, and I had to turn away.

"Because there is a natural order, Ember. And death is part of it. I intervened because you requested it and requests made on behalf of another are powerful. But it can't always be that way." Cinder looked apologetic as he spoke, as if he disliked telling it like it was.

"Makes sense," Rowen said.

Cinder tapped his fingers against the doorframe in a rhythm that sounded a little bit like our song, 'Daughters of Disaster'. "I'm going to leave you two now. I'll be back after you've gotten some sleep. I want to talk to you about what happened tonight. The three of you with Jett, it's given me an idea I'd like share with you. When you're of sound mind. Goodnight."

Gone. Just like that, he vanished. Sometimes I envied that ability.

Rowen stretched and stifled a yawn. "Sleep sounds really good right now. After I blow your mind of course. I have a congratulatory orgasm to give you."

My cheeks burned as I blushed to the tips of my toes. "Well, how can I say no to that?"

It wasn't our finest intimate encounter by any means. We literally fell into my bed together. Intoxication botched our normally smooth moves. We laughed it off, which increased our closeness.

Joining the light hadn't come with fireworks, balloons, or a big welcome party. I hadn't really expected it to, but finally choosing was rather anticlimactic overall. However, not every choice needed to be celebrated to make it real. Perhaps the most poignant choices were the ones made in the privacy of one's own heart and soul.

As I lay curled in Rowen's arms, I found myself whispering words of thanks. Choosing the light didn't make anything any easier or less frightening, but it did mean that Rowen was my ally, a partner in more than just love. We had dedicated ourselves to the greater good even though we were so far from perfect ourselves. Venturing into this endeavor with him made it far less intimidating.

"You know, I got a new ability too," Rowen said, his voice thick with sleep. "I can enter other people's dreams."

I listened in bewilderment as he described his new talent. Entering the dreams of another person sounded both intriguing and terrifying.

"Can you do it at will? Are you forced into it? Sounds scary."

"It's only happened a couple of times. With Arrow, actually. I think I did it accidentally. It didn't feel scary, just confusing." He yawned, causing me to yawn as well. "I'll have to ask Cinder about it sometime. I'm not sure I know anyone else who would know."

I knew then that Cinder's declaration was true. This was only the beginning. We would likely face Dash again. He had seemed so intent on having Rhine's boys among his kind. A demon required more than a decapitation to keep him down. Even if he didn't prove to be a further threat, then there would most certainly be others like him.

The world could be a dark, ugly place. We would find the beauty and help others to see it too.

I had thought that I needed to be ready to declare my choice, but I would never have been ready. Having my back against the wall as a demon threatened to harm my friends and me, that was what I'd needed. It forced me to choose by stripping away my uncertainty. Danger itself had given me the courage to be bold.

Good things could come from evil. It was a tough concept to grasp sometimes, but it was perhaps the biggest affront to evil. As much as evil sought to breed more of itself, it often planted the seed of goodness.

My commitment phobia was by no means over. Even lying there with Rowen, part of my mind whispered: *What if it doesn't last? What if he just breaks your heart?* What-ifs are total bullshit, the lies we tell ourselves to foster a fear we shouldn't have to live with. I'd just made two significant commitments: one to Rowen and one to the light. Maybe that didn't mean I was cured of my fears, but it was a damn good start.

* * * *

The mouthwatering aroma of freshly baked cookies drew me to the kitchen. Cinder had just taken them out of the oven. He flapped an oven mitt at me, herding me out of the small space.

"Go sit down, Ember. They need to cool for a few minutes."

When he turned back to the oven to grab another tray, I swiped one from the counter anyway. Crazy hot, I juggled it back and forth between my hands as I returned to the dining room table.

Rowen and Arrow sat on one side, Jett on the other. I took the seat next to her, frowning when she swiped the cookie from my grasp.

It hadn't been easy getting Arrow over here. He'd been reluctant to say the least. He sat there with a hand clenched on the handle of a mug of coffee. Since arriving with Rowen twenty minutes ago, he'd barely spoken more than a few words.

Around a mouthful of cookie, Jett exclaimed, "Holy shit, Cinder, these are good!"

That earned her a nasty glare from Arrow whom she rewarded by showing him a mouthful of chewed food.

"Does anyone want more coffee?" Cinder asked. With an apron and oven mitts, he looked hilariously cute. He was more in his element than I ever would be in such attire.

"Only if you have some Irish cream to go with," Arrow said, frowning into his mug.

"No thanks, we're good," Rowen interjected.

Cinder joined us, setting a plate of cookies in the middle of the table. Then he pulled out the chair at the head of the table and sat down. He waited expectantly for us to try his baked goods. Even Arrow couldn't resist nabbing a few. They were shortbread, my favorite, and tasted absolutely, melt-in-your-mouth fantastic.

"The reason I've asked you all here," Cinder began once we were all happily munching away, "is to discuss the possibility of arranging a team, if you will. You all have various strengths and gifts. Combined together, you were able to drive off a very powerful demon. Your teamwork was impressive. Together you can accomplish so much more than you can accomplish working alone."

"Wait a minute," Jett broke in, her cookie paused halfway to her mouth. "You want the four of us to work together? As a team?"

Cinder gave a nod of his shaggy, blond head. "Yes. A run in like you had with Dash won't be the norm I'm sure, or so I hope. However, in many other scenarios, the four of you could truly complement one another."

Arrow began to laugh, a bitter sound that drew everyone's eyes to him. "Have you conveniently forgotten that I'm dark? I'm a drug dealer who takes orders from those in direct opposition to you. How do you expect me to be part of your little band of merry men?"

Unfazed by Arrow's snark, Cinder met his gaze evenly. In a gentle tone, he said, "Arrow, I would never ask you to do anything you're not comfortable with. I merely thought perhaps you would be interested in working with your brother at times. You are dark, yes, but you still have free will. And I did not ask you here to count your sins, merely to invite you to be a part of something special."

Arrow leaned back in his chair, crossed his arms, and muttered, "Special."

"Even me?" Jett asked. "I'm not an angel baby like these three. What can I do?"

Cinder graced her with a smile that revealed his even, white teeth. "No, an angel baby you certainly are not. You are fierce with the exceptional strength and healing that a human does not possess. Even these three can't heal as fast as you can. Your dedication to Ember is admirable. You have more to offer than you think."

Munching on her cookie, Jett pondered this, nodding silently. Then she said, "I'm in. As long as it doesn't interfere with band stuff."

"I'm definitely in," Rowen added. He slid a sidelong glance at his brother who glowered at nobody in particular. "Arrow? You can say no, but I think you should at least consider it."

With a screech, Arrow shoved his chair back. "Yeah, I'll do that." He grabbed a handful of cookies before storming for the door. He paused on his way out to add, "Thanks for the cookies."

"Well, that went well," I said when he was gone.

Cinder shrugged, unfazed by Arrow's attitude. "He'll come around."

"So, what about you, Spike?" Jett's elbow found its way between my ribs, making me squeal. "Are you in?"

I thought about the demons I'd faced down. They existed to offer unsuspecting humans choices that would swallow them whole. They slunk from person to person, breathing lies and deception into the ear of any who would listen. I recalled the poisonous smile on every one of their faces when they saw me, so sure that little old me couldn't do a damn thing to throw a wrench into their plans. Then I thought of Dash and Koda.

"Yeah, I'm in."

Epilogue

We hadn't seen much of Arrow lately. In the week since our talk with Cinder, he'd kept to himself, preferring to stay home and write music while locked away in his basement. He had barely reacted when Rowen announced that he was moving out. Though it was safer for them both that way, Arrow's lack of emotion was worrisome. I knew that Rowen was more concerned than he let on.

Jett and I were back at The Spirit Room to watch a friend's band play. We'd decided to use tonight's outing as an opportunity to find out if we were up for the challenge Cinder had presented to us.

"There's a demon behind you," I told Jett. "Don't turn around. You won't see him. He's incorporeal."

"Ok, so what now? What's he doing?"

"He's giving me the finger."

And he was. He knew we were on to him. We'd caught him whispering in the ear of a guy already strung out on drugs, encouraging him to take it further, to test the limits of life and death. The guy was oblivious to the literal monkey on his back. With bloodshot, sunken eyes, he scanned the bar, most likely looking for Arrow or one of the many other dealers who frequently passed through.

"Well, give it right back." Jett spun around with both middle fingers up. The people standing behind her gave her a dirty look, which she ignored. "What does he think of this?"

"Stop that." I grabbed her hands, trying to stop the werewolf from antagonizing the demon.

"Hey, buddy." Rowen swooped in out of nowhere, sauntering up to the bleary-eyed guy. "Want to come outside for a smoke?"

The guy tried to focus on Rowen, but he had a hard time and shook his head in confusion. "Yeah, sure, whatever. Thanks, man."

Crimson Sin

The demon moved as if to follow them, but I stepped into his path. "Not tonight, dude. Leave that guy alone."

To anyone who was paying attention, I appeared to be talking to nobody. However, in a rock bar where everyone was getting a drunk on, nobody was watching me that closely.

The demon sneered at me. Even though he wasn't corporeal, he had a human appearance. Not all of them chose to look that way. Some of them chose to be downright ugly and terrifying.

"You think a couple of nephilim brats are going to get in my way?" With an exaggerated sigh, the demon suddenly turned visible. He remained relatively emotionless, as if I was so low on his awareness scale that I wasn't even worthy of his disdain.

"Not just us." I pointed at Jett who was made a show of flexing as if prepping for a brawl. "Trust me, you don't want to tangle with her. She's an eye gouger." To emphasize my threat, Jett held up a hand tipped with claws and smiled. "Of course, if you don't have it in you to take us, I guess you could just jump on out of here and there wouldn't be anything I could do about it."

"Do you think I'm an idiot?" He did muster a glare for me then.

"Yes," I nodded. "I do."

He held up both hands in a 'bring it on' gesture. "Alright. Let's have it. Show me what you've got."

Without wasting a second, Jett grabbed him by an arm, spun him around, and wrenched his arm up behind him so hard he grunted. Then she shoved him up against a nearby pillar and put her free arm across the back of his neck.

"I can slit your throat in a split second," she snarled. "Take your business elsewhere. You're done here."

I placed a hand on his shoulder, pulled some of his dark power into me and then thrust it right back into him. "Listen to the wolf. We can't kill you, but I can guarantee that we'll have fun trying anyway."

"Are you for fucking real, little thief?" The demon chuckled. When he followed that up with a sigh, I wasn't sure I liked his bored response. "I don't need this crap tonight. I'm far too busy to piss around here with half-breeds. You want the junkie so bad, fine. Have him. There's always more where he came from."

The demon vanished, which pleased me but lacked true satisfaction. Unfortunately, he was right. There were always more. For every person we aided, there would be hundreds more we couldn't. That realization startled me even though Cinder had warned me not to entertain such ideas.

"You do what you can do, Ember," he'd said. "And leave the rest in God's hands."

I knew he was trying to ease the perfectionism that I'd felt since choosing the light. In a way he did. Still, there was so much to mull over.

Jett scoffed, "Where was the challenge in that? I expected more of a fight."

"Sometimes they give in because it's easier to move on than to engage. It's not a good thing. He's just moved on to another target."

We headed outside to find Rowen. He was sitting on a bench, sharing a smoke with the guy, and talking him through what appeared to be a bad trip. We hung back and watched without being obvious.

"Too bad all guys aren't like that." Jett nodded toward Rowen. "You nabbed a good one. It's about time I guess. Your track record sucks."

"Tell me about it. I think Rowen and I were meant to meet now. I don't want to read too much into it, but it feels destined."

Jett cackled and tossed a purple lock out of her eyes as she lit a cigarette. "You? Read too much into things? No way."

I had to smile at her sarcasm. I couldn't help that I was an over-thinker. Since our meeting with the Dark Mountain Records reps a few days prior, all I'd done was think. About juggling music, keeping up on my graphic design business, and being available to act on behalf of the light. This juggling act was going to require some work.

The Dark Mountain rep booked some time for Crimson Sin at one of the better studios in the city. We would be recording twelve of our original songs. We currently had an indie record available for download, but this was the real deal. Dark Mountain was going to back our record and had already committed to a small, promotional tour.

I was thrilled. We all were. This was the start of our dream come true. Still, I hoped like hell that it didn't drive a wedge between Rowen and me. He'd been nothing but supportive. I wondered if I would have been as supportive if our roles were reversed.

Of course Dark Mountain didn't forget Molly's Chamber. They too had been contacted for a meeting. They were offered the chance to record an EP, which would be promoted by the label. According to Rowen, Arrow had barely surfaced since then. He stayed in the basement writing.

Rowen found an apartment downtown already. Living at Arrow's had become too dangerous. This way Cinder could put a ward on Rowen's place, giving him some sanctuary from demons. Cinder had also put his seal on Rowen. As a Dominion, he supervised other angelkind, the light nephilim included. His constant guidance and presence in my life made more sense to me now. Of course, Cinder's seal wouldn't stop all demons from messing with us. Some of them would be encouraged by it.

Koda for one was not deterred by it. Though we hadn't spoken since the last time he showed up at the jam space, he'd been around. I saw him lurking in the parking lot outside the vampire bar when we played there a few nights ago. He kept his distance, but he made certain that I knew he was there.

Dash, on the other hand, hadn't bothered Rowen or me, though from what I heard, Arrow had been in contact with him. Dash had offered him a chance to earn his way back into the family. Arrow had been reluctant to share the entire conversation with Rowen.

Demons were unpredictable. Like tonight, some of them would go out of their way to avoid a run-in with a white lighter. Others sought us out. I still wasn't sure which Dash was. Would he give up on Rowen? I didn't know, but if not, I was more than willing to hack his head off again.

"Wanna head over to the jam space? I think I'm done with this scene for tonight. I'd rather work on some new material." Jett's gaze followed a guy with liberty spikes and a studded leather jacket. "Or maybe I'll see what he's doing."

"What happened to the dude with the dreads?"

She scrunched her face up and shook her head. "No go. He was engaged. Alas, my hunt for a boy toy that can keep up with me continues."

"Your pack is huge. Why not hook up with another wolf?" I refused the cigarette when she offered it. I was down to just a few a day. Good for me.

"Been there, done that. It just leads to awkward shit within the pack. I prefer to keep my personal life personal. And I kind of like human guys. They're always so surprised when I throw them down and rip their clothes off." She chuckled to herself at a naughty memory.

I watched as Rowen flagged down a cab and got the guy safely inside. They exchanged a few words, and the cab drove off. Running a hand through his blue 'hawk, Rowen flashed me the smile that always made me weak.

"Go get laid," Jett quipped. "You reek like lust."

Despite her ribbing, I knew she was happy for me. She just showed her happiness through snarky remarks.

When he rejoined us, Rowen said, "I convinced him to head home and get some sleep. We had a good talk. I may have got him thinking about rehab."

"In ten minutes you managed that?" Jett asked. "Shit. You're good. No wonder you have wings already."

Rowen grinned and ducked his head, embarrassed by her praise. Taking his hand, I slipped my fingers between his and squeezed. He squeezed back, and we shared a look.

With a nudge, I asked Jett, "Do you still want to jam?"

She cast a last glance at the punk rocker with the spikes. "Yeah, let's go. Bring lover boy. He can play bass."

"You sure that's ok?" Rowen's grin was teasing. "Our bands might consider that some kind of treason."

"Aw, screw 'em. I happen to know for a fact that Tash song writes with Mr. Country. I don't suppose Arrow would want to come by, hang out, and have a drink."

Rowen's smile faltered. "I doubt it. I'll text him though."

My heart ached as his smile faded. Rowen didn't like to discuss his relationship with Arrow in too much detail. They were still friends, though embracing each other as brothers would take time. Being on opposing sides wasn't going to make that easy.

We headed for the parking lot with Jett chattering up a storm. She was great at lightening a dark mood. In no time she had us laughing and joking along with her. When Rowen and I showed her the song we'd written together, she didn't even get mad. She just wanted to steal it for Crimson Sin.

After we ran through the song a few times, she admitted, "I kind of hate to say it, but you two make a pretty good team."

I exchanged a look with Rowen, who gave me a sexy wink. My heart fluttered the way it always did when he looked at me like that.

"Yeah." I fiddled with the pegs on my guitar, hoping to hide my goofy blush. "We really do."

~ ~ ~ ~

Spike's story continues in Rebel Heart Book Two, *The Spirit Room*.

~ ~ ~ ~

About the Author

I live in Alberta, Canada with my husband, daughter and three annoying but super cute cats. I love to hear from readers so don't hesitate to drop me a line.

Website
TrinaMLee.net

Facebook
Facebook.com/AuthorTrinaMLee

Instagram
Instagram.com/TrinaMLeeAuthor

Printed in Great Britain
by Amazon